T0116470

LIVING
for the LAMB
of GOD

THE SEQUEL

JAMEY O'DONNELL

authorHOUSE®

AuthorHouse™
1663 Liberty Drive
Bloomington, IN 47403
www.authorhouse.com
Phone: 833-262-8899

*This is a work of fiction. All of the characters, names, incidents, organizations, and dialogue
in this novel are either the products of the author's imagination or are used fictitiously.*

Published by AuthorHouse 07/28/2023

ISBN: 979-8-8230-1146-4 (sc)
ISBN: 979-8-8230-1147-1 (e)

Library of Congress Control Number: 2023913038

Print information available on the last page.

*Any people depicted in stock imagery provided by Getty Images are models,
and such images are being used for illustrative purposes only.
Certain stock imagery © Getty Images.*

This book is printed on acid-free paper.

DEDICATED TO MY FRIEND AND ADVISOR
GEORGE "BUDDY" DOW

CONTENTS

*L*iving for the Lamb of God begins where *Hunting for the Lamb of God* ends, with the Hunters discovering the settlement of New Hope, which is a collection of families and individuals who have banded together with the hope of restarting civilization after much of the Northwest Hemisphere is decimated by a super EMP at the hands of Iran and North Korea.

Their encampment is located next to the Cherry Creek Reservoir in Denver, Colorado, providing fresh water and opportunities for game hunting. It also provides tree cover to camouflage them from the Hunters…humans who have resorted to hunting and killing other humans for food.

When the EMP hit the previous year in 2022, all electricity stopped and electrical wiring was fried, eliminating cars, airplanes, computers, internet, phones, running water, television, and radio.

Elevators stopped working, trapping hundreds of thousands, all dying within days. Pacemakers stopped working, causing millions to drop dead where they stood. Over 3000 jet airliners fell from the sky, killing close to a million people. Anyone relying on oxygen died within hours.

In a nanosecond, the world changed as America changed, and the initial survivors of the bright light and the big swoosh had to rely on their survival skills and pre-planning for a disaster such as this.

In *Hunting for the Lamb of God*, the book tracks the footsteps of the Jenkins and Price families, who have both joined together to traverse the terrain. With laden shopping carts, they make the days' trek to Cherry Creek Reservoir after surviving for months in their homes in a suburb of Denver, fighting off cannibalistic neighbors wanting to kill and eat them.

There, they find communion with other God-fearing folks and life was as good as could be expected until the day the Hunters drive through their camp. The Hunters do not stop to talk with them as would be expected, thereby tipping off New Hope as to who they were and their intentions.

What used to be normal people living normal lives, all had been stretched to their limits while finding their inner strengths and discovering their flaws, all while trying to maintain some semblance of their humanity in a world that was seemingly bereft of feelings and charity.

To a man, they came to an understanding that the America they had known would never be what they remembered.

To have any kind of future, they had to be willing to do things they'd never had to do before and not lose themselves while doing them.

The key component to their survival would be their faith in God.

He that dwelleth in the secret place of the most High shall abide under the shadow of the Almighty.

I will say of the LORD, *He is* my refuge and my fortress: my God; in him will I trust.

Surely he shall deliver thee from the snare of the fowler, *and* from the noisome pestilence.

He shall cover thee with his feathers, and under his wings shalt thou trust: his truth *shall be thy* shield and buckler.

Thou shalt not be afraid for the terror by night; *nor* for the arrow *that* flieth by day;

Nor for the pestilence *that* walketh in darkness; *nor* for the destruction *that* wasteth at noonday.

A thousand shall fall at thy side, and ten thousand at thy right hand; *but* it shall not come nigh thee.

Only with thine eyes shalt thou behold and see the reward of the wicked. because thou hast made the LORD, *which is* my refuge, *even* the most High, thy habitation;

There shall no evil befall thee, neither shall any plague come nigh thy dwelling.

For he shall give his angels charge over thee, to keep thee in all thy ways.

They shall bear thee up in *their* hands, lest thou dash thy foot against a stone.

Thou shalt tread upon the lion and adder: the young lion and the dragon shalt thou trample under feet.

Because he hath set his love upon me, therefore will I deliver him: I will set him on high, because he hath known my name.

He shall call upon me, and I will answer him: I *will be* with him in trouble; I will deliver him, and honour him.

With long life will I satisfy him, and shew him my salvation.

Psalm 91 KJV

ONE

Everything is
Different Now

"If they have cars, then there have to be other cars that survived the blast," Bill Jenkins said.

"The difficult thing will be to find them."

He rubbed his chin as he contemplated the where of it all.

"My guess is that the vehicles we saw were underground somewhere when the EMP hit. The Sheriff's vehicle was probably in their underground garage, so that's a no-brainer, but the other vehicle was an old classic car. Wherever it was when the blast hit, it had to be underground, otherwise, it was rewired and re-equipped with an ignition switch, generator, spark plug wires, and battery that was either underground or in a Faraday cage, and I think that's highly unlikely.

My point is this…we start looking for cars underground and hope we can get the keys to whatever vehicle we find, or we are going to have to hotwire it, which I'm not familiar with how to do to a newer car. Getting gas won't be a problem because we can just siphon it out of cars along the roadways" Bill added.

"Having a vehicle would change everything for us. Having more than one would be a game-changer for sure," offered Bob Hawkins. "We need to start brainstorming possible locations where we might find these underground places that would have cars, and quite frankly,

I have no idea where to start, except for downtown Denver, and that's a good fifteen-mile walk away."

"There are other buildings closer, off of Orchard and I-25, and there's some up Parker Road where the freeways meet, so I think that's where we go first," said Terry Pryor.

"What about car lots? Do they have underground facilities, you know, where they would keep cars?" asked Mark.

"I've never heard of a car lot having an underground garage," said Bill as he continued.

"Whatever we do, we have to do it quickly, because I don't think we have much time. If those cars that drove through here were not hunters, they would have stopped and identified themselves. They would have been glad to see that there were other people alive and surviving. They were scouting, looking for a food source, and now I'm sure they believe they've found one in us, so it won't be long before they come back, and it will be a sneak attack at night. Everything has changed now, and we must be vigilant like never before. If we are lucky, it will just be those two cars, but we can't count on that. What we have in our favor are numbers. We have a lot of men here, and we are armed.

Anyone that has their tent set up away from the rest of us needs to move their tent closer, otherwise, they will be the first ones targeted. We must remain together as one big group so everyone can be safer," Bill recommended. "Make sense?"

"We can be sure they are coming back. Who knows when the last time they've eaten was, so if it's been a while, they could be back as early as tonight. Whatever we need to do to protect ourselves, we need to get busy and do it right now because time's a wasting."

The men all agreed, and New Hope became a buzzsaw of activity. All tents were moved closer to the activity areas, a new fire ring was created, the consolidation of all of their activities in proximity between the Great Building, the picnic tables, and the latrine and shower area was completed and made more sense for their survival.

After everything was moved, it created a whole new look that everyone would have to get used to, especially when getting up in the middle of the night to go to the bathroom.

Whiskers had become especially needy living in this new outdoor environment, clinging to Julie and Viv and following them wherever they went, alternating between the tents of both women. Whiskers was in tune with the wildlife surrounding them along the perimeter of New Hope and would never go outside the activity area under any circumstances.

Everyone in the camp gathered around the new fire ring that was now ablaze, and the men of the camp picked up their conversation where they had left off, bringing everyone else up to speed with what they had discussed earlier.

The women were terrified at the thought they may be under attack in the near future, but not like they would have been almost a year ago when their lives were still certain. They had become hardened to the world around them, circumstances making it a priority. Viv knew firsthand how evil could disrupt their daily lives, remembering full well her episode in the Whole Foods that could have ended badly for her, but thanks to the sheriff's deputies, she escaped a tragic outcome, giving her the strength to overcome an attack on her family in their front yard not long after.

She often wondered about whatever happened to Officers Tipton and Engleart, hoping they were still surviving and navigating their way through this horrific life the world was now providing. She owed a debt of gratitude to them that she knew she could never fully repay. The patrol car that had come through New Hope earlier in the day looked to be a lot like their vehicle, so a part of her thought the worst, causing her sadness thinking about it.

One thing she knew for sure.

It wasn't a sheriff driving that car and neither was its passenger.

The men decided that any plans to go looking for a vehicle would have to wait.

With the possibility of an attack looming large, they would need every able-bodied man to be at the ready on site.

That night and all of the next day, there was a nervous buzzing around the camp, with people very nervous about an imminent attack, and everyone stayed close within the confines of New Hope. Even the fishing was done exclusively on shore, as no one wanted to be too far out on the lake should they be needed to fight.

The nervous tension in the air was not good for Kate, with a baby on the way. She tried her best not to dwell on the hunters, but she knew she would be an optimum prize for them, considering the extra weight she was beginning to put on with her pregnancy.

Mark kept his eye on her wherever she went in camp, so she knew there were more than her eyes watching out for her, giving her some comfort in a world of uncertainty.

There would be no drinking alcohol by any of the men, at least not until they knew where they stood with the hunters, making sure everyone would be on the alert.

Bob Hawkins wanted it to come sooner rather than later if it was going to come, feeling that the more time that went by, the less diligent his constituency would be. He was the elected lawman for New Hope, and he'd be damned if any of his flock were harmed in any way.

He made sure that everyone got familiar with their weapons and knew how to use them. He instructed those that did not know how to clean them how to do so because a clean weapon was a trusted weapon and could be counted on in your hour of need.

They also agreed to stand watch over the camp throughout the night, with a man taking an hour watch, then relieved by the next man doing the same, continuing through the night.

Jack Price was the spiritual leader of New Hope and led the group prayers before every meal and before they bedded down for the night, and he believed probably more than most that they were protected, and no harm would come to them. Since he was fairly new in his faith, his optimism was strong and his resolve unwavering.

His optimism was not shared by most of the others, as they had been on this Earth longer and seen the ways of the world, but it was shared with the children, and for that reason alone, his attitude was appreciated by all.

The last thing the inhabitants of New Hope wanted was for their kids to live in fear.

It was good for them to be alert to the outside world but growing up being scared of everything around them did them no good at all, so it was natural that the children gravitated around Jack, and he kept them all busy by delegating small chores for the camp, small but necessary chores to keep things running smoothly. In between, he would lead Bible studies and games to be played.

In the back of Bill's mind, he thought a great deal about the army base underneath Denver International Airport and the resources they possessed, wishing he could get his hands on one of those MRAPs, which would put them in a whole different category regarding protection.

A big part of him wished the soldiers had agreed to take the Price family so they would be in a secure location, even though he didn't have much hope that they were even in existence now, but another part of him felt an allegiance to his new neighbors and he couldn't imagine leaving them behind. They were all in this together, and all of them would survive this new threat from the hunters if they worked together and kept their heads on straight.

If America were to continue, it would be because of small communities like New Hope that sprung up across the land, incorporating the same frontier spirit our ancestors had shown when traversing across the Rocky Mountains and settling in the West.

Bill knew there had to be more just like them, good people banding together and surviving the best way they knew how, without resorting to hunting down their neighbors and eating them, and maybe one day they could come together as one. That was Bill's hope for the future, and up until this latest scare from the hunters, that hope was alive and well in his heart and his actions.

The hunters would be nothing more than a momentary setback if Bill had anything to say about it. His belief was if they came for them, New Hope should show them no mercy and extinguish the threat immediately, meaning they should all be killed with extreme prejudice. There was no room for mercy in this new world and none should be given, especially to those with the intent of killing those in New Hope and eating them.

Though they were not technically zombies, it was paramount they were treated as if they were, because they had acquired the taste for human flesh, and their appetites would not be sated by normal food. Eventually, they would turn on the community and begin their old habits again, and New Hope could not afford to have a killer amongst them.

The night after the hunters had made their appearance and the camp had transformed itself, everyone gathered after dinner around the new fire ring, as was their custom, but now a roll call was done before everyone began socializing, as it was done first thing after breakfast in the morning and would continue to be done without fail from that point on.

"Tonight, we are going to begin our night watch, with the adult male members of New Hope standing guard, each for an hour, continuing until sunrise, and everyone for tonight's watch has been notified, so the rest of us can sleep peacefully, which is the whole point.

This will be the new way we do things around here, and it will continue until we are sure the threat is gone. No one leaves the perimeter of the camp unless you are fishing on the lake or hunting, especially the children. We have to insist that everyone follows this rule for all of us to be safe. If you are outside the perimeter and run into trouble, chances are we will not get to you in time to save you, so if you break the rules, know that you are gambling with your life. Understood?" asked Bob Hawkins.

Everyone in the camp acknowledged Bob and went about their socializing, thinking about what Bob Hawkins had just said to them, and incorporating it into their conversations. All were on board with the new way things would be done, and everybody would do whatever was asked of them to contribute to the well-being of the camp as a rule.

Bob and Viv had each other to lean on, as did Mark and Kate, Brian and Rocky, and just about everyone else in New Hope had that someone, even Jack had the kids, but the one person in the camp that was all alone was Julie Price. Though she missed her husband every day since he'd been gone, she never missed him as much as she did that night.

After everyone had finally gone to bed after extinguishing the fire, it was Julie alone in her tent with Whiskers, but he could not give Julie the comfort that she needed, so she lay alone in her sleeping bag, sailing off in her mind to happier times when she and Paul would laugh and talk halfway through the night, with Paul making her giggle like a little girl at the funny things he would say to her. He always had a captive audience in Julie and loved to make her laugh, and it was no hard feat to bring her to tears from laughter.

When it was time to sleep, he always put his arm under her neck so she could breathe him in, knowing she was protected from everything out in the great big world that could ever hurt her, but now he was gone.

Jack had told her about the time on the couch with his dad and his dad's wish for Jack to relay to his mother how much she was loved by him, and it crumbled her. It also gave her solace to know that Paul was in heaven waiting for her, and she would someday be with him for eternity, never to be apart again.

This is where she always ended up at night in the throes of slumber, enabling her to go to sleep and dream of him, always with a tear in her eye and a song in her heart. It was Paul's favorite song, *Dream a Little Dream of Me*, and he used to sing it to Julie in her ear.

Tonight was different, however, because the threat of a horrible death was something the whole camp faced, and she being the most vulnerable beside the children, it would be Julie that would be the easiest prey. She understood this without anyone having to tell her, which is why they made sure Julie's tent was the closest to the inside of the group of tents banded together.

Everyone had the responsibility of watching out for themselves and their children, but they also kept an eye out for her.

Julie was starting to come around, and there were moments she could even be seen laughing at something in camp, taking her away from her inner misery, even if for a moment, and it was wonderful to see her smile. She was beginning to let her guard down and see how beautiful life is beyond her pain and suffering, and most of all, her loneliness.

Whiskers had turned out to be a Godsend for her. Even though the cat loved Viv too, he gravitated more toward Julie, maybe because he knew she needed him more than Viv did.

⚒

Bill Sigler and his family hadn't eaten for days, and their stomachs were rumbling. Their last kill was 2 weeks prior; a homeless guy not more than skin and bones because he had not eaten for a while himself.

Most everyone had died off, either from being hunted by the hunters or from starvation and dehydration. The sick died soon after the EMP struck, cutting off their ventilators and dialysis machines, and the diabetics had no insulin to keep them alive because it went bad with no refrigeration.

The ones that lived longer than a month were of hearty stock, and they foraged through every store and house they could find for food and water. There were still a few people left, but they were few and far between and got good at avoiding the hunters, so Bill Sigler's food supply had begun to dwindle.

He was most worried about the General. If he had not found that camp at Cherry Creek State Park, it was a sure bet the General and his two soldiers would be cutting Bill and his family up into steaks.

Bill was cooking up one of the two guys on the grill that tried to ambush him when the General pulled up to his house with his men. Had Bill not offered them a place at his table, they probably would have killed him and his family right then and there, then proceeded to eat the two men Bill had killed, cutting the family up for later.

Bill was a smooth talker and talked his way into the General's good graces while chomping down on a rib, but the General was a different sort of fellow. Bill may have thought he had the upper hand at first with the bodies on the cart in his front yard, but he soon realized how severely overmatched he was.

The General appeared to be alive, but when you looked into his eyes, it seemed like he was dead. At least he gave that impression. His eyes had no soul behind them, and when you got close to him in proximity, your blood began to run cold from his negative energy. He made it clear to Bill Sigler in no uncertain terms that if Bill did not start to work for him in finding food for him and his men, they would be on a plate in front of the General during his next meal, so from that night on, Bill and his son Will would scout the territory looking for families instead of individuals, as one man or woman would not be enough to feed all of them.

Granted, they would kill anyone they saw whether they were alone or with others. Killing just one meant they'd be going out for more.

This new bunch of people they found at the reservoir was enough to keep the General fed and happy for at least a couple of weeks, maybe longer.

Bill thought it wasn't smart to drive up to them and alert them to his presence, but that wasn't his call to make. The General insisted they get a head count to make a plan of attack, and thankfully, Bill would not have to plan this himself, so if anything went wrong, it wouldn't be on Bill.

The General and his men had left Sigler's house half an hour prior with his agenda made known. Tomorrow night would be when they made their assault on the compound. They planned on taking at least four of them in the trunk to be slaughtered and grilled.

They would lay and wait in the weeds by the reservoir on the other side of the latrine and shower house so they wouldn't be seen, then they would snag them one by one as they got up to go to the bathroom. When they came out of the latrine, they would be snuck up on and chloroformed, putting them to sleep, then be stabbed dead, dragging them over to the road and put into a pile until they had enough of them, then push the sheriff's vehicle over to the pile and quietly load them into the vehicle, then start the car and drive away.

This would take the four of them, with the General sitting in the old classic car up on the hill, while Bill, his son, and the two soldiers did the dirty work.

TWO

First Line of Defense

They parked on Parker Road, not wanting to alert New Hope of their presence and proximity to them, hours before their planned attack. Even if their cars were heard from a distance, they would be forgotten after a few hours. The Sigler's were weak from hunger and could not go another day without eating, and the General and his two soldiers were not any better off, sitting in the car behind them.

Though they were visible in the pale moonlight that shined down on the reservoir, the four men waited in their cars for the early morning hours, when they would make the mile-long trek to the compound to begin their murder spree. All would have to walk softly in the dark, not making a sound so their sneak attack would succeed. Any noise at all would be like sending up a flare to warn the campground of their arrival, ruining everything they had planned.

People were still up and socializing around the fire, with only half of them to bed at 11:00, leaving another three hours before they would begin their descent into the perimeter of the camp. By then, everyone should be fast asleep.

Bill Sigler was extremely nervous about this assault they were about to make. He was dead set against driving through the camp a few days earlier, alerting its residents to their presence, but what's done was done, and he would have to make the best of a bad situation. He had no idea what kind of people he was dealing with, but he did know they were probably not as weak from hunger as he and his son were, so if any hand-to-hand combat were to take place, he did not like his chances, nor his son's.

Part of him entertained the thought of killing the soldiers when they were not expecting it, then killing the General, but they seemed invincible to him, and he was frightened of what would happen if they failed.

Bill Sigler was tasked with the chloroforming, while Will had to do the stabbing, leaving the two soldiers to carry the bodies to the pile. Why was it that Bill and his son had to do the hardest and most dangerous part, while the soldiers only had to carry the bodies? It was apparent to Bill Sigler that he and his son were the expendable ones, and until they got out from under the thumb of the General, things would never change and only get worse.

It was close to 2:00 A.M. now, and the four men began their walk down the road into the park, quietly and slowly, leaving the General behind. This was probably the worst night they could have chosen because the full moon was so bright, and to make matters worse, Bill Sigler was wearing a white shirt, not thinking clearly from the hunger. He was almost like a neon sign and could be seen at least half a mile away, and as they got close to the weeds surrounding the reservoir, they were spotted by Bill Jenkins through the trees, who was on guard duty, and he wasted no time in waking Bob Hawkins from his sleep, alerting him to the oncoming attack.

Bob stood behind the great building, while Bill was on the side of the shower house, and both men could see the four intruders coming up behind the trees and into the weeds in the shallow of the reservoir.

The air was so thick you could have cut it with a knife, and Bill and Bob were doing everything they could do to regulate their breathing, not knowing for sure what they were up against. The only ones to have guns of the four were the two soldiers, as Bill had the bottle of chloroform with a rag and his son Will had a big hunting knife. The name of their game was stealth, so they had no use for guns.

If Bill and Bob had thought correctly, the attackers would either go for people as they went to the bathroom or be more brazen and attack the outer perimeter tents, so anticipating their attack mode correctly would be crucial to their success in thwarting their assailants. Both men were completely in the dark of the structures they stood by, while the four men, which could be seen now in the moonlight, headed for their positions. The biggest man of the bunch wearing the white shirt, who seemed to be carrying something other than a weapon, was standing behind the latrine, not more than twenty feet from Bill Jenkins standing on the side of the shower house. The big man was partially in the moonlight, but out of view of the tents, while Bill Jenkins stood completely in the dark. As long as he didn't make any noise, he would not be detected by the big man.

The big man was easy to see because of his white shirt, and it was him that Bill first saw through the trees coming up the road.

Off to the side away from the big man, Bill Jenkins could see a younger man standing under a tree, partially camouflaged, but holding a big knife with the blade glinting in the moonlight. Not far from him, Bill could tell there were at least two other men back behind him in the trees but could not make out anything definitive about them.

There was no denying what these ghouls were there for, and this is what it all came down to. These men were not there to steal from them, but instead, they were there to kill them, and this would be their first defense of New Hope since its inception.

Bob Hawkins, Bill Jenkins, Terry Pryor, Mark, Jack, and the rest of the men in camp had prepared for this ad infinitum, but no preparation could duplicate the real thing when it comes calling.

The four men seemed to get into position, and it didn't seem like they were interested in advancing on the tents, so it was clear to Bill that they intended to get people as they went to the bathroom during the night, and just like that, Julie started to unzip her tent, meaning she was heading for the latrine.

The four marauders were alerted, and all crouched down to be as inconspicuous as they could be as Julie navigated her way around the tents and headed for the latrine, with the big man hiding behind it in full view of Bill Jenkins, who had his rifle trained on him, ready to fire on him at the first sign of an attack.

Julie walked into the outhouse and shut the door behind her, unknowing what awaited her when she walked out of that door, and Bill Jenkins could see the big man that was crouched down start pouring a liquid into a rag, and that's when it became obvious to him how they planned to take their victims, so he now concentrated his attention to the younger man with the knife standing at the edge of the weeds by the trees. The big man would put Julie to sleep as she walked out the door, while the younger man would do the killing, so he would have to be the first one taken out.

Bob Hawkins was more interested in the two men hiding in the shadows of the trees and had his weapon trained in that general direction.

There were more than enough men in camp to overtake all of them, but they were all asleep, so this intervention would be left up to Bob Hawkins and Bill Jenkins alone.

Julie was making rustling noises in the outhouse, then exited through the door, and just as she was outside the outhouse, the big man snuck up from behind her and put the chloroform-soaked rag over her mouth, knocking her out instantly without so much as a peep from her, and that is when Bill Jenkins squeezed off a round into the neck of the younger man, causing him to drop his knife and fall to the ground screaming, with blood squirting viciously out of his neck, obviously severing one of his carotid arteries, and he then finally stopped moving, bleeding out to his death.

Immediately upon seeing this, Bob Hawkins started firing into the trees, hoping to hit the hidden figures that were in there, but the two men began to run back toward the road behind the trees, with neither of them firing a single shot, leaving Bob Hawkins no opportunity to shoot the men as they quickly left his line of sight.

Bill immediately ran over to the big man, still kneeling with an unconscious Julie. He ordered him to release her and put his hands up, and by this time all the men were out of their tents with their weapons, all surrounding Bill Sigler with their guns pointed at him, and all Bill Sigler could do at that point was stare at his dead son twenty feet away in the moonlight, knowing something bad was bound to happen on that night he felt so apprehensive about, seeing his only son in the weeds not moving a muscle and wishing he were dead himself.

While all the commotion was going on, the boys in camp re-lit the fire in the common area to provide some light for what was to come next.

"Get up you bastard! Brian! Bring me a roll of duct tape out of the great building!" said Mark, standing there with a rifle touching the back of Bill Sigler's skull, ready to blow his head off at the slightest inclination.

When Brian returned with the duct tape, Bob Hawkins took it from him and began to duct tape Bill Sigler's hands behind his back, then his feet together, then taped his feet to his hands, essentially hog-tying him, and it took four men to drag him around the tents to lay him on the ground next to the fire in the dirt.

"What are we going to do with him?" asked Terry, wondering what good he could be worth to them alive.

"We're going to interrogate the hell out of him. That's what we're going to do Terry" Bob Hawkins said forcefully, challenging anyone to disagree with him by his tone.

"What about the boy dead in the weeds?" asked Terry, sounding more compliant and onboard with whatever was to come next.

The men thought about it for a moment, then Bill offered "We have to drag him away from camp. I don't think anyone believes this piece of shit deserves a proper burial, and I certainly don't want to expend a lick of my energy digging a hole deep enough to bury him in. We can't throw him in the reservoir because he'll taint the water, so let's all drag him over across the road to that group of trees back about a hundred yards. We won't have to look at him over there, and he'll be far enough away for us not to smell him".

Everyone thought that was a good idea and decided that would be the first thing they did after interrogating the big man.

Bill Sigler was crying now, weeping for his son, but also weeping for his own life.

Bob Hawkins was trying his best to not squeeze the trigger on him, making sure his safety was on, so he didn't shoot him accidentally on purpose.

"Who are those other two guys that got away?" asked Bob, just as they heard a car start up and drive away from the top at Parker Road.

Bill Sigler didn't answer and got kicked in the face by Bob Hawkins for his silence.

"You better start talking! "said Bob.

Jack, Kate, and Viv were tending to Julie by the outhouse, trying to bring her around to consciousness, applying cold compresses of water-soaked rags on her forehead, until finally, she began to stir.

"How do you feel?" asked Viv.

"Like I have a splitting headache" Julie answered. "What happened?"

"You were attacked by one of the hunters. They came into camp and knocked you out with this" said Viv, showing her the rag. "They must have put something in it, but you are back with us now."

"Bill said they were getting ready to stab you," said Jack. "Thank God they didn't."

"Come on mom. Let's get you back to bed" said Kate, so Jack and Viv both helped her up and walked her back to her tent, only a few feet away from the monster that attacked her.

"Look. I didn't want to do this. We were ordered to by the General." said Bill Sigler, spitting out blood from the kick in the face he took from Bob.

"Who's the General?" asked Bill Jenkins.

"He's evil and made us do these things. He would have killed us if we didn't obey him," said Sigler.

"Bullshit. Do you mean to tell me you don't eat people? Cut the crap. There's no way you are out here to kill us and not eat us. You mean to tell us that you have been killing people for someone else to eat, but not you eating them too? You better start telling us the truth." said Terry, getting more fired up by the minute.

"No, I'm not saying that either, but we wouldn't have come here if not for him," said Sigler.

"You're the one that was driving that sheriff's cruiser a couple of days ago, aren't you?" asked Bill.

"Yeah, that was me," said Sigler.

"Where is that cruiser now?" asked Bob.

"It's up on top of the road by Parker Road. Should still be there. Is my son dead?" Sigler asked, not wanting to hear the answer he knew was coming.

"Yes. Deader than a doornail. What kind of a father are you, bringing your son out here to do this kind of horrible thing?" asked Bill in disbelief.

Bill Sigler could only stare down at the dirt, as he had nothing to say in his defense.

"The truth of the matter is you've been eating human beings for a while, isn't that so? Isn't that how you got your hands on that police cruiser? How did you make it a whole year and not eat people? What did you eat if you didn't eat people? The only people alive now are people like us that have fished and hunted game, and the others are people like you that have resorted to cannibalism, which is one of the reasons there are hardly any people left because you've killed them." said Bill Jenkins.

"Where're the keys to that car up there?" asked Bob.

"In my pocket," said Bill Sigler, spitting out blood.

Bob Hawkins reached into Bill Sigler's pants pocket and fished them out, then tossed them to Mark.

"Mark, you should grab a couple of men and go up there and bring that police car down here," said Bob Hawkins.

Mark didn't need to be told twice. He grabbed two guys from the reservoir, and all three headed up the road to retrieve the cruiser.

"What are you guys going to do with me?" asked Bill Sigler.

"What do you think we ought to do with you?" asked Bill Jenkins.

"You could let me go. I won't be any trouble for you anymore. I just want to get back to my wife and daughter," replied Sigler.

Terry looked at Bob and Bob looked at Bill, wondering what they should do with him, but Bill had no questions on that subject, as he knew full well what should happen to him.

"There's no way we can believe a damn word that comes out of your mouth. You'll be back again, only next time you'll figure out a way to get to us. As long as you're still alive, we're always going to have to look over our shoulders. There are not too many people left alive, so if you're going to eat, you'll have to come back," said Bill.

Bill then pulled out the revolver that was given to Viv by one of the police officers, put it against the ear of Bill Sigler, then pulled the trigger, exploding the side of Bill Sigler's head all over him, watching one of his eyes shoot and bounce off the side of one of the tents, leaving him to fall sideways into the embers, catching his hair and cap on fire.

The men looked at Bill Jenkins with mouths open wide, not believing what they had just seen. Most men have never seen a man killed, let alone a man have his head blown off at point-blank range within hands reach.

"Dayum," said Terry. "I can go the rest of my life and never want to see that again."

Some of the men came over to the fire to see the body, and one man pulled his head out of the fire, stomping the head out with his foot.

The women were naturally horrified, all except Viv, because she knew Bill did what needed to be done.

A few of the men drug Bill Sigler over to where they had just dragged his son moments before, across the road to the trees.

It would be weeks until the bodies had decomposed enough to the point of unrecognizability, but maybe with the help of some of the indigenous animals in the area, the process would go a little quicker.

※※

"What in the hell happened back there" yelled the General at his two soldiers in the front seat as they drove down Parker Road to Arapahoe Road.

"They were waiting for us as if they knew we were coming Sir," said one of his soldiers. "They shot Sigler's son and killed him on the spot and captured Bill."

"Now they have his car! I wonder how much Bill told them, like where he lives?" said the General. "I'm starving to death. There's only one thing left to do, and that's to go back to his house and kill his wife and daughter. As soon as we get there, I want one of you to shoot the mother and tie up the daughter for later. Whichever one of you shoots the mother, I want you to cut her up and put her on the grill, and you can start with her ass. There's a lot of meat to be had there."

As soon as the men pulled up to the house, both soldiers kicked in the door, and you could hear the wife and daughter scream bloody murder from upstairs, well before the soldiers got up there. When the wife's bedroom door was opened, she was waiting for them and the soldier got a face full of buckshot, damn near severing his head from his body. He then fell backward over the banister, already dead before crashing through the glass kitchen tabletop. When she went to reload, she in return was shot dead by the other soldier, taking a round to her forehead and killing her instantly.

The daughter was frozen in fear seeing her mother brutally killed in this way, fearing she would be next, and she pleaded with the soldier not to kill her as he duct-taped her to her bed, out of sight of her freshly killed mother.

THREE

Dreaming of a New Horizon

The morning after the thwarted attack on New Hope, all the citizens gathered around the picnic tables after eating breakfast to discuss and debate what their next moves should be.

"We have a vehicle now, and this changes things. Instead of taking all day to retrieve supplies that we need, we are only looking at an hour now, and our reach has expanded exponentially. We can go farther out now than we could before, meaning we can now replenish supplies that we have exhausted in the stores around us," said Terry. "How much gas is in the cruiser?"

"There looks to be about half a tank," answered Mark, who drove the car down to the campsite. "There are two five-gallon gas cans and a hose they must have used to siphon gas in the back of the cruiser, and assuming it has a twenty gallon tank, it would take four cans to fill it up."

Bill had been thinking long and hard about what their options were from the moment they arrived at New Hope, mostly because that's how his mind operated. As great as things had been there, he was always thinking of a plan B or C.

"Have any of you considered that there might be a better place for us?" asked Bill.

There was a long pause amongst everyone at the table, with thoughts about what Bill had just asked them.

"What I mean to say is, we are very exposed here. We've just had that proven to us last night. Who's to say this won't happen again? Maybe the next time we're not so lucky to get tipped off by someone knowing we are here. Had we not been ready for them, they would have probably succeeded in what they were trying to do, and we wouldn't have known or understood what exactly happened last night.

We would have woken up to fewer people in camp and not known why.

We can be seen plain as day from the dam road up there.

What I'm suggesting is there might be a place better suited for us. Before we had no options in that regard, but now we do, and it starts with that car. Gas will not be a problem, because there are thousands of cars everywhere around us, so as long as we can siphon gas, we have fuel," said Bill.

"OK, but the car is just one vehicle. Assuming there is a better place for us, how do we get everyone there?' said a voice from one of the men.

"Let's put that question aside for a moment. Let's concentrate on another place that would work for us. Do any of you know of a better place than this because I do?" asked Bill.

"How about Lake McConaughey," asked Bob Hawkins.

"In Nebraska?" asked Bill.

"Yeah. It's a big freshwater lake, and it's out in the middle of nowhere. There would be no hunters out there, and we'd be safe" Hawkins answered.

"Man Bob, that's 200 miles from here. Assuming we didn't break down along the way, which is a possibility, how would we survive? Would it be fish alone? If I remember right, there's not a lot of game to be had out there, and if we did break down along the way, we'd be screwed. Besides, any kind of stores to replenish us would be hundreds of miles away. I'm thinking somewhere closer to where we are now, but off the beaten path" answered Bill.

"Do any of you know where Elbert is?"

None of them knew for sure but knew it was somewhere in Colorado.

"Elbert is an hour's drive from here. It's down past Elizabeth and Franktown, down by Kiowa, and not too far from Colorado Springs.

Mark knew exactly what his dad was going to suggest and thought it would be a great place to plant roots and settle down.

"There's a place along the back roads where Mark and I have been to many times. It's nothing but alfalfa fields and cattle ranches. As some of you know, Mark is an Eagle Scout, and we spent many days and nights down there camping.

The Boy Scouts have their biggest campground in the state there, and it's called Peaceful Valley.

They have about 300 acres of land with a campground on each side of the main road.

One is reserved for Boy Scouts, and across the road is for Cub Scouts. On the Boy Scout side, there is a small lake that is stocked with fish, and it would be perfect for our group. There are also cabins throughout the campground which would serve us well if we were there.

The best part about this place is the game. It's full of elk and they roam throughout the campground on both sides of the road. There are a lot more elk to be had out there than there are here, I can tell you that for sure.

As far as being away from major stores, it's only ten to fifteen miles away from supermarkets, lumber yards, and society in general.

I can't see there being any hunters out there because of the cattle. There would be no reason for anyone out there to be hunting humans for food. How many people are out there that are still alive I obviously can't tell you, but I can almost guarantee that the people we would find out there, if any, would be a lot more hospitable than any we would find out here," said Bill.

"My dad's right. It would be the perfect place for us. The EMP hit us last year. It'll be a year next month in May. They would have been preparing for summer camp all summer, meaning they should be stocked up with all kinds of canned goods and paper products that haven't been used. It might be a gold mine for us" Mark exclaimed.

"Peaceful Valley, huh?" asked Terry.

All the residents were intrigued by this new information presented to them by Bill and Mark. Even Brian knew of this place, as he had spent many nights there himself on the Cub Scout side.

After some discussion amongst them, they all seemed to be open to the idea of pulling up stakes and trying something new, but the question remained on how they would get there.

"This place sounds great Bill, but how would we get there? I mean, we've got over thirty people here, and moving us, along with our gear, would be a gigantic undertaking. We have one vehicle and that's it. We would have to get a bunch more vehicles, or some vans to get us there. It's taken us a year to get our hands on the vehicle we have now, so what ideas do you have for that?" asked another of the men.

"That would be the lynchpin for us making that move. Of that, there is no doubt, which means our main focus right now should be procuring other means of transportation. Without it, our dreams of going somewhere else are just dreams. Our search has to be in underground garages, and the only place I think we even have a chance is in Downtown Denver. What would be optimum is to find a school bus or two or three vans."

"Agreed. I propose we begin our search tomorrow morning, but who goes?" asked Terry.

The group debated about who should make the trip downtown, and it was decided that Bill, Terry, and two of the other men would make the drive to Downtown Denver.

The first thing that needed to be done was to fill up the car and get their hands on as many 5-gallon gas cans as they could get their hands on, so Mark and one of the other men were tasked to make that happen.

They left shortly thereafter to the Home Depot, where they found all the gas cans they needed, and grabbed fifteen of them, then they began siphoning gas out of cars they found in the parking lot, filling up the cruiser, preparing the men for their adventure in the morning.

⁓⁓⁓

The General and his soldier had eaten their fill the night before after barbequing up Bill Sigler's wife, all while the daughter was restricted to her room, crying her eyes out most of the night.

The General knew the road was coming to an end for them, and he was beginning to think about what options were left to him and his soldier.

The reality was the world was beginning to be devoid of people, so their hunting expeditions would be less fruitful, especially with Sigler and his son, and now one of his soldiers was gone.

It had been a rough go of it these last ten months, ever since he had left Ft. Carson with two of his soldiers, looking for greener pastures after the Fort had turned to shit and begun cannibalizing each other.

Ft. Carson had not been hardened to prevent the effects of an EMP, so everything shut down there, along with everything else in the world.

Had the General not had his 1950 Chevy Styleline Sedan parked in the underground garage on base, he would not have had a means of transportation to escape the Fort before they had become a meal on some of the other soldiers' plates.

They had initially gone to NORAD at Cheyenne Mountain for entry but were denied, much to the protestations of the General, but looking back in hindsight, they had probably turned to cannibalism by now as well, he thought.

In reality, NORAD had been supplied up until recently by way of the underground train system, which the General did not know of, so all was still up and running at NORAD.

He sat on the couch in the living room, just off the banister where one of his soldiers had crashed through the night before and ruminated over the last few years of his life, remembering his illustrious career, then ending when he found his wife murdered in their home by one of the soldiers on base and thinking to himself that America had come to an end without a single shot being fired because now it was every man for himself.

They would be finished eating on Sigler's wife in a couple of weeks, and he had a decision to make on whether to cook up the soldier that had died before his flesh began to rot or leave him be, and instead kill the daughter when the time came.

It would be a tall task to ask of the other soldier since he was grieving his loss of him. Maybe too much to ask, and certainly too much to expect of the remaining soldier to eat his friend.

And what would they do after that? Where would they go?

The General started to make a contingency plan in his mind that involved no one other than him, and that would be putting his service revolver to his head, ending the misery of living this nonexistent life, putting an end to it once and for all.

Once a religious man that believed in the Hereafter, General Lawrence O'Ryan questioned his faith in God and could not rectify why God could let this happen to such a great country as America and its citizens, leaving those that remained after the event searching for their place in the world, but more importantly, their standing with God. If God was still watching over his flock, how could it be that his children were now faced with killing men to eat and survive, and how would that be looked at by God?

Was all of this a test, to see how far we would go before we started breaking God's laws to make it to the next day? Have we failed that test? What's more, the General and those like him that resorted to eating human flesh, what about their taste for it? Taking place of ordinary food they used to eat, the food that now induced vomiting at the thought of eating it, preferring a leg or arm portion of a freshly killed human being?

How would this be judged by God?

Had they all turned their backs on Christ and signed a pact with the Devil?

The only thing that made sense in the mind of the General was there would be no hereafter for any of them, that they would all burn in hell, making the idea of blowing his brains out more palpable.

He stared at the soldier as he slept on the other couch across from him and wondered how long it would take for him to turn on the General out of starvation, putting himself on a barbeque grill for one of his last meals.

The time was coming closer to having to decide about him.

He wasn't there yet, but probably soon would be.

He then thought about the sweet girl upstairs and what her life must look like through her eyes. It had been such a long time since he had thought of how anyone felt. He could not afford to have any empathy for anyone, or any mercy, yet here he was doing exactly that, a mere few hours after dining on her mother.

Whatever he used to believe in, he had betrayed that long ago and would now suffer at the hands of God for his betrayal.

His rank meant nothing to anyone left in the world except himself, because he was now a hunter hunting the hunted, not for God or country, but himself.

In the blink of an eye, he went from being one of the highest-ranked officers in arguably the mightiest military in the world to just another man wearing a uniform, trying to make his way by using his made-up power that no longer existed.

Soon he would be all alone, one way or another, and it somewhat frightened him.

Not because of the end that awaited him, but because he would not be remembered for the sacrifices he made for his country. His loss of both legs at the knees in the Vietnam war, and more importantly, the loss of living a normal life serving his country.

When he passed, he would not be given the military funeral with full honors so many of his fellow officers had received after their passing, and he would not be buried somewhere like Arlington National Cemetery, or even Fort Logan Cemetery here in Colorado.

He would lay to rest wherever it was he eventually died, maybe even on the couch, he was sitting on in that suburb south of Denver, all alone with no one saying any last words or eulogizing him over his flag-draped casket.

It didn't occur to him that once he was dead, it would not matter.

Not to America, not to the United States Army, and certainly not to him, as the deaths of all those before him mattered not, because there was no one left to remember them, just as there was no one left to remember him.

At that point in his thought process, the sudden realization of his nothingness overwhelmed him, and he bent his head down into his hands and began to weep, feeling the pain of no tomorrow and no yesterday.

Across from him on the other couch, the soldier pretended to still be asleep but could see out of his squinted eyes the General weeping in his hands, creating an uneasy feeling deep inside of him, wondering how long it would take for the General to crack.

He thought to himself that time might have already arrived, and he was witnessing it while making sure his revolver was close at hand and at the ready.

He saw the telltale signs well before that moment and was expecting something extraordinary to happen with the General, though he had no idea how that would manifest. All he knew is that the General seemed to lose some spring in his step with each passing day, and his strength in command seemed to wane, appearing non focused on the task at hand, whether it be directing the soldiers to possible hunting grounds, or giving them the orders to kill, though the night before he had no reservations in ordering the death of the woman they had just eaten.

Hunger must have played a deciding factor in his decision, but other than last night, he saw the General becoming weaker by the hour, and he knew he was heading toward a decision he would have to make regarding the direction he would have to go, with or without the General at the helm.

※

Some of the women were scrubbing the front and back seats of the cruiser, trying to get as much of the dried blood off the seats and the floor with the limited cleaning supplies they had. It wouldn't have been so bad, but it was more than blood. There were pieces of skin and brain as well, causing some to stop for a minute and take a drink of water, while some others vomited.

Found under the front seat was a wallet, and when opened, it revealed the identity of the sheriff it belonged to. One of the women placed it at the end of the picnic tables and continued to scrub away, putting as much elbow grease into it as she could.

After a couple of hours, they decided they had done all they could do to clean up the bloody mess that had been inside, and when looking at it after they were done, Bill was beyond impressed.

"You ladies sure did a bang-up job cleaning this car. Thank you! Thank you very much" Bill exclaimed.

"Shirley found that wallet under the front seat, over there on the table. It belonged to one of the police officers the car belonged to" said one of the women.

Bill picked it up and looked inside of it, not remembering the name of the officer that saved Viv from being raped in the Whole Foods, but he was fairly confident this belonged to one of the two officers. There couldn't be many more police officers driving around after things went to hell in a handbasket.

He decided not to tell Viv about the wallet and placed it back on the table. If she happened to see it and opened it, so be it, but it wasn't going to be him that showed it to her.

He knew his wife to be a strong woman with a stout heart, but everyone has their breaking point, and she hadn't reached hers yet.

He wasn't about to be the one that helped her get there.

Bill, Terry, and the other two men decided they would leave when the sun came up.

They fit as many of the gas cans in the back of the SUV cruiser as they could, along with some tools they may need for anything unexpected along the way.

Viv had made the men some venison sandwiches and boiled a couple of gallon jugs of water for them and put those in the back seat in a plastic bag.

Bill also put the service revolver given to Viv by one of the officers in the console just in case they ran into trouble.

The men would be leaving in the morning before most of the community would have woken, so everyone gathered around the fire and held hands before retiring for the night with Jack leading a prayer for the men, asking Christ to watch over them and guide them in finding what they were looking for.

Jack Price was becoming more confident by the day in God's will for New Hope, and it showed in his manner and his speech.

Every day he was knee-deep in his father's Bible, cross-referencing with a reference book he had picked up along the way, trying to understand every word, phrase, and reference made regarding one book referencing the other.

His thirst for knowledge in that book was that of a man dying of thirst in the desert, needing to know everything about Christ and his father that he could know and understand.

He was truly living for the Lamb of God now, living a life fuller than he could have ever imagined. With all the heartache and tragedy he was surrounded by in the world, he found himself never happier than he was in those times, as he was living the life of a truth-seeker being filled with the word, and the word was enough because it gave him sustenance and all the strength he would need to carry on.

"Bill...be careful out there. I've already lost one father. I don't want to lose another" said Jack to Bill, then he embraced him, giving him a massive hug and not wanting to let go.

"I'm proud of you Jack. Proud of the man in Christ you are becoming, and your mother is proud of you, and most of all, your dad is proud of you too. He is looking down on you right now and he is smiling. I'm sure of it! I don't know if you realize how important you are to New Hope. You give comfort to so many of us, and even though you are new to your faith, it is obvious to everyone that your connection to God is real, and it is genuine.

We are all in good hands with you.

This community needs God, more than any of us ever have, and you help us to find our way to him, keeping him ever-present in our heads and our hearts" Bill said in the most heartfelt way he could think to express himself.

They hugged again, with Bill giving Jack an all-knowing wink, assuring him that they would be careful and come back alive.

At a distance, Mark could see the embrace his father and Jack shared and was happy their families were becoming one. He considered Jack more than his brother-in-law, but considered him a brother, the same as Brian, and felt somewhat responsible for Jack's journey to Christ.

It was different now with his father back with them from D.C, and the months they had survived without him were a testament to that.

They never would have arrived at New Hope without his idea, forethought, and planning.

FOUR

Last Chance in Boulder

B ill and Terry were on the road now, joined by Jim Eberle and Max Johnston, two of the men from camp traveling north on Parker Road until it turned into Leetsdale Drive, leading them into Downtown Denver.

All of the men were armed except Terry, him having no desire to fire a weapon for any reason, even in these apocalyptic times.

Every few blocks they drove, they would see some evidence of a human being, whether it be skeletal remains at the side of the road or sitting behind the wheel of a car, or the body part of someone, half-eaten by the remaining dogs still alive, but what they did not see were any living people anywhere.

The drive downtown would normally take no more than half an hour but having to drive around so many cars in the middle of the road added another half hour to their drive.

Everyone for the most part was dead now, with many dying within the first month of the EMP. The rest had died due to exposure or were hunted.

They passed many stores along the way and stopping to search for supplies would have been fruitless, as all the stores would have been picked clean by those that were living in this much denser urban area of the city.

Besides, that was not their mission this time around.

They all had to be laser-focused on why they were going to Denver, and that was to find vehicles that ran and could be driven back to New Hope.

After turning onto Colorado Blvd, they headed for Colfax Avenue, the main road that traversed east and west through Denver, where they would be turning left toward downtown.

It sickened Bill to see what this once lively street had become, a virtual wasteland with no signs of human life, or any life for that matter. All the storefronts either had their doors propped open or their storefront windows crashed in, emptied of all their possessions related to food and water.

If there were people still alive down here, they would have to be hunters or ultimate survivalists, being the fittest to ward off any marauders that would try to take from them what was theirs, leaving them not much better off than those that had succumbed to the elements or another human being.

Bill pulled over to the side of the road, leaving the car running.

"Well...where do you think we should begin? Any suggestions?" he asked.

"What are we looking for exactly?" asked Jim Eberle.

"We are looking for garage doors tall enough to allow a bus or any type of tall vehicle to go through them, otherwise we are wasting our time searching in that particular garage," Bill answered. "I guess maybe we should just drive around until we spot one."

They drove down every street downtown, looking for that type of entrance and they were few and far between. When they did find one, they would get out and search the garage, provided they could get inside, as most of the garage doors were shut and could not be opened without electricity.

This went on for most of the morning, not finding one vehicle that would suit their purpose, but it then hit Bill like a ton of bricks.

They had driven by so many city buses parked alongside the streets they had traveled, it had not occurred to him that's what they needed to be looking for.

He remembered driving by a huge bus station on the corner of Colfax and Broadway, so they doubled back to it, driving down the ramp to an underground facility big enough for a bus to go into.

There were no doors to prevent them from driving inside, and much to his excitement, they found several buses parked underneath, so they began their search down there.

Bill grabbed his weapon from the console, making sure it was on the safety setting before putting it in his pants pocket. He didn't want it going off, possibly shooting himself in the leg.

The first bus they walked over to was locked. Bill remembered seeing bus drivers open their doors by reaching in through the driver's side window and hitting a switch, but this switch was battery operated and none of the doors could be opened by it a year later, so they had to pull the doors open with brute strength to gain entry.

They must have spent two hours down in that garage, trying to find keys to match the buses by going into the RTD office to retrieve the keys off of the keyboard hanging on the wall, then looking in the pants pockets of dead bus drivers for keys they could not find on the board and were able to find three sets of keys that matched the buses they were able to pry open.

All three buses did not even register on the dash once they were put into the ignition switch, confounding Bill because he knew that even with a year that had gone by, the buses should have at least had their dashboards light up and possible turn the engine, but all three were dead as a doornail.

He stood outside of the last bus he had tried, scratching his head in frustration, and then he realized the problem. Though they were technically underground, they were on the first and only level, with no doors on either side of the facility, which would have enabled the electromagnetic pulse to enter the garage and kill everything electrical inside, just as if they were out on the street.

He walked over to the bus scheduling board, trying to come up with a plan that would work for them, and then he saw it.

Boulder Junction.

A new underground facility underneath the new Hyatt Hotel in Boulder, thirty-five miles to the northwest of where they were currently was big enough for six bus bays.

By the description of the facility on the board, this was a real underground station, whereas the location they were at was nothing more than a transfer station, meaning the Boulder Junction station might be deep enough underground to prevent the EMP from entering.

After Bill showed this to the other three men, they began to discuss if it was worth the risk of driving up there, but Bill convinced them it was their only shot at getting a vehicle big enough to transport everyone.

It was just after noon, so they dove into the bag of sandwiches to refuel for the afternoon.

The whole time they had been downtown, they'd seen nary a trace of human activity, making them feel as if they were the last men standing in the world, and then they saw *him.*

He was standing at the edge of the bus entrance, looking around for anything to sustain him, and then he saw the four men in the cruiser and pointed his rifle toward them.

Bill jumped out of his seat and exited the vehicle, pistol in hand, and pointed it toward the man.

"Hey, you! Drop your rifle and walk slowly over here toward me!" Bill barked.

The man at first did not know what to do, but then Bill squeezed off a shot, with it ricocheting off the concrete next to the man and exiting to the outside.

He immediately set his rifle down and walked toward Bill.

"Hold off on firing that weapon," said the man.

The man looked like hell, as would be expected of someone living on the streets in a city where life had passed by long ago.

"I'm not going to hurt you. I just don't want you having that rifle in your hands while we are here. We are leaving in a minute, and then you can go pick up your rifle after we leave. Fair enough?" asked Bill of the man.

"Fair enough. Where are you going?" asked the man.

"That doesn't concern you mister" answered Bill.

"Can I go with you?" he asked.

Bill looked him over as he now stood ten feet from the man, noticing he was covered almost from head to toe in dried blood.

"I don't think so. You're a hunter and we don't need your kind anywhere around us," said Bill. "You're lucky I don't shoot you right where you stand."

The man looked like he hadn't eaten for at least a week.

"I'm not a hunter. I just carry that rifle for protection. There's a lot of bad people around here," said the man.

Bill had Terry hand him a sandwich from the bag, then tossed it to the man, who did not attempt to catch it.

"I just threw you a sandwich. Go ahead and eat it," ordered Bill.

"I'm not hungry, but thanks anyway," said the man.

"What do you mean? Everybody's hungry. Eat the damn sandwich!"

Bill was now getting agitated.

"No thanks. Maybe later" answered the man.

"You're a damn liar when you say you aren't hungry. You haven't eaten for days. I can see it in your eyes. You're a goddamn hunter sure as I'm standing here. You've got blood all over you" Bill said to the man, barely able to stand from weakness.

"I'm going to walk over and pick up your rifle. If you move even a little bit, I'm going to shoot you. When we drive out of here, we'll leave your rifle on the street. Understand?" Bill said to the man as he walked toward the rifle.

After picking it up, he walked back to the cruiser and handed it to Max in the back seat, then got behind the wheel and drove through the exit onto the street, where Max laid it down by the curb, and they then drove away.

In the rear-view mirror, Bill could see the man run to the rifle, pick it up, and aim the gun toward them as they drove away, but they were too far down the road for the man to hit anything, choosing instead to conserve his ammo for a better opportunity.

"Good Lord. That is why we are armed gentlemen," said Bill as he headed for the I-25 freeway entrance ramp toward Boulder.

Driving on Highway 36 toward Boulder was like a breath of fresh air. Other than the occasional car stalled, all you saw were the Flatirons, with the Rocky Mountains back behind them, still snowcapped from the previous winter, and for a moment, you could forget about the hunters and all the dead, because you saw nothing to remind you.

It took them about an hour to arrive at Boulder and Bill had a good idea of where the bus terminal was, just off of Highway 28 to the right after making their turn into town.

Everyone had their eyes out for a Hyatt Hotel, and sure enough, there it was off to the right a couple of blocks away.

When they came upon the garage door of the facility, it was closed, causing the men's hearts to sink, because they were fresh out of ideas.

Bill parked in front of the hotel, and all four men got out of the car, weapons in hand.

"There's got to be a way into the garage through the hotel. Those glass doors should be unlocked" Bill said.

As luck would have it, they were light-sensor sliding doors, so they had to push them in to gain entrance, with no help from electricity.

Once inside, it looked like a bomb had gone off. Chairs and tables were strewn everywhere, and the juice machines in the breakfast area were all tipped over on their sides as if someone had tried getting the last little bit of juice out of them at one time.

There was no cereal left in the cereal dispensers, and all the cabinet drawers were opened and ransacked. Even the non-dairy creamers had all been opened, with their contents sucked out of them, littering the floor in front of where they had been displayed.

"Damn. Whoever did this was starving to death," said Max.

It was dark in parts of the hotel, so they had a hard time finding where the stairwell that led to the garage below them, but eventually, they found the elevators, and around the corner from them was the stairwell, with a sign indicating that the RTD buses were below.

"It's going to be pitch black in there. We need to make some torches so we can see where we're going. Grab a few of those rope posts over there" Bill said, referring to the posts holding the decorative ropes that distinguished the lines for people to stand in, waiting to be seen at the front desk.

After unscrewing the bases from the poles, they began to tear down the curtains from the windows to be used as fuel for the flames.

Bill went behind the front desk and started rifling through the drawers, looking for tape, preferably duct tape, to secure the curtains to the poles.

What he did find was a couple of rolls of packaging tape, which would suffice in the absence of anything better to use.

It took every bit of the tape that he had, but he was able to make three good size torches out of the poles and the curtains, which would probably only last them fifteen minutes at the most before burning out, so he decided they would only use one at a time, saving the other two for when they were needed.

"Who's got a match or a lighter?" asked Bill.

No one did, and why would they? None of them were smokers, so who else would carry a lighter or matches? No one thought of bringing any matches from New Hope, which were used to light the campfire.

Bill ran back over to the front desk and started looking for a means to light a fire, even though he didn't remember seeing anything he could use when he was looking for tape.

"Jim. Go out to the car and see if there is anything out there in the console or the glove box. Max, go with him to help him with the door." Bill asked.

Bill went through everything and found nothing. He even went through the desk in the back office.

"Nada. Not a damn thing" said Jim, a little out of breath from running.

"There has to be a lighter or some matches somewhere in this hotel. If not in here, then maybe in one of the cars out in the lot. Let's start looking" Bill said.

The four men split up going in all directions.

Jim and Max went back outside to look through the vehicles, while Bill tried to find the maintenance closet, and Terry headed toward the hotel laundry.

Twenty minutes later they all showed back up to the stairwell leading downstairs, all with their hands full of lighters and matches.

"Excellent. Let's put all of these in our pockets. "We will need them somewhere down the road, I'm sure" said Terry.

Bill handed one of the torches to Max and another to Jim, then lit the one he was holding, and it burst into flame.

They opened the stairwell door with Bill leading the way, then descended the stairwell several stories down until it dead-ended into the door leading to the bus depot, which was wide open.

As they entered the cavernous room, it took them a minute for their eyes to adjust, and the first thing Bill smelled was diesel, giving him a big spiritual lift because a lot of the buses nowadays were running completely on battery-powered electricity, which would have meant failure for their expedition. The smell of diesel fuel meant diesel-operated buses.

Alongside the room where they were standing, they could see a bus platform for passengers, and to their left, they could see six bus bays, with three of them occupied by buses.

They began to walk toward the buses when they came upon a plate glass window and a door next to it that said *"RTD Employees Only"*, so they stopped when Bill stopped.

"The keys to these buses are going to be in there. We need to get in there to find the board where the keys are hanging," said Bill.

Naturally, the door was locked, so they busted the plate glass window with one of the torch poles. Jim climbed in and opened the door from the inside, letting everyone else in.

It didn't take long for the board holding the keys to be found, as it was hanging on the wall to the left of the main desk. There were three sets of keys, so Bill grabbed all of them.

The torch was beginning to go out, so they lit a second one, and Max had the idea to start looking for flashlights, and he found two of them, both working.

Because they were underground and shielded, the flashlights worked, which was an auspicious sign for the buses to work as well.

The flashlights were high-powered and provided plenty of light without the torch having to burn, so they put the torch out, then put it aside for safekeeping just in case.

Bill grabbed the keys, and the men followed him to the bays where the buses were parked, beyond excited that may have finally found their ticket to a new and safer life because, without one of these buses, their chances would drop significantly.

Bill asked one of the men to shine the light down on his hands so he could see the keys. He then grabbed the light and walked to the front of the buses to see their identification numbers so they could match the keys to their respective buses.

Bill reached into the side window by the steering wheel of the first bus and fumbled around for a bit looking for a switch, a handle, or a button to open the door, and when he found it, the door opened and the lights came on inside the bus, prompting cheers from all four.

Before the men walked into the bus, Terry told them all to stop for a minute.

"Before we start turning keys, let's all say a silent prayer."

The men then bowed their heads and clasped hands, staying silent and praying together for the same outcome.

Bill stepped up to the driver's seat, sat down, and put the key in the ignition, then turned it. The lights came on the dashboard, but the engine didn't turn because the battery was dead for sitting close to a year. Bill happened to look at the fuel gauge and it showed the tank full to the brim. Unfortunately, the bus would not start, so they walked to the next bus.

This time Bill could not get the door to open, as there wasn't even enough juice in the battery to open the door.

The last bus seemed to be their only hope, so Bill was able to open the door and the lights came on, but this time the lights were super bright, meaning there was more juice in this battery than the others.

He turned the key and the bus started right up, turning on the headlights and illuminating the cavernous garage they were in, prompting an even bigger set of cheers from the men, but Bill immediately squashed their happiness by telling them the bus was on empty, and they'd be lucky to make it out of the garage, let alone home.

"We have to take the battery out of this bus and put it in the first bus with the full tank," said Bill.

"I know where the battery compartment is. I used to drive a school bus similar to this, and the compartment is on the back left side of the bus, not by the engine, and these aren't your regular twelve-volt batteries, but twenty-four-volt instead. We are going to need some tools, like a crescent wrench, or a socket set would be even better. These batteries are big too, so it's going to take more than one of us to lift them. You think they've got any tools in that office?"

"We're going to find out," said Bill as they walked back to the office they had broken into.

In the back of the room, there was a door that led to a utility room, and that is where they kept the tools.

"Here's a socket set that should work for you," Bill said as he handed the socket set to Max. "You're the expert. I'm going to let you take charge of this operation."

Max was distracted by something else, not listening to Bill.

"Man oh, man. This is exactly what we need" said Max, holding something resembling a charging port for a cellphone, but a lot bigger, and it had two big wires coming out of it with clamps.

"Do you know what this is? This is a jump starter for those buses out there. We can jump-start the bus and not have to replace the battery.

This is a Powerall, twenty-four volts specifically made for jump-starting these buses! Let's go!" he said, leading the way out of the door and back to the buses.

When Max went to the side of the bus toward the back, he found a utility door and opened it, exposing the huge twenty-four-volt battery he talked about, then asked for someone to shine their light down on the battery so he could see what he was doing.

He clamped one of the wires to the positive terminal and the other to the negative, then flipped a switch on the Powerall charger.

"I'm going to let it charge for a minute, then you try to start the bus again Bill," said Max.

Bill walked back to the front of the bus and sat in the driver's seat, waiting for the command from Max.

After a couple of minutes of charging, Bill heard his command and turned the key, and the bus started up as if the battery had never been dead, and the cheers from the back of the bus resounded throughout the subterranean concrete cave they were in. The men were hugging each other and dancing around the bus, not having been that happy in a very long time.

"Max, I think it would be best if you drove this beast home," said Bill, almost crying from joy.

Max got behind the wheel and took a few minutes to familiarize himself with the controls, the dash, and everything else that pertained to operating the bus.

"I think I'm ready, but there's just one thing. That door to the terminal was closed and I don't think we are going to be able to open it. Unless it's like a regular garage door at home that has a disengage switch from the motor that opens and closes it, it's not going to open, and even if there is one, there's no way we can push the door up high enough to clear the top of the bus" said Max.

"He's right," said Jim. "We're going to have to drive through it. We are going to have to crash this bad boy right through it."

All the men agreed that was the only way they were going to get that bus out of the garage, so they walked up the ramp to inspect if there were any obstacles along the way, and to see how stout the garage door was.

After making an initial turn, it was a straightaway up the incline to the garage door, so Max would have to start at the other end of the garage to get up enough speed to break through, provided the door wasn't made out of solid metal, which thankfully, it wasn't.

It was nothing more than a light steel mesh, easily broken through with enough speed gathered.

All the men boarded the bus with nervous anticipation. Not only would Max have to get up enough speed, but he'd also have to stay in a straight line and not bounce off the walls going up the incline, and this is what worried them the most, though no one wanted to say anything to Max, thereby making him nervous and jinxing him.

Max started to back the bus out of its parking space and backed it up to the back wall of the garage.

He then began his ascent, with the other three men gripping the seats in front of them, hoping for the best-case scenario and not damaging the bus beyond drivability.

He was at twenty-five miles an hour when he hit the incline, and almost lost control of the bus because of the bump, but he proceeded up the ramp in a perfectly straight line. When he hit the garage door, it made a deafening crash as it came off its track and flew into the air outside of the terminal, falling back down onto the top of the bus and rolling off to the side, leaving a clear view of Boulder and the stores surrounding the hotel, and then Max stopped the bus to even more cheers from within.

"You did it, Max! You did it!" screamed Bill, as happy as he could be.

Now with a little luck, they would make it back to New Hope with a big new bus in their arsenal. A few days before, they were stranded with no transportation, but now they had two late model working vehicles.

Bill and Terry exited the bus, telling Max to wait there while they got the cruiser to lead the way home.

Five minutes later, the caravan of a city bus led by a police cruiser was traveling down Highway 36 with the sun behind them, on their way back to the only home they've known for close to a year, but now they would be making plans to leave that home for a new one.

It would be a home where their safety would be paramount, and they could live the lives they were meant to live.

FIVE

Preparing for Peaceful Valley

S ixty miles later, they were pulling into New Hope on a big shiny new bus, and all of its residents were jumping up and down at the sight of it. This was the closest thing they'd seen to freedom in the days gone by since the blast, and excitement filled the air.

The bus meant freedom. Freedom to go where they would be safe from the hunters, freedom to raise their families the best way they knew how, and the freedom to start a new civilization of God-fearing folk that still believed in America and all it once stood for.

Viv and the women began to cry, overwhelmed with joy, knowing that their days exposed in the park were numbered. None of them knew what Bill and Mark knew about their final destination, but they trusted the two men to know better than they did.

Even Julie was smiling ear to ear, never wanting to relive the close call with death she had just a few nights prior, and she saw the bus as God's blessing on them.

"We got lucky, real lucky," said Bill to Bob Hawkins as he got out of the cruiser. "We weren't finding anything in Denver and made a trip to Boulder because of an underground bus station there. That's where we found the bus, and she started right up after Max found a jump box for it. The nice part was the tank was full when we started, and there's still over four fifths of a tank. There'd probably be a little more, but the tires have lost some air from sitting for a year, so it cut down on our mileage. We're going to have to figure a way to get some more air in those tires."

The bus was plenty big enough to haul all of the inhabitants of New Hope, along with all the tents and personal effects, all the kitchen items, and even the bicycle used to pump water from the reservoir.

Everything they possessed at New Hope would be going with them, along with items they hadn't procured yet, things they would need to stock up on for their new home.

That night after dinner, they all remained at the picnic tables to discuss when they would like to leave, what they had to do to prepare, and what they could expect when arriving at Peaceful Valley.

"The very first thing we have to address is preparing the bus. Some of you may have noticed that the tires on the bus are low on air, and I have an idea of how to get air into them. We will have to use those tire repair cans, the ones you see in 7-Eleven's and auto part stores. Some people call them Fix-A-Flat. They hold about five pounds of air in each can, so we are going to need a lot of cans. There are six tires on the bus, two in front and four in back, and each tire holds about eighty-five pounds of air. I'd say the tires are about fifteen to twenty pounds light right now, so say we need four cans per tire, times six tires. That amounts to twenty four cans, so we are going to have to rustle those up and start airing up those tires" said Bill.

"The second thing is to find a semi-truck somewhere and siphon out about fifty gallons of diesel fuel. These buses hold 250 gallons of fuel. We have four fifths of a tank now, and these buses only get a couple of miles to the gallon. We've got more than enough to get where we are going now, but once we get there, our options may be very limited to refuel, so we want to make sure we have as much in the tank now that we can carry" Bill added.

"The best place to find a truck would be a loading dock with a truck already backed up to it. We also saw some semis parked alongside Arapahoe Road a few months ago when we were getting building supplies from the Home Depot" said the man instrumental in constructing the Great Building for New Hope.

"Once we get the bus ready for traveling, we can begin to load it up, which means we are going to have to sleep one night under the stars and out of our tents. Hopefully, we won't get rained on. The last things we load are our sleeping bags and ourselves in the morning, then we hit the road first thing," said Bill.

"It should only take us two hours at the most to get there. It's a straight shot down Parker Road, then we hang a left toward Elizabeth at Franktown, then hang a right when we get to Kiowa, then go south ten miles and we'll be there. I'm thinking we can plan on leaving here a week from today, as long as everything goes to plan. The first thing we load is the water pumping system, including the bike and the boards we are using for the water to travel, which means we are going to have to pump and boil extra water to hold us over for a day or two. Does anyone else have anything they want to say?" Bill asked.

"I know everyone is very excited about making this trip and thinking about what our new home will be like, but I have to stress that we are not out of the woods yet," said Bob Hawkins. "I strongly encourage all the men to be strapped while we are still here. We are not safe as far as the hunters go. We are still visible and could run into more of them before we leave, so heads up and be extra careful."

"Jack, what about you? Is there anything you want to say?" asked Bill.

"Mark tells me there is a chapel where we are going, and I was very excited to hear that. I hope all of you will continue to attend church on Sunday and Bible study during the week. We must always remember that without Jesus looking over us, our survival will not be possible. Our survival depends on our dependence on him, so let's not slack off when it comes to giving him all the glory and continuing to ask him for his protection," said Jack.

Everyone said a resounding "Amen".

Bill and Viv were in their tent, excited for the move in the coming week, and chatted about little things when Viv turned to Bill.

"I opened the wallet that was found in the police cruiser," she said.

"And?" asked Bill.

"It was Officer Tipton's. He was the one that saved me from that thug in Whole Foods. His wallet in the car probably means he is dead, right?" asked Viv.

"I think it's a pretty safe bet Viv. I'm sorry," said Bill.

"If it wasn't for him, I think you would have come home to an empty house. It was his weapon that he gave me that stopped the hunters from coming into the house and killing us that night. I cried when I saw his driver's license. I had a bad feeling about that car the minute the hunters drove up in it that day. I thought it looked like his car, but I couldn't be sure. Now I know. We owe him so much Bill, and I can never repay him for what he did for us." Viv said as she began to weep again.

Bill wrapped his arms around his wife and kissed her, being very thankful to Officer Tipton and his partner, wishing he too could thank them for what they had done, saving his wife and family more than once.

The next day was full of excitement for the camp, as many started to prepare for their trip. The men tasked to fish for the camp began early in the morning, some setting their lines offshore while others rowed their boats onto the reservoir, all catching as much fish as they could for the coming days ahead.

Others were on the ready for any sign of elk around New Hope, in hopes of bagging one of the creatures for salting and wrapping for their new home in case pickings were slim when they got there.

Max and Jim took the cruiser out to the closest locations that would be carrying the cans of Fix-A-Flat they would need to pump up the tires on the bus and look for semi-trucks to siphon diesel fuel from.

Another thing they were looking for were cleaning supplies and paper products, mainly toilet paper and paper towels, which they found in abundance at Sam's Club in Highlands Ranch.

There were still cases of toilet paper and paper towels on the shelf, but they could only fit two cases of each in the cruiser on account of the fuel cans.

They had thirty cans of Fix-A-Flat, which were enough to inflate all six of the tires on the bus, making it roadworthy for the fifty miles they would drive to Elbert.

The cases of paper towels and toilet paper were loaded onto the bus as soon as they got there, and as soon as they had pumped enough water to get them by for the next few days, they disassembled the bike and the water boards and loaded them on to the bus as well.

The day before they left, Max and Jim found the two semi-trucks discussed earlier in the week and siphoned enough diesel fuel out of the tanks to fill up ten five-gallon cans, which wasn't an easy task.

Siphoning gasoline is a tricky proposition by itself, but diesel fuel is a whole other animal. It is thicker and harder to get suction on it, so you really have to suck on the hose hard to get it moving, and almost always end up with a mouth full of diesel fuel, which you almost always end up swallowing a little bit of it, causing you to violently vomit.

Needless to say, it was the least favorite thing for anyone to do, but it was amazing the line of people that volunteered to do it for the sake of the camp.

The bus was full to the brim with fuel, along with the cruiser, and the tires were roadworthy.

On the last day in camp, everyone tore down their tents and loaded them into the bus with their personal items, along with all the dining canopies they had set up over the picnic tables, leaving only their sleeping bags out with a few ground tarps.

Everything else was loaded up, leaving more than enough seats on the bus for its passengers.

That night, the moon was full and there wasn't a cloud in the sky, making for a good night to sleep under the stars. They had all had their fill of the last fish fry at New Hope, along with baked bread, corn on the cob, and salted jerky made from an elk a couple of months back.

All the tarps were down now, and the camp looked like a ghost town compared to what it once was, and most had a sense of sadness at leaving the only place they called home over the last year.

New Hope had been just that for all of them, a new hope that sustained them, and had they not found their way there, most, if not all would have surely perished. They were one big family now, counting on each other and leaning on those they became closest to in times of uncertainty and sorrow.

Miraculously, not one of them had become dangerously sick or injured in any way, leaving Jack Price not having to do much except distributing an occasional Advil or antibiotic.

The worst injury to happen to anyone was spraining an ankle or getting an infection, nothing that Pharmacist Price couldn't deal with it.

New Hope had truly been blessed with just enough know-how among the men and women to survive, improvise, and invent their way through the winter, and here they were in late spring getting ready to make a lifechanging move, leaving the confines of Cherry Creek State Park, which had served them so well.

In their own ways, everyone said goodbye to New Hope and thanked Jesus for the home he had provided for them this last year, and all slept better that night than they could remember, sleeping under the stars on a warm early May evening, barely needing to be inside their bags.

Kate and Mark slept close to Julie and the boys, with Jack, Viv, and Bill not too far away.

The only one of the bunch that didn't sleep well was Whiskers, as he was constantly distracted by the wildlife on their perimeter, making sure he was deep in Julie's sleeping bag away from any critters that could attack him.

<hr />

The General sat up on the couch he had slept on again, reached down to grab his prosthetic legs, and attached them at the knees up through his pant legs.

His uniform didn't resemble a uniform anymore, as he had worn it every day for the last year. If it were not for his medals and rank, you would never know he was a military man.

General O'Ryan had officially reached the end of the line and decided he could go no further. He hoisted himself from the couch and began quietly walking up the stairs to the daughter's bedroom, to commit his last act of decency, hoping it would sway the Lord when his time came before him.

The soldier was dead asleep on the couch across the living room and didn't hear the General as he made his way up the stairs as quietly as he could, despite his legs creaking with every step he took.

When he got to the girl's bedroom, he stood in the doorway and looked upon her sweet young face, knowing what he had to do, and he walked toward her bound body asleep on the bed, then sat down on the bed beside her, waking her up.

Her immediate reaction was to scream, but the General had his finger up to her mouth, indicating to her that she should be quiet, and she was.

He pulled his knife out of his pocket and began cutting her loose from the ties that bound her, and when he was done, he whispered to her to remain quiet.

"Whatever you hear downstairs, don't be afraid. I'm sorry about your mother, I truly am. You are going to be alone now, but there will be food for you" the General said.

"I'm not going to eat my mother" she answered.

"I'm not talking about your mother. Just trust me and be quiet" he said as he walked out of the room.

He knew that the only way the girl would be safe was if he took out his soldier downstairs, otherwise he would kill the girl and eat her too. In this horrible spider web he'd spun himself into, he tried to do one last honorable thing, and that was to save the girl.

The General slunk down the stairs the same way he ascended, quiet, with a purpose.

When he got to where his soldier lay, he stood over him and looked at him as he slept.

The soldier had obeyed every order he'd ever been given, so this wasn't about eliminating a disobedient, but was instead a mercy kill for the girl upstairs.

He had no idea what would happen to her, but she would have two weapons at her disposal when everything was said and done, and she would have a chance beyond the walls of this house, so her odds of survival would be a whole lot better without the soldier still alive.

He pulled out his service revolver and pointed it at the soldier's head and squeezed the trigger, putting a .38 caliber bullet directly in the soldier's temple, killing him instantly, not knowing what hit him.

Stoically, the General then walked to the other couch he had been sleeping on and sat down.

"What's happening down there?" she screamed from her room.

"Don't come down here, not yet" said the General.

He then put the pistol under his chin and pulled the trigger, splattering his blood and brains behind him on the wall behind, then slumped over to his side.

The daughter was officially safe now, at least for the moment. The two men that had killed and eaten her mother were now dead. Two fresh kills for the barbeque grill out in front of the house.

The daughter had come out of her room and looked down onto the living room, seeing both of the men stone cold dead.

She knew she was all alone in the world now, and all she could do was sit down at the top of the stairs, put her head in her lap, and begin to sob the tears of a lost little girl, forced to live in a world that turned completely upside down for her less than a year ago.

The only sounds she would hear from that moment on were the sounds of her breathing and the wind and rain. Everything else would be dead silent.

⊱⟶∧⟵⊰

After eating a breakfast of venison sandwiches and Tang, they all loaded up into the idling bus, ready to hit Parker Road.

Max was driving the bus, with Bill and Viv in the front seat of the cruiser, and Julie riding in the back seat with Whiskers fast asleep on her lap.

Bill led the caravan and pulled onto Parker Road driving south with the bus behind him.

The farthest they had driven south on Parker Road was to Arapahoe, so he had no idea of what to expect after that.

The driving was smooth sailing for the most part, and after they'd gone under the E-470 overpass, they found themselves driving through Parker, a thriving bedroom community that attracted a lot of people that had relocated out of the busy streets of Denver. It was a place to raise your kids the way you were raised if you grew up in the suburbs.

Little league baseball, soccer matches on Saturday mornings, picnics in the park, and neighborhood parades on the Fourth of July that ended at the neighborhood pool.

The only thing left to see out the windows now was shopping centers that had been blown out by vandals, stalled-out cars along the roadside, and an occasional skeleton laying on the side of the road.

Once they passed the city of Parker though, everything changed.

The fields were wide open, and the expanse of Colorado was on full display.

With only an occasional house off the roadway, you could see for miles on end, and the beauty of the state was as overwhelming as they remembered, and it only got better once they made their left turn at Franktown, because now they were surrounded by huge pine trees, and had they had their windows open, they would have smelled them.

Something all the passengers on the bus took note of was the air conditioning on the bus, something they had not felt for so long, and they were eating it up.

The further they drove, the more they realized how far into the back roads they were. Most of them had never been this far south of Denver and had no idea it was this beautiful. It felt like being in the mountains on parts of the drive, whereas other times felt like they were in the prairies of the wild west.

Another thing they saw was a lot of dead cattle carcasses, most just skeletons now. This was highly disconcerting to them, as they had hoped to raise cattle out there, but as hope springs eternal, they saw living steers grazing on the new grass growing just before Elizabeth.

Bill saw a Walmart up ahead and decided to pull into it, thinking there might still be canned goods inside because of the desolate area they were in.

"Max, why don't we park these vehicles, and everyone can go inside to see if there's anything in there we can use," said Bill as he stood outside the bus, talking to Max through the driver's side window. "Be sure and take the keys with you."

When they all walked into the store, they were amazed that a lot of the shelves were bare considering they were surrounded by large acre ranches, with not a lot of neighborhoods close by, but what they did find in the back of the store were cases and cases of bottled water, juice, pop, and other drinks, and they also found a whole cache of toilet paper.

Julie threw four or five fifteen-pound sacks of cat food in a shopping cart for Whiskers, hoping he would get his taste back for it. He'd been eating the same food as the people had, running out of cat food a long time ago.

It took about an hour to load everything onto the bus, piled on top of all their gear, and it was a delicacy for them to be able to pop open a bottle of juice and drink it down, something they hadn't done in a while.

"We are close now," said Bill to the group on the bus. "We're only about fifteen miles away."

After doing a head count and making sure everyone had gotten back onto the bus, Bill led the way for the caravan.

In ten minutes, they arrived at Kiowa, and they could see a road sign indicating that Peaceful Valley was eleven miles away, and all on the bus cheered as they made their turn for their new home.

It was all two-lane highway now, driving on a country road with grain silos nestled next to small ranch houses that sporadically popped up alongside the road, and every so often, they could see a steer or two in the distance, grazing away without a care in the world.

After passing through the tiny town of Elbert, they could see a ranch down off to their left, with a big barn that said Peaceful Valley Scout Ranch painted on its side, and when Bill kept driving past it, the people on the bus became confused, wondering why he was passing it.

About a mile more, Bill started to slow down and turned left at a cattle gate onto a dirt road, with a sign that said Peaceful Valley at the mouth of the road.

Bill was driving slowly now, so as to not cause the road to dust up, and everyone on the bus almost had their breath taken away.

As far as they could see in any direction, there were huge pine and spruce trees, giving them the feeling they were in the forest, far away from mankind and the hunters that sought them as prey. All had ear-to-ear smiles and could not wait for the bus to stop so they could run and play in the tree line that surrounded them.

It was then they saw him in the middle of the road with a rifle, sitting on a horse, blocking their passage any further.

Bill recognized this man. He put the cruiser in the park position and got out of the car to talk to him.

"Hey, Burt! Do you remember me?" asked Bill.

"Well hell yes I remember you! How the hell are you Bill?" Burt answered him and then climbed off his horse. "What do you have here? You've got running vehicles. I didn't think there were any more of those."

"I'll fill you in" Bill answered.

Burt was the caretaker for the scout ranch and had been for years. He lived on the ranch in a home designated for him, and he was the one that made everything operate.

He graded the dirt roads all over the ranch, made sure all the water valves on the ranch were turned off in the winter and turned on in the summer, along with working on the vehicles, and took care of everything else on the ranch, making sure it was all in working order.

"Where is Henry? Is he still in the ranch house? I looked down at it as we passed it and I didn't see any signs of life." Bill asked.

"He's down there with his wife. I see him every day when he rides up here. We all ride horses up here now, ever since the blast. So, how many people do you have with you?" asked Burt.

"There's over thirty in the bus and there's three of us in the cruiser. Let me give you the low down real quick. Things turned to hell in Denver after the blast. We finally had to leave our home and went to Cherry Creek Reservoir to set up camp, mostly because of the water supply. When we got there, these other families were already there, doing the same thing we were going to do, for the same reasons.

I don't know how much you know about what's happened, but the ones still alive are hunting people and eating them." said Bill.

"What the hell? You're kidding me, right?" asked Burt, not quite knowing what to say.

"Yeah, and they've really wiped out most of the people that initially survived. Our camp was raided a week and a half ago by hunters, but we got the jump on them and killed two of them. We decided that we were too exposed where we were, so we started thinking about uprooting and going somewhere else, and since Mark and I had been coming up here so many years, remembering the lake stocked with fish, and being so far out off the beaten path, I figured this would be the perfect place for us to relocate.

In other words, we're here to set up camp and make this our home" explained Bill, waiting for a response from Burt.

"We have a lot of resources, and we're kind of like our own little traveling township.

I'll tell you what else we've got. We've got a whole pharmacy worth of antibiotics, so that has to be worth something to you, right?" asked Bill.

Burt looked at Bill for a minute, kicked his boot in the dirt, and replied, "Tell you the truth, I'll be glad to have the company."

Bill gave out a great big whoop, then hugged Burt so hard he almost caused him to fall.

"There are a couple of Venture scouts up here that were here when the EMP hit. They were here helping us prepare for summer camp, and they are staying in the Doc Holliday cabin up the road past headquarters.

Trail Boss has a couple of bedrooms and is unoccupied, as is the bunkhouse across the way from it. Why don't you all drive up to the dining hall and park your vehicles up there? You and the missus can stay in Trail Boss, and the rest can stay in the bunkhouse, at least until you guys figure out where you want to stay.

All the forts are open, and most have bunks in them.

Let's say we all get together in the dining hall around six tonight. We've got a bunch of industrial-size cans of lasagna, more than enough to feed everyone, so if you can get a fire started in the fire ring outside and get the women to tend to the cooking, we can all have dinner together before the sun goes down and catch up," said Burt.

"Sounds like a plan. See you soon" said Bill as he walked over to the bus.

After bringing everyone up to speed, they drove over to the dining hall and parked, and this was the first time everyone exited the bus, glad to be among the trees and away from the city.

Bill walked everyone down to the bunkhouse and there were more than enough beds for everyone, then he grabbed the women to the side and asked them to go into the dining hall where they would find the cans of lasagna and pots and pans, asking them to prepare dinner, while asking the men to gather up wood and start the fire.

Bill took Mark, Kate, and Viv to the side and walked them over to Trail Boss, the cabin just across the way from the bunkhouse.

"You and Kate are going to stay with us tonight if you don't mind," said Bill to Mark.

When they walked in the door to the living room, they found their bedrooms. They were thrilled to not be sleeping on the ground, but instead on real mattresses, as would be the same for the rest of the transplanted travelers.

"I'm going to go help the women," said Viv as she strolled out the door as if she were in heaven, with Kate following behind her.

Today was a good day, better than most.

SIX

Catching Up

This was the most activity the scout ranch had seen in a couple of years, and the first time the new residents had eaten a meal underneath an actual roof, being inside of the dining hall where their voices reverberated off the walls and ceiling, making them sound like a larger group than they were.

Burt had gotten the two Venture scouts over to the dining hall to join the rest of the group for dinner, and they were both thrilled to be in the company of other kids their age.

"When everything stopped that day, we had almost 100 Venture scouts and a couple of dads up here. It took all day to figure out that something was seriously wrong, that it wasn't just the ranch that lost power. When none of the vehicles would turn over, or even have the dash lights come on, Scott whipped out a crank emergency radio he had in the Quartermaster building and heard the news of the EMP.

Needless to say, it was bedlam from that point on, and had we not had some levelheaded Venture scouts up here to corral the rest of them, who knows what would have happened? That night we all managed to come together and prepare a meal, pretty much the way we are now, but with a lot of fearful scouts.

They were all trying to use their cell phones to call their families, and naturally, none of their phones worked, so after a couple of days, they all decided, including the dads, to make the trek into Denver, or Castle Rock, Parker, wherever they lived around here.

The only one here from out of state was Zach, the tall red-headed boy you see over at the other table with the boys, so he stayed, but the rest of them left walking. Other than Jake sitting next to him, we haven't seen hide nor hair of any of them ever again," said Burt.

"But only Jake made it back?" asked Terry.

"Yes, but he was almost dead when he got here. He hadn't had any water or food for days, and the story he told us damn near curled the hair on the back of our necks.

Depending on where the boys' homes were, they split up and headed their separate ways, so Jake tagged along with one of the other scouts and his dad because they all lived in Castle Rock, which is about thirty miles west of here.

It took them a couple of days to get into Castle Rock, and they arrived at the home of the scout he was traveling with first. He spent the night with them that first night. The mother and sister were home alone and damn glad to see his buddy and father, and they all had dinner together by barbequing meat from the freezer. He left the next morning for his house, which was still another five miles of walking, and when he got to his house, no one was home. Both of his parents must have gotten stranded in Denver, which was where they worked, so he figured they would be home soon walking from downtown because it had already been five or six days since the blast.

He waited there for them for over a week, eating whatever he could find in the house, and finally decided he should go back to the other scout's house, not knowing what he should do.

He stayed with them for a week at least, and then walked back to his house, and there was still no sign of his parents. He waited again for over a week at his house and concluded that they wouldn't be coming home, so again he walked back to the other scout's house, but this time they were all gone and there was blood everywhere, and he saw what he thought were human leg bones out back by the barbeque grill.

Can you imagine, being a young man almost eighteen years old, and coming up on to a scene like that? He grabbed a few bottles of water from their basement, threw them into a day pack, and started making the hike back here to camp because he didn't have any place else to go.

On the way back, he was chased by a couple of older men in Franktown with knives, and he told us they were going to kill him. They just saw him walking along the road and came after him, yelling at him to stop running, but he didn't and the old men couldn't keep up with him, so he made it away from them, but from that point on, he was super afraid of people and managed to stay undercover on the way back. Anytime he had to pass a house, he just ran past it at full speed until it felt safe for him to stop running.

He finally got back to camp here a day later, and he was a hell of a mess when he got here, and he's been here ever since," said Burt.

"They would have eaten him had they caught him," said Bill, and he continued.

"That's what's been happening everywhere. As you can imagine, a lot of people died within the first twenty-four hours. Anyone that relied on oxygen, a ventilator, or any kind of medical device to stay alive died. As soon as the food ran out in the urban areas, people started cannibalizing each other because they were starving to death. Most of the people that died after the first month were killed and eaten by their neighbors.

It almost happened to my family.

I was in D.C. because I work for the government, and it took me three months to get out here, but when I did, Viv, Mark, Brian, and our neighbors across the street were on their last legs" said Bill.

"How did you get out here from D.C.?" asked Conrad.

"Believe it or not, I came here by underground train. This whole country is connected by an underground rail system, and because it was underground, it was unaffected by the EMP blast. Those radio announcements you were hearing on that crank radio were coming from a place called Mt. Weather, an underground city in the Blue Ridge Mountains in Virginia. It's where the President, his cabinet, all the Representatives and Senators, and their families ended up." explained Bill.

"So, I took a train from there to DIA. There's an underground military base there, and I was given permission to come out here and get my family, so they assigned two soldiers to me, and we left the base under DIA in an MRAP military vehicle and got to my house.

When I got there, I found our neighbors across the street had joined together with my family, but the soldiers were not allowed to take anyone else but my immediate family. Well, there's no way we could have left them there, so I told the soldiers I wouldn't be coming back with them. If they couldn't take all of us, they weren't going to take any of us.

I got there just in the nick of time because there was a pack of cannibals in the neighborhood and they were targeting my family, so we loaded a bunch of shopping carts with a few days' worth of supplies, and we headed for Cherry Creek State Park because we knew we couldn't stay where we were at. We needed to be close to a water supply, and that's how we got hooked up with all the people you are looking at now.

None of us resorted to cannibalism, but instead, we lived off the land the best way we knew how, and that's how we came to be here. We were too exposed where we were, with still too many people in the general vicinity, and the only people left alive were cannibals, and they were branching out looking for new food sources, which was how we were discovered.

We had it pretty good for quite a while, but all good things come to an end, and so did ours.

Now you know the story.

The bottom line is this. Things aren't going to get better than this, than what we have now.

In truth Burt, I don't have any idea how many people are still alive in America, or what kind of government is left. All I know is that it's been a year and we haven't seen any help coming at all.

Will it ever be the same as it was? No way. I don't see it happening. I think we are some of the last people alive in America. I'm sure there are pockets of survivors like us around the country, but they are going to be in the outskirts like us, not in any of the urban areas.

"How much canned goods do you have in the kitchen?" asked Bill.

"There's probably enough in there to feed all of us for a couple of months tops, but the lake was stocked right before the blast, so with a year for the fish to breed, I'd say there's enough fish in there for years to come," said Burt. "And there's been lots of elk in camp. I bagged one a month ago and field-dressed it. Had elk steaks for a week, then I salted up the rest and made a bunch of jerky.

Thankfully we have well water here, so all we have to do is hand pump it."

Bill and Mark had forgotten that Peaceful Valley was well water, meaning they would not have to drink the water from the lake.

"We brought a system up with us to pump out water from the lake using a bicycle, thinking we would have to drink lake water. Maybe we can still use it to take showers? We can probably rig something up to provide water to the shower stalls in the boathouse" exclaimed Bill.

"There's a ton of propane in camp. All the campsites have propane tanks hooked up to the latrine shower stalls, plus we've got a 500-gallon tank that was just filled before the blast, further up the road, so I'm sure we can construct something to provide hot showers. By the way, it's been a while since I've had any bread. Thank you, it's delicious" said Burt, referring to the bread made at New Hope, which they had brought with them and put out on the tables.

"I'll take the horse up to see Henry in the morning and let him know you are all here," said Conrad.

"How about I pick you up in the police cruiser and we both drive there together?" offered Bill.

"Deal" answered Burt.

After washing up all the pots and dishes, everyone retreated to their sleeping quarters for the night, using propane lanterns to guide their way down the dirt road as Burt galloped to his home quarters.

That night would prove to be the best night's sleep any of them had in a year, sleeping on real mattresses that creaked underneath them providing a welcoming sound, inside of a building with a roof, walls, and a secure door.

Day One at Peaceful Valley had lived up to everything that Bill and Mark had told them it would be, and then some.

Bill and Bob Hawkins pulled up to Burt's house opposite the lake, and Burt was sitting out on the veranda, sipping a cup of coffee, made on his Coleman stove outside.

"Coffee? I've got a fresh pot here" said Burt.

"Absolutely!" answered Bob.

"I forgot how beautiful the mornings were here. Henry is going to be surprised to see a car drive onto his property I imagine," said Bill.

"He's going to shit his pants" chuckled Burt. "He's going to think he's dreaming."

The three men sat at the table drinking their coffee under the trees, admiring the makeshift corral Burt had built for his horse.

"We had to cut loose the rest of the horses. Henry took two of them for him and his wife, but the others went off somewhere on their own. There wasn't enough hay to feed all of them, and I'm just about out of hay for Missy here. I imagine Henry's in the same shape I am," said Burt.

After finishing their coffee, the three men jumped in the cruiser and headed for Henry's house down the road.

As they pulled up, Henry was outside tending to the horses, and his face said everything.

"Hey Henry," said Bill. "Remember me?"

"Bill! Mark's dad, right?" Henry asked, amazed to see someone new on the ranch after so many months of solitude.

Henry Williams was the head guy at Peaceful Valley. He was the ranch superintendent and lived in a house about a mile from Burt.

"Good memory" answered Bill.

"I could have sworn I saw you drive by yesterday followed by a big old city bus. I thought my eyes were playing tricks on me. Was that you?" asked Henry.

"Yep. Brought a whole bunch of people with me too. We are setting up a homestead on the ranch. Hope you don't mind." Bill responded.

"The more the merrier. How did you end up with vehicles that run?" Henry asked.

"They were underground when the EMP hit. It took a little bit to get the bus started, but we got it up and running. The worst part is finding fuel for it, but that's not that bad either. There are plenty of semis around. You just have to look for them," said Bill.

"Henry, I want to open up all the forts. There are quite a few families I'd like to make the forts available to. I was hoping you could drive over with us, meet everybody, and we could go to each one of them and unlock them since you've got the keys" asked Burt.

"Sure. Let me check in on the wife though. She's got a nasty urinary tract infection we think, and she's hurting," said Henry.

"I think we can help her Henry. We have a big supply of antibiotics. Do you know if she's allergic to penicillin?" asked Bill.

"I can't remember. I'll find out though. Give me a minute and I'll be right out," said Henry.

After about five minutes, Henry came rolling out of the house with his big ranch key ring and told Bill she wasn't allergic to anything, giving the go-ahead for penicillin to treat her.

They all loaded up into the cruiser and drove back to the ranch, with Henry talking up a storm about how America was going to end up being taken over by another country, and that it was just a matter of time.

The thought had crossed Bill's mind more than once about that very thing, and he wondered how long it would take China or Russia to begin attempting to claim territory, and more importantly, what position the U.S. Military was in to do about it.

They pulled up to the dining hall where all the families congregated and heated water to make oatmeal and coffee, and some were still sleeping.

It was exciting for Henry to see all these people at camp, and the first person there he got to meet was Jack.

"Henry, this is Jack Price. He is our pastor and our pharmacist. Jack, this is Henry Williams. He is the superintendent of the ranch. His wife is suffering from a urinary tract infection, so they think, and she needs some penicillin. Why don't you grab the backpack with all the meds?" said Bill.

"I've got an idea. We passed the Health Lodge. You can see it. It's right over there" said Henry, pointing his finger through the trees to a building on the main road. "We should probably get you set up over there. Are you by yourself, or do you have a wife with you?"

After Jack confirmed that he was alone, Henry offered the Health Lodge to Jack as not only a place to dispense medicine but also as a place to stay. It had a bed in there for patients, which he could use as his own.

Jack grabbed his backpack of medicine and PDR, along with his personal belongings, and they drove the one eighth of a mile to the Health Lodge, where Henry opened it up to him.

After leaving him there, they drove to the forts, which were square cabin-like buildings sporadically situated throughout Peaceful Valley. There were six of them in all, and all had bunks in them.

Henry had gotten the full skinny on where everyone had spent the night, so he knew how to place everyone.

"You and the missus can remain in Trail Boss Bill, and we can move the Venture scouts out of Doc Holliday, so you can put a family in there. There's Cook's Roost as well, and we can put a bigger family in there. That's right over there by the pool" said Henry, pointing a finger once again through the trees.

"How many family units are there?" Henry asked.

"There's eleven total, and all the rest are single" answered Bill.

The bunkhouse was separated into five units, so five families could stay there, leaving more than enough for families to be by themselves.

"All the rest can stay in the living quarters above the kitchen in the dining hall," said Henry.

The rest of the day was spent figuring out which families wanted to be close by and which families wanted space away from everyone else. As it turned out, most of the families preferred to be close to each other, as they had become accustomed to living that way in New Hope. Once a family indicated how they wanted to live, Bill and Henry took them over to where they would be if it was one of the forts, and the rest found their havens in the bunkhouse or surrounding buildings, leaving those that were single to find a bunk in the dining hall.

Rocky and Brian would stay in the second bedroom as two brothers would with Bill and Viv, and Mark and Kate opted for one of the units in the bunkhouse across the way.

Julie found a perfect alcove in the dining hall for herself and Whiskers, giving him the run of the whole building, and keeping him busy chasing field mice that had gotten inside.

After a week, a schedule was formulated, revolving around mealtimes in the dining hall, with breakfast being the time when reports were delivered on the progress of the camp and duties that needed to be done.

It was decided that Terry would remain Mayor with special input from Henry Williams, Bob Hawkins would remain Sheriff, Bill would remain City Planner and procurer of supplies, and Jack Price would remain Camp Pharmacist and Pastor.

Burt was named Maintenance, Jim Eberle oversaw hunting and fishing, and the boys under eighteen were in charge of gathering and chopping firewood for the dining halls and removing trash. The women were tasked with all the cooking and cleanup, and any sewing that needed to be done.

With everyone contributing in some way, Peaceful Valley ran like a well-oiled machine, and all looked forward to Sundays when they would all walk the mile to the chapel on the edge of the camp and listen to Jack's timely and perfectly delivered sermons, bringing them hope for the future and gratitude for what they had.

So many had died in America, yet they were still standing thanks to their cohesiveness, with no egos out of check or personal agendas at play.

It was a communal life for sure, which could only work under the circumstances they all found themselves in.

Their mission was simple and clear-cut, and that was to stay alive and healthy.

With those two things at the forefront, everything else fell into place.

It was springtime, with summer right around the corner, and they had what they needed to master their mission.

All things considered; life was good.

SEVEN

A New Kid in Town

A month had gone by and they were well into the summer of 2023. The first week they arrived at Peaceful Valley, they tilled a big patch of ground close to the lake, then seeded the ground with a variety of vegetables and fruit, with mostly tomatoes accounting for the fruit, and they constructed an irrigation system thanks to the bike and the water boards they had brought with them.

The garden was starting to sprout, and all were excited at the possible yield to be added to their menu.

When not watering the garden, a lever was pulled, directing the water to the showers at the boat house, providing hot showers all day on Fridays, thanks to Burt's installation of a water heater fueled by a propane tank, keeping the residents of Peaceful Valley cleaner than they had been for a long time.

It was only one shower per week, but it was the most glorious of showers, providing hot water for a good five minutes per shower.

Kate was visibly pregnant now with her first child, and Mark was proud to be the father, hoping to be as good a father to this child as his dad Bill was to him.

No one knew what the future held for mankind and bringing a child into the world was a scary proposition, even before the bright light and the big swoosh, but they were bound and determined to raise their child with all the love they could and teach their baby to know and love Jesus Christ.

Each day, an hour would be allocated by those under eighteen toward chopping wood for the winter. The few cabins that did not have a fireplace or pot belly stove initially now had a wood-burning stove inside, thanks to Burt.

It was amazing all the things they had at their disposal on the boy scout ranch, and the quartermaster building was the source of most of it. Anything and everything you could imagine could be found there, and if you couldn't find what you were looking for there, it would most likely be in the junk graveyard at the outer perimeter of the camp.

Years and years of construction project materials would end up there, along with everything else that was not useful at some point, sometimes proving to be a treasure trove for the most unusual projects.

Then there was the barn next to Henry Williams's house, which was another cornucopia of odds and ends.

Henry Williams's wife made a dramatic recovery from her infection after a couple of weeks on penicillin, and was back up to snuff, spending most of her time with the women on the ranch, so much so, that she and Henry made a second home of one of the leftover cabins on the ranch, making them closer and more a part of the community that had been created.

The kids started to become very creative, hosting elaborate skits at night around the campfire, entertaining the adults, except the one night they elected to do a skit on the hunters eating people, which did not go over as well as they had hoped.

For some, it was all too real, such as Viv, Mark, Kate, Julie, Jack, Rocky, and Brian, as they had firsthand experience with them in the old neighborhood.

Others in camp had experience with them as well, but all kept their experiences close to the vest. They didn't want to dwell on the evil they had witnessed, which kept it alive for them, so they instead concentrated on how good it was not to be afraid anymore and not have to constantly look over their shoulders.

This was the newfound freedom they found in Peaceful Valley.

Instead of living in a populated place before the blast, where there could be up to 200,000 people living within a square mile, they were now in a place where there had only been just a few people in every square mile, with folks sometimes miles apart from each other.

The downside of all of this was their new ambivalence toward people in general unless you were one of them.

They changed with the times because the times demanded it.

It had been a while since the bus had been driven, so they decided it was time to make a supply run. The nearest Walmart other than the one in Elizabeth was in Monument, so they decided to make the thirty-mile drive there. The fuel tank still showed between three-quarters full and full, so they still had miles to go before they would need to think about refueling, but they took fifteen cans with them in case they ran up on a semi-truck on their way.

Bill, Mark, Max, Bob Hawkins, Burt, and Henry were the ones who decided to make the trip. Viv and another woman in camp went as well because they had a laundry list of things needed for the camp, along with stuff the women needed specifically.

The big thing on the list for Viv was a crib, bassinet, diapers, and baby clothes.

After all, she was going to be a grandmother soon, and her grandbaby would not want for anything. She also had formula on the back of her mind in case Kate would not be able to breastfeed, but it would depend on if there was an expiration date, even on the powdered stuff.

All the men were strapped as well, not familiar with the territory they were headed into.

Should they run into any kind of trouble, they would have more than enough firepower to take care of the situation.

It was so different now in these times because whatever direction they went, it felt like they were the only ones in the world left alive, and to a degree, that was true.

Mostly everyone was dead now, and it was up to them to keep civilization alive.

Mark and Kate were doing their part, and if all went well, there would be more children on the way.

Before they left, Burt opened up the trading post to let each of the kids grab a candy bar, something they had not had in over a year, much to their delight.

It felt amazing to the two women on the bus to feel air conditioning, reminding them of days gone by.

The best way for them to get where they were going was to travel north a mile to Kiowa Creek Road, then go south, traveling on the back roads, as there was no straight-line route to get there, but after forty-five minutes, they pulled up to the front of the Walmart along Interstate 25.

They noticed a couple of semis parked in the back by the loading dock, so after dropping off the women, along with Mark, Bob, Burt, and Henry, Bill and Max drove around to the back to siphon fuel for the bus.

Viv was like a kid in a candy store, picking out the baby clothes, while the other woman started filling up carts with the stuff on their list.

The men found a lot of canned goods that hadn't been taken, plus a bunch of bottled water out front and in the back of the store. When someone filled up a cart, they would bring it to the front of the store for loading into the bus, then grab another cart and begin the process all over again.

Bill and Max found all the fuel they needed in the semis parked out in the back and the semis would continue to be a fuel source for the next time. Each of the semis had two 100-gallon tanks that were both practically full, and they only needed fifty gallons to fill the 250-gallon tank on the bus, leaving them a couple of five-gallon cans to take back with them to Peaceful Valley.

When they pulled back up to the front of the store, they were amazed at all the carts waiting for them to be loaded onto the bus. This was a very profitable supply run for them, and they were able to procure just about everything on the list and then some.

When the shoppers inside came to the front of the store with more full carts, they all agreed they had gotten everything they came for and began to help Bill and Max load the bus, and that's when they heard the sound of engines.

"What is that?" asked Max, who heard them first.

They all stopped what they were doing, and they all could hear the engines far off in the distance, getting louder with each passing minute.

After five minutes, the cause of the sound came into view.

Traveling south on I-25 was a caravan of military vehicles, fifteen in all, creating excitement among the group.

"It's the army! Finally, things are on the right track!" yelled Bob.

"Hold up. There are no American markings on them other than the one in front. Look closely!" yelled Bill.

Immediately their excitement turned to fear, as they could now see Chinese flags displayed on the side doors of the vehicles, meaning that these were Chinese Army and not American.

The MRAP upfront was American, but all the rest following were Chinese.

"They must be heading to Fort Carson," said Henry. "Son of a bitch. It's happening."

"What's happening?" said Max.

"The Chinese are here in country, which could mean they're here to carve out a piece of America." answered Henry.

"You don't know that for sure Henry. They could be here to help us. I wouldn't get yourself wrapped up in a tizzy over this, not yet anyway," said Bill.

"Chinese here to help us? That's a good one," said Henry. "I hope you're right."

They waited for the caravan to be down the highway and out of sight before loading anything more onto the bus. There was no telling what the intentions were of the Chinese, but it was better to be safe than sorry, not attract their attention.

Whether they were spotted by the caravan or not, their intent seemed to be a direct path south, and the only destination that made sense was Fort Carson, or maybe even NORAD.

After everything was loaded, they all got back on the bus and headed back from where they came. The discussion on the way back was tense, laced with worry and angst.

Though it seemed that America would never recover and be what it once was, the thought of being under Chinese rule was horrifying to anyone that understood what that represented.

China is a communist country that impedes and suppresses the progress of its people and is antithetical to anything American, with freedom taking a back seat to the will of the Chinese government.

If the Chinese were on American soil to exploit its resources, it would only be a matter of time before their reach would extend to Peaceful Valley and its inhabitants, and there would be nothing they could do about it.

"I imagine we've got lots of time before we have to worry about them if their intentions are not good, but we have to ask ourselves what we can do about it if they aren't," said Burt.

"We're just a ragtag bunch of families and no match for an army. That's for sure"

Burt's words were sobering because they were the truth.

They had children to consider, and a firefight would only end up getting all of them killed.

At this point, however, it would be putting the cart before the horse adopting the mindset they needed to prepare for battle, as no one knew what their intent was.

To remedy that, Burt would crank up his emergency radio when they got back to camp, to see if there was any news about this or anything else.

They had not listened to the radio for a while because it was always the same abbreviated nonsense that help was on the way, but it would be months or years before it got to you.

"I almost forgot. We brought a HAM radio and a car battery with us. It should still have enough juice in it to hook up the radio. Maybe we can find out what's going on in the area?" said Bill.

Burt and Henry's ears perked up at that suggestion, giving them a little hope for some information to guide what the residents of Peaceful Valley should do next.

When they arrived back at camp, there was no shortage of helpers to unload the bus, and Viv had not lost her excitement at setting up the crib and bassinet in Mark and Kate's cabin, bringing some normalcy back into her mentally interrupted routine.

Burt, Henry, and Bill were on Burt's veranda, listening for any news regarding what was happening in America, and what they heard was not encouraging.

The announcement acknowledged the presence of Chinese troops on American soil, under the pretense of humanitarian aid, but also spoke of martial law being imposed in the cities of Los Angeles, Portland, San Diego, and Seattle, where the Chinese army had taken control of the few people left alive, monitoring their whereabouts and actions to better facilitate aid, which sounded like total bullshit on its face. The fact that an American emergency airwave would be reporting on this as business as usual had the smell of a takeover.

"This doesn't sound like they are here to help," said Henry.

Burt was up on the roof wiring his antenna to the HAM radio while Bill was connecting the radio to the car battery.

Just as Burt had gotten off the roof, Bill had turned on the radio and was shuffling through the dial to find a transmission and came upon a conversation being had.

"The caravan turned off the freeway at Manitou Springs, so I imagine they're heading up to NORAD. Have no idea what they'd want up there, unless they're up to no good" the voice said over the radio.

"This is Bill, talking to you from Monument," said Bill, not wanting to give their location in case others with ill intent were listing in.

"We saw the caravan going south your way, just past Walmart. Could you make out anything in particular about the trucks you saw?".

"Just that they were Chinese, and they seemed to have a lot of soldiers riding in them," said the voice. "Fort Carson is a ghost town, so I didn't think they'd be going there. None of this looks good."

Bill looked over to Henry and Burt, shaking his head in disbelief at what he was hearing.

"I don't see that we can or should do anything different than what we are doing now, and I don't see any good that can come from us alarming the rest of the people here. What do you guys think?" asked Bill.

"I tend to agree with you, Bill. There's nothing we can do except work ourselves into a lather about something that may not happen. We still don't know what's going on, and we may not until it happens, whatever that might be. For all we know, we might fly totally under their radar, and we might not be an issue for them. I think our goal must be the same as it was yesterday, to stay alive and live our lives the best way we know how, starting from scratch" said Burt, with Henry nodding his head in agreement.

What else could they do?

To the best of their knowledge, no one knew of their existence, and the best way to move forward would be to remain as discreet as possible, doing exactly what they had been doing.

From the main road, you'd never know anyone was alive on the property because nothing started until you got a mile back on the road into the trees. The first sign of civilization was the lake and the boathouse, where only the garden, the pumping apparatus for the garden, and the showers were visible, and it was another mile before you hit the living quarters and the dining hall.

You would have to be actively looking for signs of life, which was the beauty of being at Peaceful Valley, which brought so much comfort to the people living there. It was like living in a hidden canyon of trees.

They decided that any campfires should be behind the dining hall, instead of being in the front where they had previously been, taking extra precaution not to be seen from the road, and all swimming in the lake would be done only with a couple of adults present, during scheduled hours of the day.

In case any vehicles were seen coming up the dirt road, the children could be corralled out of the lake, and everyone could make their escape and run through the trees to the rest of the population.

The trick would be to make these changes without raising suspicions as to why.

They all agreed that life there must not change for any of the residents. The last thing they wanted was for people to live in fear, just as they had done after the hunters had made their attack on them at New Hope.

That night, Burt had once again brought out candy bars from the Trading Post for the kids after dinner. He knew a secret, and that was they had cases of candy bars locked away, to be sold to the scouts camping there that never came.

If he passed them out only occasionally, he could make them last all summer, and maybe through next summer as well.

"I saw a whole herd of elk this morning by the chapel while I was sweeping off the benches for the next service this Sunday," said Jack to Burt as they sat around the fire after dinner drinking coffee.

"Really? Did you hear that fellas?" said Burt.

"How many were there?" asked Bob Hawkins.

"Ten or eleven for sure, maybe more. There were two bulls, a bunch of cows, and some young ones," said Jack.

"I think we should make our way over there first thing in the morning. Would be nice to bag one of them this time of year. They usually don't come around until the beginning of fall. Does anyone want to join me?" asked Burt.

Bob Hawkins and Jim Eberle said they'd go, so the three of them got up before sunrise the next morning and walked to the chapel on the edge of Peaceful Valley and sat sporadically throughout the trees surrounding it, each of them hoping to be the one that fired off the kill shot.

EIGHT

The Way Things Are Now

When America ceased to exist on the global stage, the world went into a global recession, and hyperinflation was one of the results.

Alaska and Hawaii suffered catastrophically, as the dollar lost all of its worth overnight.

The world's economy was based on the U.S. dollar, with it being the world's reserve currency. With America no longer existing on a banking level, it made the Chinese yuan the new American dollar.

China lost half a trillion dollars a year due to lost exports to America.

The euro came close to crumbling, and the yen did not fare much better than China, losing a lot of its exports to the U.S. as well.

All the countries around the world being propped up by the American government no longer had billions of dollars thrown their way, severely hampering their economies as well.

Iran and North Korea suffered the most, having crippling sanctions from the rest of the world for their part, having been behind the demise of America.

China, who had once seen to it that North Korea got everything it needed, suddenly turned its back on them, partly for what they had done to the world's economy, but also because their economy was suffering greatly. They could no longer afford to be so generous with their southern neighbor.

South Korea and Japan formed an alliance with the European Union, and they all relied heavily upon each other for the importing of goods, and some companies did quite well filling the vacuum, but overall, the world was suffering.

Canada and Mexico, both of which were also affected by the EMP, were trying to rebuild the infrastructures they had lost, and though their people were working, they had no reserves left to thrive, barely keeping their governments afloat, thereby creating an unsustainable tax burden on its constituents to keep their doors open for business.

The one country least affected was Russia, selling their oil through their pipeline to Germany, and now selling even more to make up for what America had provided.

The lower forty-eight of the United States was prime fertile ground for the taking and had America not had its missile silos hardened against an EMP attack, China and Russia both would have moved in a long time ago to take their piece of the pie.

The U.S. military was nowhere near its capability as it once was, and their active reserve force was nonexistent, but still having the capability to nuke either of these countries kept them at bay, until now.

The Chinese were on a reconnaissance mission, exercising their power where they could, but for the most part, they were trying to find a way to breach America's inner sanctum, taking the U.S from within.

Russia also had reconnaissance missions underway, but not to the degree that China had. They were aware of each other's intent and were playing a chess game with each other, to see who would be able to get the upper hand first.

Whoever took control of America's resources would be the true superpower of the world, and the number one resource China was interested in was oil, which meant their primary focus was on North Dakota, Wyoming, and Colorado.

China is the number one importer of oil, and with the ability to come up with their own, it would make them rich beyond their wildest dreams, making up for all the lost revenue from exports to the U.S., putting them on top to be the number one supplier of oil in the world.

All the drilling was in place, so all they would need to do is retrofit the power plants and electrical infrastructure in the areas where drilling occurred, and they could drill their own oil.

It would be significantly cheaper than if they had to start from scratch, and the timeframe would be cut in half. All they would have to do was pick up the pieces that America had left behind.

Russia's plans were a bit more nefarious, as they were eyeballing Alaska as a potential source for oil, even though Alaska was up and running, and technically still part of the United States.

Being just a hop, skip, and a jump from Russia, with Alaska once owned by them, they had designs on taking over the state and making it once again part of their country and their economy. Four of America's military branches had bases in Alaska, so it would be an act of war should Russia make that move, and they severely outmanned and outgunned the United States as far as Alaska was concerned. A real response from the U.S. would require help from their naval ships, now all stationed in Hawaii, and limited air support from D.C., but in the end, it would not take much for Russia to overtake Alaska.

The Chinese were in Colorado for several reasons, mostly to do reconnaissance on the military bases there, but also to see if there was any infrastructure up and running, and to inspect the drilling wells that could be put into operation.

Their presence was mainly in North Dakota because that's where the bulk of the oil was, and should they begin to extract oil from the ground, it would be there they would begin.

Kate was in the sixth month of her pregnancy, and the baby was expected to show up in late September or early October. Everything that could be done to prepare had been done, and the camp was super excited to have a new member on the way.

Their cabin was full of baby furniture, diapers, baby clothes, and blankets.

For all anyone knew, this could be the last baby born on Earth, and everyone was treating it that way.

Henry and his wife had a rocking chair in their living room, and they gave it to Kate as a gift, thinking she would get a lot more use out of it, which she would.

The men had done an excellent job of keeping their secret regarding the presence of the Chinese Army in Colorado, enabling the camp to live its best days without the worry of the unknown effect it would have on them down the road.

The freedom of the children to frolic and play was the biggest benefit, allowing them to be kids, not having to grow up before their time and take on the worries of the world.

It was a balancing act between that and keeping them vigilant, but the men had their backs, so no harm would come to them if they had anything to say about it.

Jack had been busy that summer, treating toothaches and sunburns the best he could. Luck had been on their side so far, keeping broken bones and disease away from the camp, but he knew eventually something more serious that required hospitalization would come before him, and he would need the help of all the adults in camp to deal with it when it arose.

His faith in God had become so strong over the last year, he could not see anything coming his way that he could not handle, mostly because his faith had not yet been put to the test.

Brian and Rocky had grown closer than ever, living as brothers and sharing a bedroom, staying with Bill and Viv, spending most of their time fishing on a boat on the lake, or hunting ground squirrels with slingshots.

Schooling was a sketchy thing facilitated by some of the women in the camp, making sure the kids didn't grow up illiterate and knew their ABCs, teaching them to read and write the old school way, using pen and paper, not computers and smartphones.

They also learned basic rudimentary math skills, like addition, subtraction, multiplication, and division.

It was a good thing that some of the adults still remembered how to do these things, as most had lost their abilities because of calculators.

In so many ways, the world had gone back to the way it was before the electronic revolution changed the way people learned, and this was how America was built.

Burt and Henry had decided to take on the project of rewiring an old generator they had in the barn over at Scott's place, hoping to get it up and running to provide electricity where they believed it would come in handy the most.

There was plenty of gasoline on the ranch because of all the ranch vehicles, and it would be some time before they would need to look for other gasoline sources off the ranch, so if they were successful in rebuilding the generator, they had plenty of fuel in house to run it.

Bill was sad for his son Brian, as he would not be able to follow in the footsteps of his older brother, becoming an Eagle Scout.

Sure, he could do all the same things that Mark did, and it could be documented, and he could even have a uniform with an Eagle badge sewn onto it, but it wouldn't be the same and there would be no pomp and circumstance around it like there was for Mark when he received his, and there would be no troop to support and celebrate him.

Bill had spent a lot of time with Mark on his scouting journey, and it created a bond with him. He wanted Brian to have the same experience with him, but such would not be the case, so Bill would have to find other ways to create that bond with his son.

Julie Price was beginning to find her place in this new world, but the process had been agonizingly slow for her.

Kate's pregnancy had helped a lot, getting her ready for childbirth, teaching her, and Mark the Lamaze Method of childbirth, as there would be no epidural or nitrous oxide to help her with the pain.

This got Julie out of her head, but at the same time, she thought of her husband being able to assist in the process, reminding her that he was not around anymore. The only thing that would truly heal Julie and allow her to move on with her life was time, time to grieve, and time to figure out that she had to move on to survive, that life goes on no matter how hard the road becomes.

Whiskers was a great comfort to her, and she became dependent on the cat the same way he had become dependent on her.

Thank God for Whiskers.

Viv wished she could be more supportive of Julie, wishing she could give Julie all the time she needed, but she had a family that needed her too, and so the majority of Viv's time was spent between her husband, her son Brian, and her daughter-in-law's preparation for childbirth, leaving the rest for Julie and virtually none for herself.

This was typical of Vivian Jenkins and why everyone that knew her loved her.

She could always be counted on to be the rock in the stream of humanity that flowed throughout the residents of Peaceful Valley.

It was just after 2:00 in the afternoon when everyone in the camp heard the jets in the sky coming from the west. It was a sound they had not heard since everything began, and with the quiet they had become accustomed to, it felt like thunder precursing an oncoming storm ready to pummel them below.

It was a magnificent sight to behold, as the formation of seven jets flew overhead, leaving a jetstream behind them as if to say they had arrived and were there to stay.

After the jets passed overhead and trailed off into the quiet of the afternoon, a new sound was approaching, but this sound was different. It sounded closer and they could feel its vibration. By this time, everyone else in the camp gathered by the bunk house, with Bill and Burt instructing everyone to get under the trees or inside of a building, to get out of sight of what was coming, which was a caravan of military helicopters flying super low, approaching the camp.

These were not our helicopters. They were Chinese, and there were many of them, flying in formation. Bill counted seventeen of them as they flew overhead, and he was pretty sure none of the camp patrons were spotted, though he couldn't be sure.

These came as no surprise to the men and women that had made the last trip to Walmart, but to everyone else, it was a mixture of wonder, excitement, and fear.

They passed overhead and out of sight just as quickly as they appeared, obviously on their way to parts unknown, not appearing to slow down to inspect what was below them or even know they were over a camp.

When it became apparent they had seen the last of their flying intruders, the residents came out from hiding, filled with more questions than answers, and the few had to admit that the jig was up, that something significant was underfoot in their home state, as this was not the first time they had been seen in the area.

"What in the hell are the Chinese doing on American soil, and where is our military to engage with them?" asked one of the men in the crowd.

No one had an answer for him, but instead wild speculation that had no root in reality.

None of them were military men, and no one knew how bad things were in America. They had no idea what was up and running and what wasn't.

"We should all keep our ears tuned to our surroundings. I don't think they saw us, and even if they did, I highly doubt we would be on their radar, but better to be safe than sorry. We didn't want to spook any of you and saw no value in it, so we elected to keep them to ourselves. Now you know, so there's no point in keeping it from you. I have no idea why they are here, but I don't think it's because they are here to help.

If they start coming down the back roads to where we are, then we might have something to worry about, but as it stands now, I think we are OK.

Most of you know I worked for the Department of Agriculture, and I was stationed in D.C. when all of this happened. What many of you don't know is how I got to Denver from there. There is an underground rail system a mile below, with a train connecting different parts of the U.S.

One of those connecting stations is underneath DIA, where there is a massive underground military installation. The thing I'm most concerned with is what the status of that base is now. It is not encouraging to see foreign countries on our land with no presence of our military. Hell, we haven't seen any of our guys other than the MRAP that was leading the caravan a couple of weeks ago.

Are they here to take over America? If so, why would they be here instead of New York City, Chicago, or especially Los Angeles, which would be closest to them? Taking over America doesn't seem like something any country, even China, would want to do, especially when you consider how much land mass China has. Though they have over a billion people, most of their country is populated the way ours is, with most in the urban and coastal areas.

My suspicion is they are here for another reason entirely, and that would be to exploit our resources, and what does Colorado have that they would want? Though there's more of it in other states, I think it has to be oil. NORAD is also here, so maybe they are trying to infiltrate that. The truth is, it could be several things, and none of them have anything to do with us, and there's nothing that we are getting in their way of, so why should we be paranoid or overly concerned about them as long as they are not bothering us?" said Bill.

"If anything, they might be more concerned about us if they knew of our presence. I think if we remain as discreet and incognito as we can, we won't be having any dealings with them. That's my opinion. Let's face the facts. America as we knew it is gone, and there is nothing we can do about that. Someone was eventually going to come in here and take what is left of a dead nation. Even our allies would do the same. I'd be surprised if there are even a million people left alive."

Though everyone had their own opinions of the state of America, Bill's words were sobering and had the ring of truth to them, but to hear their thoughts the way Bill had spoken them out loud had a sickening sadness attached to them, forcing every one of these people to acknowledge that the voices in their heads were real and not the boogeyman whispering to them from the dark recesses of the closet.

In the back of their minds, they had hoped and prayed that someone would eventually come to their rescue, making this nightmare of frontier living come to an end.

They wanted to be able to drive to a McDonald's again and order a Big Mac with large fries, those tasty succulent oil-soaked fries that still lived on in their memories of a more self-indulgent time or make a mad dash to the local 7-Eleven to get that Cherry Slurpee they'd been craving for most of the day.

Those were the days my friend.

We thought they'd never end…but they did, and they were never coming back.

Not ever. Not in this lifetime.

The free world had always seen America as the shining city on a hill, just as Ronald Reagan had described it so many years ago, and now it was gone from them, with no other country to take its place.

Now the free world would have to contend with the likes of China, Russia, Cuba, North Korea, and Iran on their own, using their limited resources to quell the dictatorships they represented, keeping them from knocking on their doors and selling their wares to their dumbed-down constituencies, not knowing or remembering the mistakes of the past, destined to repeat them.

Call it ignorance or stupidity, there was no country left in the world with the fortitude to smack down what had grown to be a disease within themselves, soon to be revealed as a bandage ripped off of the skin revealing a gaping wound.

Bleeding out would be a blessing, but they would choose to die a slow death, leaving the most diseased to pick up what is left in the world they created.

NINE

Mandy Sigler

Mandy Sigler had survived thus far, making it a whole month without her father, mother, and her brother. When the General and his men came back that night without her father and brother and shot her mother, her world ceased and life lost all meaning, but she still had the desire to live.

After spending two days up in her bedroom crying her eyes out, she finally made her way out of the bedroom and out of the house because the smell of the dead general and his men were becoming unbearable.

She went through all the homes in her general vicinity and was able to survive on bottles of water and assorted cans of food and crackers she had found, sleeping in different beds every night. There was no way she was going back into her home.

All the homes she had gone into were empty, as her father and brother had killed everyone to put meat on the grill, so she had her pick of places to lay her head at night.

Of the four family members, she was the one that almost starved to death because she could not acquire a taste for human flesh like the others had, no matter how hungry she became, so for months after the blast, she lived on pork and beans and whatever else came in a can while the others feasted on human flesh.

In one of the homes she entered, there was a girl she knew from high school that lived there but ended up on the family's grill. They both shared the same pants size, so she was able to find an unworn pair of pants and a t-shirt to wear, enabling her to change her clothes out of the ones she had been wearing for close to a month.

Mandy had just turned nineteen, and a year earlier had just graduated from high school before the blast. She had become one of the first girl Eagle Scouts in America since the Boy Scouts started allowing girls, which was a testament to her resourcefulness.

She knew how to survive, and she was racking her food-starved brain on what her next move would be. She kept flashing on the summer camps she had been a part of in the past, thinking of Peaceful Valley.

She wondered if anyone else was still alive there, knowing that the camp would have had people there setting up for the summer sessions. She knew they had well water and she also knew there would be a ton of food there as well, and if she could make it there, she knew she had a better chance of surviving, but the camp was so far away, probably a good fifty miles from where she was.

She also knew that her father could not have been the only one hunting human beings for food, as the General and his men did as well, so there must be more of his kind out there somewhere, and it would be her job to avoid them at all costs.

What Mandy didn't know was almost everyone was dead, including the hunters, because the hunters eventually became the hunted, as their food sources were running extremely low after killing everyone else off, with the others dying of natural causes.

After weeks of indecision, she decided that she could not live in Highlands Ranch anymore, and if she didn't make a move regardless of how dangerous it would be to expose herself, she would surely starve or die of dehydration.

In one of the homes that she had been in, she had seen a beautiful bicycle that would make the trip to Peaceful Valley, so she decided to pack a backpack with as many bottles of water and food that she could find, along with a sleeping bag, and load everything on to the bike and peddle her ass to Peaceful Valley.

This meant she would have to go back to her house one last time to get her backpack, sleeping bag, and other things she would need for the trip. She also knew that the General's car was parked out front, and she thought about taking it instead of a bike, but it was a stick shift, and she had no idea how to drive one.

The smell of the bodies was now overwhelming, but she had to go inside up to her bedroom to get a few things, holding a rag up to her nose and mouth, which did little to block the stench.

After getting the things out of her room, she took one last look at her bedroom, scanned the living room to see the rotting bodies of the General and his men, and had she looked out of the backdoor into the backyard, she would have seen her mother's rotting head and other body parts that had not been eaten.

She then went into the garage to retrieve her backpack and sleeping bag, tied them onto the bike, and headed back to the last house she'd been occupying. After arriving there, she began a house-to-house search with her backpack, filling it up with bottles of water, sodas, anything she could drink, along with any cans of food, and managed to think about grabbing a can opener out of one of the kitchens as well.

If she didn't make it, at least she would die trying to survive, which sounded a whole lot better than doing nothing at all.

It was summertime now, and the days were getting hotter under the Colorado sun, so she would leave at sunup, ride until noon, then find a place along the way that had shade and rest until the late afternoon, then ride again until sundown and rest again until the following morning.

She figured she might be able to ride twenty to twenty-five miles a day, giving her a two- day arrival time to the scout ranch.

She would also pack her industrial-size pepper spray and scout knife in case bad people tried to get her along the way.

It never occurred to her that there might be bad people waiting for her at the scout ranch, or people there in general. She had visions of being all alone there, thinking no one there would still be alive.

After preparing the bike for her departure, tying everything but the backpack down, she went into the house and up to the second floor, and opened all the windows to get a cross current of air flowing throughout the house to cool it down, enabling her to sleep as peacefully as she could throughout the night.

So many things raced through her mind as she laid down to sleep for the last time in her neighborhood, hoping to get enough rest to make the arduous trip first thing in the morning.

The neighborhood was all that she knew, as she had grown up there since birth.

※※※

Jack had been rearranging his medicines, taking inventory of what he had, but more importantly what he didn't have.

Other than ibuprofen and acetaminophen, he had absolutely nothing for pain, and this would not do if someone in the camp was in extreme distress over the pain they were having.

He began to make a list of things he needed to put on the shelves in the Health Lodge, such as Oxycodone, Hydrocodone, Oxycontin, Demerol, Morphine, Dilaudid, and Lidocaine for toothaches, along with an assortment of hypodermic syringes to administer the pain relief.

He had been studying his PDR to bone up on dosages, when to and when not to administer pain relief, and which pain reliefs to prescribe upon the maladies.

He also needed a bigger assortment of bandages, tape, and other items found in an emergency room or a paramedic's first aid kit.

He also needed a defibrillator, if he could find one in working condition, but that was more a pie-in-the-sky wish than anything based on reality.

To find one that had not been fried would be a miracle.

The camp was contemplating a run to Walmart again for supplies, so he would make sure he was on the bus as well to hit up the pharmacy in the store.

Hopefully, it had not been ransacked by marauding drug addicts, leaving the shelves bare.

Jack had also reflected on their good fortune that no one was a diabetic, meaning they would have died long ago with no insulin to keep them alive.

"Hey, Jack. What are you doing?" asked Rocky as he walked inside the Health Lodge.

"Nothing little brother. Just making a list of things I need to have if someone gets really sick" Jack answered. "How's mom doing?"

"She's lying down in her bed in the dining hall, playing with Whiskers. She sure loves that cat" Rocky said.

"Yes, she does indeed. It's a good thing Mark brought him over from Mr. Parsons's house. She needed something to keep her mind off Dad, that's for sure," said Jack.

"Do you miss him, Jack? I sure do" asked Rocky. Tears were starting to well up in his eyes.

Jack stopped what he was doing and asked Rocky to sit down next to him, then put his arm around him.

"Yes, Rocky. I miss him very much. He was always there when I needed to talk to him about something. I remember once when I was dating a girl in high school, and I asked him about a lot of things, things like when should I have sex, stuff like that. He was awesome to talk to about it, and he set me straight on some things, mostly on what would I do if I got a girl pregnant. It wasn't something I had ever considered, but after talking with him about it, it changed my whole attitude.

The last thing I wanted to do was be a father, especially when I was still in high school.

I decided right then and there that I would stay a virgin until I was married to someone I loved. It really put things in perspective for me" Jack said. "Those conversations are what I miss the most about him."

"I see Brian talking with his dad all the time about all kinds of things. Brian always goes to him to ask how to do something or find out what his dad knows about this or that. I wish I could do that" said Rocky.

"You can Rocky. You can go to him and ask him those same things, just as if he were Dad. He's not your dad, but you can still ask him anything you would have asked Dad. Bill loves you and wants the best for you, just like he wants the best for Brian. You can also ask me. I don't know as much as Bill does, but I know about a lot of things. You'd be surprised," said Jack. "Dad is watching over us right now in heaven, and he loves all of us. He knows you miss him, Rocky. Believe me, he knows."

Rocky was looking to be comforted and Jack did not disappoint. His older brother was still there for him, and he knew he could depend on him when things felt empty to him, just as they did at that moment.

❧❧

Mandy had ridden her bike about ten miles by noon the following morning, and if she had any doubts about the devastation of mankind, they were erased by the time she got to Parker, where she holed up under the awning of a store in the strip mall just off of Main Street.

All she saw on the way there were skeletons of the dead in every possible way, hunched over the wheel of the car they were driving, some laying on the side of the road, with a few even missing body parts.

It was horrific until it wasn't, as she became inured to seeing these things along the way as if seeing her neighbors being grilled on the family barbeque hadn't been enough.

Her dad had always been a good man, so it was a complete shock to see him barbequing the next-door neighbor that day, then watching him, her brother, and her mother eating the person at the dinner table.

She knew the lady next door as far back as she could remember.

They tried to get her to eat, telling her she had to if she wanted to survive, but she refused.

After a couple of days of not eating, her starvation got the best of her and she picked up an arm, but she couldn't go through with it, throwing it back down onto the dining room table. It was then that the family started ransacking other houses in the neighborhood for canned goods for her while they had no interest in normal food anymore, having acquired a taste for human flesh because nothing else would sate them.

She missed her dad and wondered whatever happened to him and her brother but was highly suspicious that the General and his men killed them since they were with them the last time she saw them.

Crying was something she did quite a lot of since the night her mother was murdered, and it was her tears that would lull her to sleep on that hot, late June afternoon, on the concrete walkway under the awning of the store.

Burt and Henry had done everything they could do to refurbish the generator they had begun working on, but nothing they did could make it run, mostly because they had no spark.

There were no unaffected spark plugs to be found on the ranch, so the project was mostly nothing more than something to keep them busy, which wasn't a bad thing entirely.

They were ready to make their run to Walmart, so Burt, Henry, Bill, and Bob Hawkins loaded up onto the bus, with Jack tagging along with two big empty backpacks waiting to be filled, looking to find his goldmine in the pharmacy department.

They traveled the same roads they had the first time, and all noticed not a single solitary thing had changed. Not one thing had moved, nor were there any signs of life in any direction they looked, and the town of Monument was no different.

They pulled up to the Walmart and Jack made a beeline to the pharmacy in the back of the store, while the others each had a shopping list to fill.

When Jack got to the pharmacy, he was dismayed to see that the metal screen had been pulled down and the door was locked, preventing him from entering.

He began kicking the door to the pharmacy, hoping to open it, then started to bull rush the door, but was not even making a dent in it.

After a few minutes, the other men in the store came running, wondering what all the noise was about. When they saw Jack's quandary, they began brainstorming ideas to get inside the pharmacy. The only thing good about this was the pharmacy should be fully stocked, having not been robbed of its contents.

Bob Hawkins had gone over to the hardware section to grab the biggest hammer he could find and a pry bar. He found a sledgehammer, which was better than he had hoped for, and a pry bar, which he brought both back to the pharmacy.

They tried the pry bar first on the door, but it had a deadbolt, so the pry bar didn't do much, then they tried the pry bar on the locks holding the metal screen in place, and those didn't budge either.

The only thing left to do was take the sledgehammer to the locking mechanism on the door. Bob Hawkins was the biggest man of the bunch, so he tried first, and after a few hefty whacks on the door lock, he was able to cave in the wall next to the lock enough to open the door, giving Jack entry.

Jack thanked them all profusely, then made his way inside for his shopping spree while the men went back to filling up their carts to complete their shopping lists.

Everything on Jack's list was in the pharmacy, including drugs he didn't have on the list, making their way into his backpacks with everything else. He took every bit of every drug he needed, along with every syringe he could find, a few thermometers he needed as well but forgot to put on the list, and every bandage, roll of tape, antiseptic, and anything else he thought he would need but hadn't thought of.

He completed his shopping by taking every bottle of ibuprofen and Tylenol off the shelves, keeping them in simple pain relievers for years to come.

He didn't want to have to make a second trip because of something he'd forgotten to include.

Burt was tasked with opening the five-gallon propane canister cage in front of the store, and he was able to get twenty-three canisters, which would come in handy. He also picked up as many lighters, stick matches, and lantern mantels he could put his hands on, and even a few heaters he could screw onto the propane canisters in case of an especially brutal winter.

Bill was asked to pick up any bottled water, juices, basically anything that could be drunk.

Bob oversaw any kind of food items, focusing on vegetables and desserts, but anything else that could be eaten.

Bill and Henry were assigned to winter clothing, but pickings were slim because at that time of year of the blast, it was late spring and there would be little to choose from, so they would have to go somewhere else later to find those items. They instead grabbed all the socks, boots, and shoes they could find, and grabbed more baby formula and baby food.

All in all, it was a good haul they took out of the Walmart, with plenty still left to grab at a later date, but the most important things they had gotten were the items Jack loaded up on from the pharmacy, making his health lodge more complete.

The last thing Jack ever wanted to do was dispense narcotics, but if he had to, at least he would have them at his disposal.

The other things that Jack wanted were Bibles, enough to give to every man, woman, and child in Peaceful Valley.

Those were the things sorely missing from his Sunday sermons.

Bill had also grabbed all the disposable razors in the store, along with all the shaving cream. All of their beards had become a thing of the past since arriving in New Hope and they continued to be cleanly shaven at Peaceful Valley, all of them except Bob Hawkins, who liked his full beard.

❧⁓⁓❧

Mandy woke up around four in the afternoon thirsty for water and she drank down a bottle from her backpack, ready for the next leg of her journey. She had a good four hours of daylight left to ride, so she hopped on her bike and headed south down Parker Road toward her turnoff at Franktown where she planned to spend the night, but she would have to make better time than the first leg of her trip, as she only had four hours of daylight to ride the same ten miles it had taken her to ride in six hours that morning.

The sun was beating down on her. Four in the afternoon was the hottest part of the day, but then it would rapidly cool down as the sun got closer to the horizon. She peddled on and was making good time, and every time she stopped to drink a bottle of her water, the sun had gone down more until it had gone down behind the mountains to her west, just as she was peddling up to her turnoff at Franktown.

She looked around at the corners of the intersection, trying to determine where would be the best place to bed down for the night. She decided on an old building that used to be a carpet store, so she walked her bike inside and began to look around.

There were rolls of new carpet everywhere she looked, so she picked out one that looked the most comfortable and laid on it as if it were a big comfortable bed, then sat upright to forage through her backpack to find something to eat and pulled out another bottle of water.

She was getting low on fluids, leaving only three more bottles of water and a couple of cans of soda, so she put the water back in her backpack and opted for the soda instead, thinking she'd need the water more on her bike ride tomorrow.

She'd drank six bottles of water that day already, so even with four bottles of water and a can of soda for the next day, she'd have to ration her intake of water tomorrow if she expected to make it to her destination.

Little did Mandy know, it was almost a year ago to the day when a boy scout had almost lost his life to a hunter that had come out of the very building she was inside of, but the scout managed to get away. Lucky for her the hunter was dead now.

TEN

The New Girl

The bus pulled into Peaceful Valley as if it were one of its stops in Elbert County, but instead of stopping on the road, it continued down the dirt road toward the trees a mile away. The first stop was the Health Lodge, where they dropped off Jack and his two full-to-the-brim backpacks.

The next stop was the quartermaster building, where they dropped off the propane canisters and other supplies, then finally to the dining hall where everything else was unloaded, then the bus was parked for the evening.

Elk stew was on the menu for that evening's meal, with lots of home-baked bread.

Bob Hawkins bagged the last elk, and he was a big one. They'd been having elk steaks for supper pretty regularly, so they thought they'd change it up a little and mix in some canned carrots and potatoes for a stew that night, much to the delight of the citizens of Peaceful Valley.

Some had the idea of calling their burg New Hope, like the old campsite they'd come from, but the majority thought Peaceful Valley was what it should stay named.

The name was fitting for where they were, and it was peaceful indeed.

"Bill, what do you say we have the boys sleepover in the dining hall tonight?" Viv said with a little coquettish smile on her face.

Bill couldn't help but grin, thanking God the old girl still had it in her.

"Sounds perfect. Tell them to get their bedding and head on over there" he answered.

The boys had no idea why they were asked to spend the night in the dining hall, but they were nonetheless excited to be spending the night in a new place. It would be like spending the night for the first time at a friend's house, but hopefully far enough away from Rocky's mom, otherwise, it would be like sleeping at home.

⟫⟫ᴧᴧ⟪⟪

Mandy made it through Elizabeth and into Kiowa by 1:30 that afternoon and found plenty of water in the local gas station that had been virtually untouched for over a year.

She drank her last bottle of water half an hour prior, so she was thankful she was able to find more and restocked her supply.

She had traveled almost forty miles in the last day and a half, and she was feeling it in her legs. She only had ten more miles to go before hitting the scout ranch, so she ate a can of tuna and a can of corn, then napped on the cool concrete in front of the gas station until about 3:30.

She woke up to a little terrier dog licking her face, startling her at first, not knowing if the dog would be a threat.

As soon as she shot up from her slumber, she could see that the dog was harmless.

She could also see that it was on the borderline of starvation, and probably dehydrated as well.

She found an old can that used to hold peanuts by the trash can, wiped it out, poured half a bottle of water into the can, and placed it on the concrete for the dog.

The dog could not drink it fast enough, so she poured the other half of the bottle into the can, and the can was empty again in a matter of seconds.

"Oh, I bet you haven't eaten for a while either, have you?" she said, as she was scratching the dog's ears, with the dog loving it.

It probably had not seen a human being for a very long time.

She opened a can of tuna and emptied it on the concrete next to the can of water, and before she had it all out of the can, it was already eaten, so she opened another one and he ate that up as well.

She walked into the gas station to see if they had any cans of dog food, and there was a can of Alpo on the bottom shelf.

She brought the dog food outside and emptied that onto the concrete as well, and the dog ate it like it was a steak dinner. It was obvious the dog had not had anything to eat or drink in days.

Mandy had probably just saved this dog's life, and whether she wanted it or not, the dog had decided to hitch his wagon to Mandy and would follow her wherever she went until the day he died, and she found that out when she got on her bike and began to ride down Elbert Road toward the scout camp.

She peddled at her normal pace and the dog galloped behind her and stayed with her, and then she would back off a bit, allowing him to catch up, then she would again pick up the pace, then she would slow down a bit once again.

This went on for a few miles until she stopped for water.

The dog was panting like crazy, but he wasn't going to allow her to leave him, and it was obvious to Mandy that he would run himself to death to follow her, so she decided she had a new friend and would pace herself to allow him to keep up with her.

She found a paper cup alongside the road and gave him some more water, and after resting for a few minutes, they continued at a much slower pace.

She figured she'd better give him a name, so she began to call him Andy, which rhymed with her name. Mandy and Andy. It felt good to not be alone anymore.

It was close to 5:00 in the afternoon as they rode by the Elbert City Limits sign just past the town gas station, and she knew they were only a few miles away, so her heart skipped a beat, not knowing what she'd be running up into, but it had to be better than what she'd known thus far.

As they went through town, they crested on top of the hill and stopped to take in the scenery, and there it was, Henry's ranch house nestled down to the left, which was the beginning of Peaceful Valley.

She knew Henry personally, as she was a big deal in scouts, especially with the Denver Area Council, her being one of the first girl Eagle Scouts in America.

She wondered if he was still alive and living in the house, but since it was getting dark soon, she figured she'd have to catch up with him at another time and continue down the road another mile to the main entrance of the camp, so her and Andy proceeded the last mile.

✋∧ℒ

Jack had put away all of the goodies he had gotten from Walmart, and he was super impressed with how the Health Lodge was looking now.

He had both cabinets with glass doors and shelves packed with medicines and pain relievers, separated by their designations, such as antibiotics, pain relief, narcotics, etc., with bandages and tapes on another shelf, and syringes separated by size and cc's

The only thing he needed now was a white coat to wear when seeing a patient, which he hoped would be few and far between.

One of the benefits of being such a small, cloistered community was there had been no flu going around, and very few colds.

Everyone, for the most part, was healthy and in good shape, except maybe his mother. She wasn't sick, but she wasn't in great shape either, but he'd take it as long as she didn't need any medicine or narcotics to survive.

The stew had been on the fire all afternoon and would be ready soon, and when it was, someone would ring the dinner bell hanging outside of the dining room, which was in earshot of everything in camp except the Forts, but everyone knew what time dinner every night was regardless of the dinner bell, so there were no excuses for missing a meal at Peaceful Valley.

But if you did, no one would go hungry.

Plates would be made for those that didn't show and put aside for them, and there was always plenty more than what people ate anyway.

Everyone was family now, and you didn't let a member of your family go to bed hungry.

At last count, including the two Venture scouts, Burt, Henry, and Henry's wife, there were thirty-nine people in the camp, with another one on the way, making it forty, so everyone sitting down for a meal together was a big operation, and was noisy.

The dining hall could accommodate up to 400 people, so thirty-nine, though it may have seemed like a lot, was a drop in the bucket and only filled a small fraction of the room, but when they all sat together while talking, laughing, and eating, it felt like a lot more people.

Jack would always lead the meal with prayer and thanks for the day, then everyone would dig in. Mealtimes were always the highlights of the day, not just because you were hungry, but because you craved human interaction. You wanted to know how your neighbors were doing, both physically and mentally.

You wanted them to be ok, and if they weren't, you wanted to help.

Whenever someone had a funny story to tell, someone always made them get up and tell it to everyone, so everyone would get the joke and laugh their faces off, or not, depending on the joke or the person's delivery, but most times it was not embarrassing for the joke teller and everyone had a good laugh, sometimes at the joke teller's expense.

"Damn, this stew is delicious," said Bob Hawkins as he reached for a big slice of homemade bread.

"Damn skippy," said Burt. "My compliments to the chef"

Mrs. Jennings was the cook that night and she was full to the brim with happiness that everyone seemed to like the stew. The ladies all helped in the kitchen with every meal, with one of them being the head cook, alternating amongst them, all sharing in all the duties during the different meals, but dinner time was always the biggest of the three meals of the day.

"Saw the Chinese again on I-25. They headed south this time. That's twice we've seen them in our last two trips to Walmart," said Henry. "I wonder if they're ever going to come back here in our neck of the woods. What do you think we ought to say to them if they stop by?" asked Henry.

"Get the hell out of here?" said Burt, and the whole hall started laughing, even the children.

"I wonder what they'd do if they saw us. I'm thinking they might not even acknowledge us. They might just drive right on by like we weren't even there. I mean, what would they say? Do they even speak English? Because we certainly don't speak Chinese!" offered Terry.

Terry then pretended to speak Chinese, and that caused an uproar of laughter, especially with the children as they spit up their Kool-Aid.

Mrs. Jennings stood up from one of the tables and commanded everyone's attention.

"I'm glad you all liked the stew tonight, but we have a special treat thanks to Vivian Jenkins. Vivian made a few fantastic cherry cobblers, and when everyone is done with their dinner, we will begin serving it," said Mrs. Jennings.

The crowd in the hall began to roar with applause, leaving Viv a little beet-faced from embarrassment. Nevertheless, she stood up and took a bow at the insistence of Bill.

Mandy was at the entrance of Peaceful Valley, with Andy wagging his tail standing next to her. Being the observant Eagle Scout that she was, she couldn't help but notice the fresh tire tracks from the bus, though she couldn't tell exactly what vehicle they were from, but she knew it was a big vehicle, nonetheless.

"Well, this is it, Andy," she said out loud. "We are either home or this is going to turn out to be a horrible mistake."

Andy was good with however it turned out to be because he had no particular place to go, so they began walking down the dirt road toward the trees, with the sun setting on their backs close to an hour ago, making everything twilight.

The first thing she passed was the empty horse corral to the left, remembering two summers ago when she attended a week at camp after the camp had been closed the summer before due to the pandemic. She had done a lot of riding that week, spending part of almost every day in the horse corrals, learning how to brush the horses and feed them, and of course ride them, working on her horsemanship merit badge.

The corral, which was at that time full of horses, used to be very clean and defined, with all the weeds pulled and no trash anywhere to be found.

Now it was overgrown with growth, and looked like a ghost town for horses, with no sign of life anywhere.

The troughs were empty of water and there wasn't a stick of hay.

It saddened her to think of whatever happened to the horses, as they had probably all died as everything else had.

She couldn't have known that a year ago the corral was full, but Burt and Henry had decided to cut them loose to fend for themselves, as there was no possible way they could feed and water them anymore.

After walking past the corral, she looked to her right up another dirt road and remembered if she walked the several or so miles to the end of it, it would be the back way to the chapel after passing the old skeet shooting range that had long since been replaced by the newer one on the northeast side of camp, miles away from where she was now, but she still had a good ¾ of a mile left before she even hit the meat of Peaceful Valley, which started past the beginning of the trees.

Mandy was tired, dog tired, and she barely had the energy to continue down the road, but she knew there would be food in the dining hall, and if she and Andy were going to eat something, she had to keep trudging the happy trail to destiny, her destiny being a meal, something to drink, a swim in the lake to clean herself, and then find a bunk somewhere to sleep for the night, because her last few nights of sleep involved concrete and a roll of carpet, leaving a lot to be desired in the sleep department.

Maybe it was nothing more than a little dog food and some water, but Andy seemed to have filled out a little since they first met that afternoon, and he was certainly a happy dog, mostly because he had found his new master in Mandy. Wherever she was going, so was he.

When they came up on the lake to their left, she almost took off all her clothes right then to run to the lake and jump in it, but she didn't as she needed to stay focused on her mission for food.

It was starting to get dark now, and there was no moon in sight up in the sky above her, meaning it would be especially dark in the kitchen of the dining hall.

She was now wondering how in the hell she'd be able to see anything in there. She had no matches or lighter, and this was presuming she would find a door unlocked for her to even get inside.

Had she gotten to camp an hour earlier, she would have had daylight to figure all these things out, so now she was thinking that maybe she should skip the dining hall and the swim altogether, and instead just find a bunk somewhere, where she could put her head down for the night and start fresh the next morning.

They stopped at a well water pump, and she began pumping water out of the ground, drinking from the spigot while supplying Andy his share down below.

The water was cool and refreshing, and she thanked her lucky stars that there was still fresh water to be had at Peaceful Valley.

She sat down in the dirt next to Andy while he was still drinking from the puddle of water she had created, and other than the sound of him drinking, the night was silent, and then she heard it.

In the distance, someone had laughed, then she heard a throng of laughter.

Was she hallucinating? Was there something in the well water?

Then she heard it again, and as her eyes became adjusted to the pitch-black darkness within the trees, she saw the faintest of light coming through the trees, from the general direction of where she thought the dining hall should be.

"Oh my God!" she whispered to herself. "There are people here."

She shot up from the ground like she'd been bit by something, and Andy shot straight up from drinking as well, then barked into the darkness as if someone was out there.

"Shoosh," said Mandy to the dog.

She began to walk the bicycle fast in the dark down the road, passing the camp headquarters building, then made a left at the trading post, and she could see the light from a propane lantern on the veranda of the dining hall up ahead.

She then came up on the bus, but she was then horrified to see the police cruiser parked next to it, the same car her dad had been driving.

She was confused by an RTD bus being parked there, but she continued up the steps to the dining hall, then began to walk around the veranda outside the dining hall to the door leading inside, and through the windows, she could see more people in one place than she had seen since everything began.

Still wearing her backpack, she and Andy walked inside, with Andy trotting up to the group first, and everything became dead silent.

Mandy was standing about twenty feet away from the tables, and everyone was in shock and just stared at her until Bill got up from his seat and walked over to her.

Mandy just stood there with half a smile and a look of bewilderment.

"Hello, young lady. What's your name and where did you come from" Bill asked in a whisper.

"Mandy. Mandy Sigler. I rode my bike here from Highlands Ranch" she said.

Bill then gently grabbed her arm and asked her to come to sit down, then sat her down where he had been sitting, taking her backpack off of her first.

"Someone get this young lady a big bowl of stew and some bread, along with some Kool-Aid and some of that cherry cobbler. I'll bet she's starving," said Bill. "Get the dog a bowl of stew too."

ELEVEN

Home Is Where
Your Heart Is

M andy was sitting at the table in disbelief, surrounded by people she didn't know, but someone did know her and recognized her immediately.

"Mandy? Mandy Sigler?" asked Mark, sitting directly across from her.

She looked at Mark and smiled, nodding her head in the affirmative.

"Mandy, it's Mark. Do you remember me?" he asked.

"I remember you. You were at my ceremony at the breakfast" she said, barely able to get the words out.

"Yes. I was there" Mark said, then turned to his dad and said "Dad, Mandy is one of the first girl Eagle Scouts in America. She's almost famous. They had a big breakfast for her at the Denver Area Council a few years ago. She and a girl from the east were the first ones ever. She made history."

Henry barely recognized her, but she remembered him.

No one had left the dining hall, and everyone was amazed at her presence, then the place erupted in questions for Mandy, overwhelming her just as Viv had placed a big bowl of venison stew in front of her, with some bread, and set another bowl of stew down behind her on the floor for Andy.

Kate brought over a big glass of Kool-Aid and a bowl of cherry cobbler.

"Hey, look everyone. Let's let the girl eat in peace. You will all have time to ask her questions later. Let me and Bob, Terry, Burt, Henry, and Vivian stay here with her so we can get her situated.

Jack, why don't you open up the Health Lodge so you can look her over when she's done here? We'll bring her over to you" said Bill, and everyone got up from where they were sitting, put their dinnerware in the big bucket for dirty dishes, and walked out of the dining hall.

Mandy was famished, as was Andy, and both dug into the food placed in front of them. Mandy couldn't believe her good fortune. She had prepared herself to not eat that night. Not only was she eating, but she was eating hot delicious food with what seemed to be good people, and she felt safe.

"Burt, do you think you can turn on the heat for the showers? This girl looks like she could use one" asked Viv.

"Sure thing. I'll go down and do it now" he responded, then walked out of the dining hall.

"I'll get you some clothes and a towel," she said to Mandy.

It didn't take long for Mandy to finish the bowl of stew, and she began eating the cherry cobbler as Bill spoke to her.

"So, you said you rode here from Highlands Ranch? That's a good forty-five to fifty miles from here. How long did it take you?" Bill asked.

"I left yesterday morning. All of my family is dead, and the only place I could think of going to was here. I never imagined there would be anyone else here, but I'm sure glad you are. I picked up Andy along the way. That's the name I gave him. He followed me here from Kiowa" she answered Bill.

"I imagine that Whiskers is upstairs having a fit right now with this dog inside. Where are we going to put her?' asked Vivian.

"There's a bed over in the headquarters building," said Henry. "It will be perfect for her and her dog. When she's done with Jack, we can walk her over there and get her situated."

"There are so many questions we want to ask of you, but they can wait until tomorrow. When you are done eating, we'll walk you over to the showers. I'll bet it's been a while since you've had a hot shower," said Bill.

"Oh my God. It's been over a year. I'm not even going to know how to act having clean hair and skin again" she answered Bill.

Just then Viv walked into the dining hall after retrieving some clothes and a towel for Mandy from Trail Boss, the cabin where she and Bill stayed.

"There's soap and shampoo in the shower stall. Here you go Honey" Viv said, placing the clothes next to her on the dining room table.

Burt had brought Brian and Rocky down to the lake with him so they could peddle the bike in the water to fill up the drum suspended just over the shower stall so Mandy would have hot water to shower with.

When Mandy indicated to her hosts that she'd had enough to eat, Henry and Bill escorted her through the trees with a propane lantern, with Bob and Terry saying goodnight, going back to their families.

"My bike is up against the bus, and it has my sleeping bag," said Mandy.

"You won't need your sleeping bag. The bed in headquarters is made. You'll be fine without it for tonight" Henry answered her.

The water was hot and ready for her shower. After showing her how to dispense the water by pulling the chain and warning her that the water would be hot, Burt walked out of the shower to the men and Andy waiting outside, allowing her the privacy that she needed.

"That girl is a trooper for sure. No wonder she's one of the first girl Eagle Scouts" said Burt.

"I imagine she's got a story to tell, that's for sure. The fact that she made it here in one piece should tell us a lot about what's going on out there now. There's probably hardly anyone left alive, including the hunters, otherwise, I suspect she wouldn't have made it. Someone would have shot her and eaten her," said Bill.

A few minutes later, Mandy walked out of the shower stall dressed in the clothes that Vivian brought her, clean as a whistle and smelling a whole lot better.

They then walked over to the Health Lodge to see Jack.

Jack was waiting for her, and was shocked at her new appearance, looking and smelling a whole lot better than when he first laid eyes on her in the dining hall.

"Why don't you sit down in this chair?" Jack said, pointing to a chair by his bed.

He first took out a stethoscope from the drawer and put it on her chest, not knowing what to listen for, but he had to play the part of the doctor.

"Do you have any pain anywhere?" he asked her.

"No. Just my legs are sore from all that peddling. Other than that, I'm fine. Really" Mandy said.

"I'm not a doctor. I just play one on TV" chuckled Jack, eliciting a laugh from Mandy as well.

"I'm the closest thing to a doctor here. I'm not even a pharmacist, but I run the pharmacy here. If you get sick, I've got medicine for it. If you get an infection or a toothache, I've got medicine for that as well, and God forbid you to get seriously hurt, I can at least control the pain with some serious narcotics. Just don't get hurt, that's my advice to you" Jack said.

"I also am the pseudo pastor here in camp too, so I expect to see you in the chapel on Sunday morning."

Something was going on with Jack. He was especially attentive to Mandy, more so than normal.

"I'll be in church. It will be nice to do that after not being able to for so long" she said.

"How old are you, if you don't mind me asking?" asked Jack.

"I'm nineteen. How old are you?" she asked.

"I'm twenty-two" Jack responded.

Mandy felt very comfortable with Jack and didn't mind answering any of his questions.

Jack was a little nervous around Mandy, mostly because she was drop-dead gorgeous in his eyes. There hadn't been a female in the camp close to his age since everything began, and for the first time in a while, he felt somewhat self-conscious about his appearance, checking his breath, smelling his armpits, and making sure his hair was somewhat combed in the mirror while attending to her.

"So, you and your dog will be spending the night next door at Headquarters. If you need anything, I stay right here in the Health Lodge. Don't hesitate to wake me up if you need anything" Jack said to her, looking her dead in the eye.

"Thank you, but I'm sure I'll be fine" she answered him, somewhat deflating Jack a tiny bit. "But it's nice to know that you are close by."

This made Jack feel a little better.

Jack was smitten. There was no denying it, and Bill and Henry could tell as much.

"I think she's good to go. Ok, Mandy, I'll see you tomorrow," said Jack.

Bill, Henry, Mandy, and Andy then walked next door over to Headquarters, and after Henry unlocked the door, they walked inside to a back room that served as a bedroom, and just as was promised, there was a fully made bed with pillow, ready for Mandy to get the first good night's sleep she'd had in a long while.

"I'm going to leave this lantern here with you in case you have to get up in the night to go to the bathroom. You know where the latrines are. I'll leave this here with you as well" said Henry, pulling out a lighter from his pocket and laying it on the table next to the lantern.

"We know where we are going, so we won't need the light. Good night" said Henry and Bill as they walked out of Headquarters.

Andy stayed with Mandy, sitting down at the foot of her bed, where he would remain the rest of the night. He was her dog now, and she would not be able to get rid of him if she wanted to.

After opening the window for the fresh night air to come into the room, she got under the sheets, removed the blanket, and laid her head on the musty pillow, thanking God above for getting her there safely to a new family of people, and for Andy, her new dog.

As she drifted away into the night, her thoughts were on Jack and how cute she thought he was.

Simultaneously, Jack was laying on his bed as well, thinking about Mandy and wondering how she survived this long, wanting to get to know her, know everything there was to know about her and thanking God for bringing her to Peaceful Valley.

The next morning the camp was abuzz, with everyone wanting to get to know Mandy and ask her questions about her bike ride and what she saw on the way.

She gave them all the answers to their questions the best she could, and she felt welcome in her new home.

She was eager to participate in the running of the camp and jumped in with both feet first in cooking, cleaning, and anything else the women needed her to help with, but her skills were being wasted, as she brought so much more to Peaceful Valley than her ability to do basic chores.

She was smart as a whip, and she had to be better than the boy Eagle Scouts because of the long-standing tradition that had been broken with the introduction of girls to Boy Scouts.

Her being one of the first was a statement, and it was heard loud and clear to those in scouting before the EMP, but then everything ceased, and she became just another survivor in a world of the dead.

At Peaceful Valley, she saw a re-emergence of her status, and she became well respected among the women and the men and was treated slightly differently than the rest of the women.

Mark and Mandy talked a great deal about things only other Eagle Scouts would understand, such as Henry, Bill, and Bob Hawkins, who was also an Eagle Scout in his day.

Sitting around a table outside of the dining hall right before lunchtime, Mandy, Mark, and Bill were chatting about the ground squirrel competition the younger boys were having, seeing who could get the most by the end of the day using only slingshots.

The conversation then shifted to her, with the men wanting to know more about her family, and how she survived and they did not, and that's when the tears finally started to flow again.

She began by telling them all the sordid details, about how her dad and brother began hunting and eating people and trying to get her to eat them as well, though she couldn't bring herself to do that.

She told them that he came into possession of a police cruiser very similar to the one parked by the bus, how he hooked up with some military men that were hunters too, and how they all went out one night, but her dad and brother never came back home, but the military men did, and they killed her mother and ate her.

Then she told of how the General killed the remaining soldier and then himself, leaving her all alone.

Bill's ears were cocked the more she described her dad and brother and asked to see a photo of her family if she had one, which she did in her wallet.

When she showed Bill and Mark the photo, Mark's jaw dropped, and Bill nodded to himself in the affirmative.

The man in the photo was the same man that took a bullet from Bill's gun into his brain by the fire at New Hope. He was the same man that chloroformed Julie Price by the latrine, and her brother was the same one that Bill had shot in the throat, killing him instantly.

He would never forget the faces of the men that prompted all of them to leave New Hope and settle into Peaceful Valley.

"This is a small world indeed," said Bill under his breath, but Mandy heard him and wanted to know why he said that.

Bill and Mark looked at each other, not quite knowing what to say to her, but Bill knew that the truth would come out sooner or later, so he elected to fill her in on what she wanted to know.

"Your dad and brother came to our camp at Cherry Creek Reservoir in the middle of the night, before we came here to Peaceful Valley. They came to kill some of us. Your dad attacked one of the women coming out of the latrine, and chloroformed her, knocking her out cold, to be given to your brother to stab and kill her.

They had come into camp driving a police cruiser and another car, an old classic. That was when I first laid eyes on your dad and brother, and they were looking at all of us like steaks on the grill.

They didn't stop or say hello, but instead just drove off.

We knew they had to be hunters and that they would be back, so we laid in wait for them every night until they showed back up, and we were ready for them" said Bill, not knowing how much he should tell her.

Mandy's jaw almost hit the table, then she asked, "What happened to my dad and my brother?"

Bill looked down at the table, trying to come up with the words.

"I'm sorry Mandy. I am." said Bill.

Mandy looked away from them off into the distance, trying to process what she was being told.

"You're right. It is a very small world" she said. "So that's what happened to them. That's why they never came back. I thought the General had them killed, but no, it was you. You killed them, but you know what? They deserved it for what they were trying to do, and I understand. I couldn't believe it when they started killing people. I could understand them eating the dead, but I couldn't wrap my head around my sweet, wonderful Dad killing people to eat them, but I guess you have to kill someone before you eat them, right? Everyone that knew my dad loved him. He would have given the shirt off his back to someone if they needed help. He would have been the last person anyone would have thought could do what he was doing, yet he began to eat people and acquired a taste for it. So did my brother and mom. I tried to, but just couldn't do it, even though I was starving. The weirdest part about it was that if they had their choice of human versus regular food, they'd only eat humans. It was like they changed into addicts. They were addicted to eating human meat.

I ate a lot of pork and beans, or anything else that came in a can.

I guess what I'm saying is they became something else, kind of like monsters in a sense.

I'm right now thanking God I'm here, with all of you, and there's no place else I'd rather be, even knowing what you just told me. I don't have any bad feelings for you. I don't. I know you did what you had to do" Mandy said. "I choose to remember my family the way they used to be, not what they became. I knew them differently than all of you did. I hope we can keep this conversation between us?"

Mark and Bill both agreed that they would not say a word to anyone.

Bill could not get over how magnanimous she sounded, but he believed her. He truly believed she understood what had to be done and was good with it.

"Thank you, Mandy. I can't tell you what it means to me to hear you say this" Bill said.

"You are going to like what we are having for lunch. Canned goods. Canned spaghetti" he said with a laugh, and she laughed too.

Jack arrived at the table just as they finished their discussion, and Mandy gave him a wink.

"Hi, Jack. Thanks for getting me all fixed up last night!" she said.

"I didn't do anything, but you are welcome just the same" Jack responded.

There was a definite spark between the two of them. The air became electric when the two were in each other's company.

Kate came over to the table next and sat down next to Mark, and she began rubbing his shoulder.

"Mandy, you haven't met my wife Kate," Mark said, and the two women shook hands.

"When is your baby due?" Mandy asked Kate.

"I think sometime in September, or maybe early October" Kate answered.

"Are you nervous?" Mandy asked.

"A little. I think I'm going to drink some whiskey when the time comes" Kate said, and they all started laughing, with Bill saying "Girl, you better drink a LOT of whiskey. Don't worry though, we'll be drinking whiskey with you!"

Mark didn't know what to say, but laughed just the same, mostly because he'd never seen his dad drunk, so that alone would be worth the price of admission.

Just then one of the women rang the dinner bell, which was loud as the day is long, and right over the head of everyone at the table. "Man, that thing is loud Mary. Give me a warning next time, will you?" said Bill.

"Sorry Bill," she said. "Now get in there and eat, you old bastard."

TWELVE

Knocking on Heaven's Door

I t was a week before the Fourth of July, and this holiday would be
much different from the year before for Viv and the rest of them. Last
year at this time, Bill was still in D.C. and they were in the midst of the
hunters in their neighborhood, holed up in their house trying to survive.

Now they were all together again, and whatever was to come their
way, they would face it together as a family, not separated from each
other.

Things at Peaceful Valley had become comfortable for everyone,
even Whiskers.

Whiskers stayed in the dining hall building, and Andy had the run
of the ranch, with the two never crossing paths.

Andy was no threat to Whiskers, but Whiskers didn't know that
and preferred to not have to deal with him. He had his place and Andy
had his, and the two should never meet.

That was the deal.

Other than Andy's first and only time in the dining hall the night
of Mandy and his arrival, he always stayed outside and took his meals
out there. He knew there was a cat inside, but he was a smart enough
dog to know that the dining hall was the cat's domain and that he

didn't belong in there, so he stayed outside, oddly enough without ever having to be told.

Everyone was excited for the Fourth of July, but they were also disheartened to know that they would not be blowing off any fireworks for fear of attracting attention to themselves.

It had been weeks since they'd seen any aircraft in the sky or trucks on the roads, and because of that, some of them had a false sense of security, thinking they were all in the clear, maybe being able to shoot off a few fireworks with no repercussions, but that idea was quickly snuffed out by the hierarchy of Peaceful Valley.

All it would take was one mortar being set off to attract the attention of not only foreign entities but possibly a hunting party that didn't previously know of their existence.

Henry and his wife were the most vulnerable since they were on the very outskirts of the ranch several miles away, and then there was Burt, with his home being the first one from the main road, about a mile away from the rest in camp.

Plans were being made to celebrate the fourth in a variety of ways, such as foot races, a barbeque with the garden's first yield of lettuce and beets, meaning they would have salad added to their menu, swimming and boat races in the lake, tug of war, and anything else they could think of they could pull off.

Another thing being put together by Mark and Mandy was a patriotic skit performed by some of the kids and adults around the campfire that night, and they rehearsed for a good week beforehand.

None of them knew the danger ahead that was heading their way, led by one of the evilest men that ever walked the face of the Earth.

Lucas Frerotte.

Lucas was a manufacturer of methamphetamine that lived on the outskirts of Castle Rock when the EMP hit, and it didn't take long for him to begin hunting humans for food and acquire an overwhelming addiction to the taste of human flesh.

Within the first couple of weeks, after the blast hit, he began killing the neighbors that were near him, with the help of 5 of his closest associates.

They started close to home, but branched out into the suburbs, feasting on families that remained alive long enough to be hunted.

For the last year, his team of cannibals ate their way through the suburbs, along with other teams of cannibals that survived on the flesh as well, and they were whip-smart on where they would find people still alive.

Eventually, the only ones left in Castle Rock were the very few survivors that had hunkered down in fallout shelters with their supplies of food and water and could not be found, and the other packs of hunters, so they eventually became the hunters of the hunters, eating their competition for human flesh until they were the last ones standing.

When all their food sources had dried up and they had eaten the other hunters, they had no choice but to search out greener pastures, heading out into ranch country where Lucas knew that the only people that would still be alive would be ranchers, ranchers with a water supply, along with the cattle they would be eating.

They ate their way across Parker and to all the ranches east of there, spending months maneuvering their way across the ranches and finding lots of prey for their appetites.

In between times, and this is what made them so dangerous, they partook in the meth he had made, curbing their hunger for days on end, but when it was time to crash and go to sleep, they eventually would wake with a voracious appetite after not eating for days while being high, then sleeping.

It was as if they had become the walking dead, and they would need to eat so much to make up for the times they didn't, their killing rampages would take out two or three people at a time because they needed that much more food to be sated, where one person would have been enough to feed a normal group of people.

They were also armed to the teeth, with all of them carrying AR-15s, and enough ammo to defeat a small army, and they always traveled at night.

When coming upon a ranch, if doing so during the day, they would lose the element of surprise and not be able to see which ranch had people alive on it. At night, they could tell by campfire or lantern light, giving them the time and opportunity to plan out how they would flank the ranch and take out their prey.

There was no guilt or second-guessing from any of them.

From the beginning, they relished in the idea of killing, as they were already bent toward hell from the drug they were consuming, twisting their brains into a convoluted Celtic knot of how deep they could go into the recesses of their evil natures, devoid of God and all goodness on the planet.

This was their mission, led by dark forces unseen, yet felt inside their inner selves, and Lucas Frerotte and his devil's drug were their conduits to the flame they were drawn to and bound by.

Killing their prey was not enough.

They had to make them suffer.

As was common with these natural-born killers, they would first take tiny little pieces off their victims, throwing them into a state of shock, and the more they struggled, the better it was for the hunters.

The ultimate prize for them was the children.

They would terrify them to the point of pissing and shitting themselves, then cut their fingers off and drink the blood of the children by sucking on their bleeding stubs while they were screaming at the height of their agony and fear.

This would be when the adrenochrome in their blood would be at its highest levels and mixed with the methamphetamine still in their systems, it would create an otherworldly high only experienced by the mixture of the two.

This is why these hunters were above and beyond the most ruthless, frightening, and evil of all the hunters.

They were not hunting just for food, or even sport.

They were killing for the love of killing, and for their ethereal sense of well-being.

Their murders were purposeful and multi-faceted.

And they would not be stopped.

As if killing these children in such a horrific manner wasn't enough, they would be the first ones slaughtered, all done in front of the parents as they screamed, pled, and cried out for mercy, only to be rewarded with the slow beheading of their children after the child had passed out from the pain.

Lucas Frerotte and his ghouls had just arrived in Elbert after butchering an elderly couple in Kiowa the day before. They were old school and had a bomb shelter behind their house, and they managed to survive on survival food and water they had stored away. They could have gone another year had they not been discovered, but as luck would have it, the old man had left the bunker to take a leak and was spotted by them and was immediately shot dead.

The ghouls then went down into the bunker and killed his wife, dragging her out to the backyard where they were both cut up and thrown on a grill over a makeshift fire, and both eaten within hours of their demise.

The hunters had no use for the food they ran across in the bunker but were more than happy to partake in the bottled water they found down there, and as was their routine, they slept for three days in the old couple's house after feasting on them.

When they finally awoke, their hunger for methamphetamine ruled the day, and after getting wired to the gills, they began discussing which way they should travel.

If they went west, they would end up back in Castle Rock eventually, so since they knew that was an unfertile territory, they elected to travel south to Elbert, hoping to hit more populated ranches along the way.

Elbert was a big dead end for them, as there was no one anywhere still alive, so they continued walking south until they reached the crest of the hill overlooking Peaceful Valley and Henry's ranch house.

Lucas Frerotte and his men decided to hole up on top of the hill to study the ranch house, looking for any evidence of life, but not wanting to warn them of their presence. Their perseverance paid off, but what they saw just as the sun had gone down behind the mountains to the west defied what they had become accustomed to, which was a car traveling toward them on the road, but then turning into the ranch house.

None of them had seen a running car for over a year, and they were dumbstruck.

The car stopped at the ranch house, with Henry and his wife exiting the vehicle and going inside.

Not only was there a new opportunity to feed, but now they might have access to a vehicle as well, but their hopes were momentarily dashed when the car turned around and went back down the road in the direction it came, but then about a mile away, they saw the brake lights of the car come on, then it turned left and traveled east on a dirt road toward the trees. After that, they lost sight of it, but it told Frerotte that there were more people somewhere in that direction.

They waited until the darkness enveloped the valley before making their way down the road to the ranch house. It was going to be a full moon that night and the next night, so to not be seen, they elected to start moving through the field as soon as it became dark to avoid the moonlight that would soon follow, illuminating their presence.

Over at the main township of Peaceful Valley, they were all gathered around the fire talking about how much fun the next day would be, as it would be the Fourth of July.

The adults and kids that would be performing in the patriotic skit were off on the other side of the dining hall and out of sight of everyone else, in the middle of one of their final rehearsals by lantern light. Everyone had their parts down to a T, and they were now just mainly going through the motions because they all knew their parts backward and forward, as they had been rehearsing now for over a week.

Jack was trying to work up the nerve to get Mandy alone somewhere, so they could be more intimate if that was something she desired as well, but he would never know unless he had that opportunity with her.

It was safe to say that Jack was now completely smitten with her and he was having a hard time focusing on anything else, especially the sermon he would be giving that Sunday.

He felt guilty because his thoughts were now so consumed with her. He felt he was straying away from Christ and his teachings, that this girl was becoming more important than Jesus to him, but he could not help it.

Everything seemed secondary to him, taking a back seat to this wonderful, beautiful girl that strolled into his life a little more than a week ago.

When he was around her, she was all he could see. Someone could be talking to him, and he wouldn't hear a word they were saying to him until they broke his concentration with a tap on his shoulder or a flash of their hands in front of his face.

Had he not been so enthralled, he probably would have been embarrassed, but he was too far gone to even notice his detachment.

Love had come to Peaceful Valley in the shape of a beautiful girl named Mandy with long brown hair, and he would not be able to sleep soundly until he made his move on her, and hopefully, she would respond in kind.

Unbeknownst to Jack, Mandy felt the same way about him as he did her, but it was different for her than it was for Jack because she was the newest member of the camp family, and she did not want to overstep her boundary if there was one to overstep.

She still did not fully know the lay of the land and didn't know anyone well enough yet to even inquire about Jack.

She knew little about his past, or what his likes and dislikes were, and because she was so nervous about the potential of hurting someone's feelings or making someone mad, she missed all the signals that Jack was throwing out.

The last thing she wanted was to make an enemy of someone there, not knowing if someone else had designs on him. She just had not been there long enough to know.

The one thing both of them felt they had was time, because no one was going anywhere.

It would remain this way between them until one or the other made the first move, and it appeared it would have to be Jack. Her desire for him would be stuffed inside, but once he made his move, she would respond to him the way he had hoped she would.

Lucas Frerotte and his five monsters had surrounded the ranch house now, all in stealth mode, waiting for the sign from their leader to commence an attack on the two people they could see sitting at a table by lantern light through the window at the back of the house.

Lucas carefully opened the back door, as it was left unlocked, and quietly slipped inside, but not quiet enough, because Henry heard him entering, thinking it was Burt trying to play a trick on him. Had he been more suspicious, he would have had time enough to grab his rifle and thwart the attack from his intruder, but Lucas stepped around the doorway into the room where the two were sitting, giving him no time to reach for his rifle, and his wife screamed out in terror.

Lucas had his AR-15's laser pointer trained on Scott's forehead and making one false move would have asked for a bullet right between the eyes, so Henry didn't make a move.

"What do you want?' Henry asked, more calmly than you would have expected.

"Good evening," said Frerotte, then yelling for his men to come inside.

Henry and his wife both knew they were in big trouble when they saw the other five men come inside.

"Who drove you home? We saw a car pull up and drop you off. Who was that? Do they live over there where I saw them drive to?" asked Frerotte.

Henry clammed up and didn't say a word. One of the men then put the nose of his rifle against Henry's temple, with Henry's wife screaming and pleading for them to stop.

"There's no one living over there. I don't know what you think you saw, but it wasn't a car driving over there" Henry said.

"I'm not going to play with you. I'm only going to ask you once more. Who lives over there?" Frerotte asked again.

On the table between Henry and his wife was a heavy meat cleaver, and Frerotte picked it up.

"I told you, there's no one over there," said Henry.

With the speed of a film set on fast forward, Frerotte brought the cleaver down onto Henry's hand, severing all of Henry's four fingers at the knuckle, eliciting a scream from Henry and his wife both, with not an ounce of mercy from Frerotte or his men.

"YES!!! THEY LIVE OVER THERE!!!" screamed his wife, not wanting to see her husband hurt anymore.

"How many people live over there?" asked Frerotte.

"A lot, over thirty people for sure!" she yelled. "Please don't hurt my husband anymore!"

Frerotte leaned his rifle against the wall, then walked over to behind Henry as he was holding his wrist where his fingers had been chopped off, trying to quell the blood squirting out of them.

Frerotte then grabbed Henry's head by the hair, tilting it backward, and began sawing off his head with the cleaver in full view of his wife, creating a horrific bloody mess of blood squirting out from his neck in every direction until his head was completely severed from his body, then placed on the table in front of her.

In a fit of panic, she jumped from the table, only to be shot in the chest by one of his monster men.

"Damn you. If people are living over there, you just alerted them to us being here" yelled Frerotte.

THIRTEEN

Waiting in the Moonlight

❧

"Morning. Let's go get Henry and the wife" said Burt as he got in the car with Bill. "What do you think he was shooting at last night? A coyote or a raccoon?"

"Maybe a bird, who knows" answered Bill.

It was the morning of the Fourth of July 2023.

As was the ritual, a car went to pick up Henry and his wife first thing in the morning for breakfast with the rest of the camp, then the couple would spend the day there until after dinner.

It was only a mile away, but too far to walk, and saddling up the horses to only go a mile seemed like a whole lot of trouble when they could be picked up a lot easier.

As they pulled off the road and drove down to the ranch past the horse corral, the horses seemed uneasy and were acting skittish.

When they drove to the back of the house, they could see why.

On the back firepit, there was the body of Henry's wife, fully barbequed with both of her legs missing, and the two men started screaming, with Burt falling out of the car and onto his knees, violently throwing up on the side of the car.

"Oh God no, Oh my God, oh my God" Burt kept saying over and over.

Bill was beside himself with grief and horror, and he ran to the back door and into the house, where he found Henry's head on the kitchen table and his body on the floor just underneath it.

"He's in here. He's dead. They cut his head off!" yelled Bill.

Bill came out of the house with a big blanket he'd gotten off of their couch and covered up Henry's wife where she lay on the grill.

"A pack of hunters did this. The question is, where are they now?" asked Bill. "They wouldn't have left them here half-eaten unless they were going after a bigger score. Get in the car Burt. We've got to get back to camp NOW!"

They didn't bother to look in the barn because they knew whoever had done this had left the premises.

They pulled the car onto the road and raced back to camp, praying that they were not too late. They almost ran over one of the boys as they screeched into the parking spot by the dining hall, sending up a huge cloud of dust and dirt into the air, alerting everyone in camp that something was seriously afoot.

They got out of the car and yelled for anyone in earshot to come over to them, which was about half of the camp's residents.

"We have a big problem. Henry and his wife were attacked last night by hunters!" announced Bill.

"What!" said Viv.

Those standing around Bill were immediately abuzz with horrified excitement.

"We just left Henry's house, and they were both murdered last night. That was the gunshot we heard. It was one of them being shot," said Burt.

"Terry, you need to take the car and alert everyone else that's not here. Go over to the Forts, and Cook's Roost, and anywhere else. We need everyone here right now present and accounted for," said Bill.

Terry was on it and drove the car to the farthest fort away, hoping to get to everyone before something bad happened.

The floodgates of bad memories had opened, and Viv, Julie, and the rest that were in the Cherry Knolls neighborhood began to relive those awful memories of the hunters in their front yard that fateful night.

Everyone near Bill kept pounding him and Burt with questions, but they were put off until everyone was there in order not to repeat themselves, having to speak of the grisly details over and over.

From the distance around the camp, there could be seen people running toward them from many directions, eager to know what was so important that they had to run to the dining hall and not at their leisure. After all, it was the Fourth of July.

The scout camp on the east side of Elbert Road was the boy scout side, with the cub scout side being across the street, but the boy scout side was actually two camps in one.

The camp they were in was the main camp, Camp Cris Dobbins, whereas the other camp was north of them toward Scott's house, which was more of a high adventure camp, where boys cooked for themselves instead of getting their meals in a dining hall. This camp was called Camp Cortland Dietler.

This was where the hunters were currently searching for them, not knowing for sure how many they were looking for, but they knew there was a vehicle involved, and that alone was reason enough for the hunt.

In the wee hours of the morning after they had cooked up the woman. They had their fill of meat and began walking through the trees toward the general vicinity where they saw the car travel to the night before, and that is why Bill and Burt never saw them.

Instead of walking down the road, they figured going in a straight line through the woods would be better and left them less exposed to detection.

It was 8:00 in the morning, and they were all sitting in the shade of the trees and the awning around Camp Dietler headquarters. They still had not discovered the other campers but were bound and determined to do so before it got dark when they would make their move to attack whoever there was to be attacked.

After they had all done a hefty dose of methamphetamine distributed by their leader, Lucas Frerotte, they all began to become very industrious, looking for entry points through the trees to resume their search, and after deciding on one, they all gathered around Frerotte.

"We don't know how many of them there are, but if the woman was telling the truth, there are at least thirty, so that means we are seriously outmanned, which means we are going to have to be particularly smart about this. They probably already know that their friends are dead, but they don't know where we are, or even if we know about them, so we have the advantage" Frerotte said to his men.

"We are going to move slowly through these trees, and we need to stick close together in order not to be seen."

And so, they began their trek through the woods, taking their time, heading in the direction of Camp Cris Dobbins.

When all the residents of Peaceful Valley were surrounding Bill and Burt behind the dining hall, Bill took inventory of everyone that should be there, and when he was satisfied everyone was in attendance, he began to speak.

"For those of you that don't know, Burt and I discovered the camp superintendent and his wife dead this morning."

The crowd let out a big burst of questions, with everyone talking over each other.

"The children need to hear this too, so I'm going to tell all of you. They were killed and eaten last night, so there are hunters in the neighborhood, and they are probably heading our way" he said.

This time there were shrieks from the crowd, and some of the children began to cry.

"Needless to say, we are going to have to cancel our Fourth of July celebration today, because we need to prepare for them when they come. We don't know how many of them there are, but I'm pretty sure there are at least two of them, maybe more" Bill said.

"Where do you think they are now?" asked someone from the crowd.

"Not sure, but my guess is they are in the woods to the north of us. We saw no trace of anyone on the road, so they must be in the woods. There is also the possibility they know nothing about us and are headed in a different direction, but we must assume they are coming our way, so everyone in camp needs to gather their bedding and head over to the bunkhouse. Those families living there now need to make room for the others. We cannot be separated and all spread out.

Those in the dining hall need to get out of there as well and head to the bunkhouse.

Today we will go about our business like a regular day, except I don't want to see anyone leaving this part of the camp. Everyone needs to stay here between the dining hall and the bunkhouse so we can see everyone. Now go to your homes and grab your bedding and come back here. Do it now" ordered Bill, and the crowd dispersed, feeling very frightened, a feeling none of them had felt since being at Peaceful Valley.

"So, what's the plan?" asked Bob Hawkins.

"I figured I'd leave that up to you. You are the law enforcement around here, so this would be in your wheelhouse," said Bill.

What none of them knew about Bob Hawkins was that he was a sniper when he was enlisted with the Army Rangers many years ago, so he had a rudimentary knowledge of how to prepare for an enemy assault like this one.

First and foremost, they needed a tactical advantage, and they would have that by being on top of the roof of the dining hall.

"Last night was a full moon and tonight will be as well. We're going to need every man out here tonight. Some of us should be on the roof, some of us hiding on the ground by the trees, and others close to the bunkhouse. Rifles will be our weapons of choice. Who's the best shot among all of you?" asked Bob Hawkins.

"I'm a pretty good shot for distance shooting?' said Mark.

"So am I," said Mandy.

"I've got a rifle for each of you. You can join me up on the roof" Bob said.

It would figure the two Eagle Scouts would be the best shots, other than Bob Hawkins himself.

"The rest of you can figure out where you want to be positioned. We want to lure them over here, to the dining hall, so we will leave a propane lantern lit on the inside.

With the moon being full tonight, we should be able to see them from the roof well before they get to us. We've done this before, and we can do it again. They won't get the jump on us if we are ready for them," said Bob.

With everything happening all at once, no one had started to prepare breakfast, so Viv, Julie, and some of the women went into the kitchen of the dining hall to rustle up some oatmeal for the camp.

Even though plans had changed for the day, they could not forgo any meals, especially for the children.

Rocky and Brian wanted to help the men by using their slingshots, thinking they were both really good shots, and they could take out an eye possibly of one of the intruders. Bill thought that would be a bad idea and made them promise they would stay in the bunk house once it got dark, much to their chagrin.

Mandy would be up on the roof with Mark and Bob, leaving Jack on the ground behind one of the trees. Jack was worried about her, but he didn't need to be. She was a crack shot.

"I'm going to worry about you the whole time you are up there," Jack said to Mandy. "I don't know what I'd do if something happened to you."

Mandy looked at him with curious eyes, wondering if he felt about her the way she felt about him, but then suddenly her question was answered when Jack leaned over and kissed her right on the lips.

She didn't know how to react for a split second as she didn't see it coming, but then she kissed him back, and it was a long, wet kiss.

They both looked each other in the eyes and they both knew what each of them had been longing to know, that this was a two-way street, that they loved each other and wanted to be closer.

If it would have been possible for bells to have rung, they would have, and butterflies were flying around inside of each of them.

"I've been wanting to do that ever since I first saw you. I had to kiss you," said Jack.

"I've been wanting you to," said Mandy, looking adoringly at Jack with love in her eyes.

No one was paying any attention to them, so they kissed again, and it was like the heavens opened up and the angels were singing.

There was no doubt they were in love and there'd be no turning back.

"Please be careful up there," he said to her.

"I will. You too, ok?" she answered.

The day was not the day they had planned out, but everyone was safe and accounted for, except Henry and his wife.

They would not be with them on that day, or any day going forward.

Jack inquired what the plan was for them, if they were going to be buried or burned.

He asked Burt first what he thought since he knew them the best.

Burt thought they would want to be burned, which turned out to be what would be done with them.

The ground at Peaceful Valley was not easy to dig. If they had a backhoe, that would be one thing, but shovels would only break because of the rocky ground, and they wouldn't be able to dig a hole deep enough for them, so it was decided that they would be burned over at the ranch house where they currently were.

Burt, Bob, Terry, and Bill would take care of it as soon as this fiasco was over with the hunters, and Jack would preside over the burning, offering up his prayers and asking the Lord for their entrance into heaven.

It would be a sad and anxious day for him, but he would stand for them with the Lord.

The rest of the camp would not be part of that, as it would be too traumatic to see them in the condition they were in.

They would hold a memorial service afterward at the chapel.

It was getting close to dinner time, and after they'd eaten, the men and Mandy were all sitting at the picnic tables on the side of the dining hall, preparing for the sun to go down.

On the other side of the valley across the lake, the hunters were hunkered down behind a campsite through the trees, looking on across the valley at the huge dining hall at least a mile away, seeing all the people, along with a car and a city bus, which shocked them.

They'd been there most of the day, just sitting and waiting, doing methamphetamine, licking their chops at all the food running around across the valley, seeing children for the first time in a while, anticipating the adrenochrome they hoped to be drinking in just a few hours.

Lucas Frerotte decided that they needed to take as many of them alive as possible since there were so many. There would be no way they could eat all of them before they started to rot if they killed them all outright, so the plan was only to eat the ones that got killed in the takeover and keep the rest locked away somewhere until they had finished off the first ones eaten.

How they would do that was anyone's guess, but they were confident they would figure something out. They knew the children would be the first ones eaten regardless because their fingers would be chopped off immediately for blood drinking, and their flesh would be the tastiest and most succulent.

If they did this right, they could be fed for a month or more, but they would have to make sure the only ones killed in the beginning were those putting up a fight.

In truth, the hunters rarely encountered those with the ability or desire to fight them, as most of their attacks were on the unsuspecting, those unprepared to fight against a sneak attack in the dark.

It all depended on what their prey knew, and how well armed they were, but they still had to be prepared for an attack, which Lucas Frerotte highly doubted they were.

They had yet to run into any that had prepared themselves, but they couldn't know what the other people across the valley had already seen in this last year. Had Frerotte been thinking, he would have considered that these people had managed to live through hunters before them and not been eaten.

These were not ordinary people they were getting ready to attack, and he couldn't know what he was ready to put himself and his men up against, but he would soon be finding out.

The sun had gone down about an hour prior, and it would soon be dark enough to climb the ladders up onto the roof without the danger of them being seen up there by the hunters.

Bob Hawkins had already cleaned and prepared his Remington 700 with scope, his go-to rifle for any hunting expedition he'd ever been on.

He had given Mandy his Ruger, also with scope, and another accurate rifle that was lightweight, which was the biggest reason he'd given it to her.

He gave Mark his Weatherby Vanguard, another super accurate rifle, so all on the roof were armed with top-notch weaponry.

The men on the ground had a combination of rifles and handguns, some with both, and all were ready for anything that came their way.

The number one rule was to make sure you were not firing on another person in camp, making sure it was the enemy you were ready to put a kill shot in.

Though they could not be sure what direction the hunters would be coming from, they assumed the most likely place would be from the trees across the valley, north of where they were.

Bob had Mark lay down just behind the ridge of the roof, giving him some protection against incoming fire, and had Mandy do the same about fifty feet down from Mark.

Since Bob was such a big target, he elected to stay behind the massive chimney, giving him plenty of cover to stand behind.

Bob was much more accustomed and prepared to take out a target farther away than the other two were, so his positioning only made sense, giving him a stand-up position behind the chimney, being able to rest his rifle on top of it and focus on a target much farther away.

The lantern had been lit and was sitting on a table inside the dining hall, illuminating enough of it to show some of its contents, but not enough to be a clear indicator that the room was completely devoid of people.

Not even Whiskers was in the building, as Julie had taken him with her to one of the cabins in the bunk house, and the kids were more than happy to have him there. The same could not be said for Whiskers. He wasn't used to kids and didn't much care for them, so the kids were well advised to not try to play with him and be careful about petting him. There was no way to know if he would bite or scratch them.

The moon was not yet overhead, and probably would not make an appearance for another hour, so long as the hunters did not make their move immediately, they felt they would be all right.

One hour of darkness went by, and then another.

It wasn't until close to midnight when Mandy thought she saw something glint across the valley at the base of the trees. She whispered to Mark, who whispered to Bob, who then whispered to Terry, who was halfway across the roof to the ladders that they thought they saw something.

Terry was up there primarily to relay to the ground what they were seeing up on the roof, and vice versa, to relay to the roof what they were seeing on the ground.

The moon was in full bloom across the valley and there wasn't a cloud in the sky, almost as if a streetlight were shining down from above, and soon all doubt would be erased that the camp would be under attack.

Through his binoculars, Bob counted six of them walking across the valley from the other side of the lake through the trees, all carrying what looked to be assault rifles, walking very slowly to not make any noise.

They were still a good half a mile away, so it would take a while before any of them were in range.

The camp had the tactical advantage, as they could see the hunters approaching, but they could not be seen themselves, as long as no one did anything stupid or made any noise to attract attention to themselves.

The rifles on the roof were also shaded from the moonlight by the trees surrounding them, giving them extra camouflage, but that was only momentary and would change as the Earth shifted its axis.

The hunters were not looking for anyone on the roof, or anyone else, and believed as always that they had the upper hand and the element of surprise.

They could not have been more wrong this time around.

Every dog has its day, and if it hadn't been for Andy barking from the dining room veranda, they would not have been the least concerned about their exposure or discovery.

Someone forgot to tend to Andy.

With Mandy on the roof, someone else should have taken control of him, but she never thought to assign him to someone.

FOURTEEN

Shooting Gallery

The hunters were at the lake now, coming toward the dining hall from the northwest.

Bob Hawkins already had one of them in his sights, waiting for them to get close enough for Mandy and Mark to each pick one out to fire upon. When they affirmed to Bob they were ready, they would all shoot simultaneously, seriously hampering the hunter's chances for any kind of success, but it would all depend on the marksmanship of Mark and Mandy.

Andy had stopped barking because one of the men down below grabbed him and brought him back to the bunkhouse.

The hunters were now roughly a hundred yards away from the dining hall, and it was becoming now or never time.

Mandy and Mark both signaled to Bob that they had their sights on someone, so Bob counted to three, then they would all fire.

When his count reached three, they all fired at once, dropping two of them in their tracks.

As luck would have it, both Mark and Mandy had their sights on the same guy.

One of them missed, but the other hit the man dead on in his chest.

Bob had taken the last man bringing up the rear, hitting him in the forehead.

That's when the real shooting started.

The remaining hunters hit the ground immediately upon hearing the gunfire, but before they all hit the ground, Bob hit another guy in the throat, dropping him as well.

That left three hunters down below, with Lucas Frerotte being one of them.

Bill was hiding behind a tree, waiting for one of them laying in the tall grass a few feet away from him to stick his head up, and when he did, Bill blasted him right in the face, killing him instantly.

Now there were two.

Frerotte and the other man found themselves seriously outgunned and exposed, causing them both to hightail it back the way they came, and that's when Bob Hawkins put a bullet in the man farthest away again, splitting the back of his skull.

There was only one man left now, and that was Frerotte.

Though he had a multitude of shots buzzing by his head as he ran back toward the lake and the trees, none struck him and he made it far enough away to where he was eventually out of range, and then he slunk back into the trees from where they came.

"We've got to chase him down, otherwise he'll come back when we have our guards down," said Bill.

"We've got time to get him. We just took out all his buddies. He's got nowhere to go" said Bob, as he stepped off the ladder. "Besides, I'm not going to go chasing after him in the dark. If we chase him, he'll have the upper hand and be able to pick us off. It's best just to let him run like the dog that he is."

"I hope you are right. Something tells me we'll be seeing that guy again, as soon as he gets hungry," said Bill.

Frerotte was safe in the trees for the moment, and he could not believe what had just happened.

Fifteen minutes ago he had five men with him, and now they were all gone.

He had seriously miscalculated his prey.

They had laid in wait for him and his men, making them the hunted.

Five of his men had been killed without any of them firing a single shot, and now he was stuck between a rock and a hard place.

He could start walking, but where to? In what direction should he go?

He could always go back to the ranch house and feast on the woman on the grill, but they had a car and would be going back there because they would expect him to go there. For all he knew, they were already there waiting for him.

If he got on the road, they would find him.

His only option was to walk east through the trees, but to where? Out into the middle of nowhere, where no living being was, with no chance of acquiring food or water?

It never once occurred to him that something like this would or could happen.

They'd been invincible for so long, he never saw it ending, not like this.

Frerotte closed his eyes, trying to ease his mind and collect himself, then hopefully think of a way out of the jam he was in.

He was tired of living now, probably because he couldn't see how much longer he could survive with no food or water.

He had one bottle left, and he drank it down like an alcoholic drinking his last drink.

He laid back on the boulder he was propped up against, and slowly began to drift away into a long-awaited sleep, one that he hoped he would never awake from.

The truth of the matter was that he had stopped living a long time ago, even before the blast, when methamphetamine had completely taken over his life and everyone around him, when it took hold of him and destroyed what little good he had in him, and then becoming addicted to the killing of people and eating their flesh, turning him into a subhuman with no connection to God.

Here he was now in a group of trees that hid him from the moonlight, languishing in the darkness where he belonged, with not one person in the world that cared about his existence, about whether he lived or died, mostly because he had probably killed anyone that had ever cared about him.

Once he drifted to sleep, his dreams against that boulder would be so horrifying that he would wake up abruptly and stick the business end of his AR-15 in his mouth and pull the trigger one last time, leaving technicolor red all over the rock behind him, with his brains to be eaten by coyotes that stumbled on him a day later.

The men in Peaceful Valley were sitting around the campfire they made, and they all heard the shot that reverberated through the valley.

They knew who had fired it but didn't know why.

They expected to see Frerotte again at some point, but he never came, and eventually, he was forgotten.

They never bothered to look for him in the trees either.

They didn't have any reason to go over there because they didn't inhabit that part of Peaceful Valley.

Mandy and Mark didn't know which one of them had taken a life, because after inspecting all the men they had gunned down that night, they discovered that the man they killed only had one bullet wound, so they knew that one of them had missed.

Secretly, they both wished it was themselves that had missed their target, not wanting to be responsible for taking a human life, even as despicable a life as the one that was taken.

They would go to their graves never knowing if they had blood on their hands or not, but in the scheme of things, it mattered not in how they lived their lives, nor did it change a thing.

They would both continue to live under the Eagle Scout code, hunters be damned.

Jack's faith in the Lord was even stronger now.

They had been attacked twice in the night, yet not one of their people had been killed or even wounded. God was looking out for them.

The same couldn't be said for Henry and his wife, and though they were killed the night before, Jack rationalized it as Providence, that it had to be that way, that without their discovery, the whole camp could have been slaughtered by ignorance.

He prayed for all the dead, even the hunters.

The next day the bodies were drug to a spot farther away than where they lay dead, away from the tall grass and onto a dirt patch, all put in a pile and lit on fire.

Later that day, a ceremony was held for Henry and his wife away from their bodies where everyone could attend at the chapel, and they too were cremated, only this time at the ranch house. Scott's wife was brought into the house, then the house was lit on fire, burning everything to the ground.

Burt was especially broken up. He had known Henry for all the years Burt had been the caretaker of Peaceful Valley before Henry had become the superintendent and was a scoutmaster for one of the local troops.

In hindsight, they were all very surprised that there were still hunters out there, wondering how they could have stayed alive for so long with just about everyone being dead now.

The most amazing thing that was happening at Peaceful Valley was the collective growth in their faith. In times like these, people would ask themselves where is God? How could God allow this to happen to his children? Where was his mercy?

But God rarely intervenes in what happens on Earth, because the greatest gift he has given us prevents his intervention, the gift of free will.

He gave us free will to do as we please, and it was the free will of the leaders of Iran and North Korea that exploded those bombs into space, just like it was that same free will that allowed Hitler to murder six million Jews.

Though they would never acknowledge it, they too were God's children, and it was God's children that did these things, not God.

It wasn't God punishing us for turning our backs on him as so many have done.

It was free will and nothing more.

Man is capable of the most beautiful and compassionate things, but he is also capable of the most heinous and vile things, and sometimes it feels like evil is winning, but it's not, because if evil was winning, evil would be the last one standing.

This instance was a prime example of evil losing the battle.

Goodness prevailed, and for that, everyone in Peaceful Valley was truly thankful.

Thankful for the foresight of their leadership and their ability to fight the foes of darkness, to smote them down like the evil dragons that they were.

It felt like God was on their side, and as always, he was, so their faith was fortified.

They celebrated the Fourth of July a week later, and it was just as grand a time as they would have had on an actual day, except for the absence of Henry and his wife.

There was a massive tug of war with all the ages dispersed on both sides of the rope, and the muddy pit saw its victims covered in mud and filth, with all jumping into the lake to get clean and to cool off.

Burt and Bill both abstained from the physical stuff because of their age, but they had just as much fun rooting for either side of the rope.

The barbeque was marvelous, thanks to the bull elk bagged earlier in the week, with fresh produce from the garden, and the Kool-Aid flowed as if it was from the heavens.

For dessert, there was a canned peach cobbler made and more than enough for seconds.

That night the crowd was treated to an excellent rendition of Yankee Doodle Dandy, the skit they had been working on, which was more of a musical play than anything else, and everyone loved it. It felt like America was still alive and thriving, and for just a minute or two, they all forgot about their stations in life in the middle of a country that felt dead.

It was good to be alive on that day, and it would be used as a springboard, taking them into an uncertain future.

Jack and Mandy were totally in love and spent most of the day sneaking away from the crowd to be alone with each other, kissing each other passionately until they had to stop, for fear they might take it to the next level.

It was starting to become obvious to anyone that was paying attention that they had become an item, especially to Julie, who looked on from a distance.

She was happy that Jack had found love but was also melancholy that she could be losing her oldest son to another woman, every mother's lament.

Julie was already alone without her husband Paul, gone now for over a year, and she wasn't looking forward to being replaced by someone else as the most important woman in Jack's life, but she knew this day would come eventually and hoped it would be with a woman of good stock and upbringing, and Mandy obviously was that.

Julie had no idea it was Mandy's father that attacked her outside of the latrine that night at New Hope, nor did anyone else but a couple of people.

Mark and Bill would never say a word, as it would do no good and would be breaking their promise to Mandy.

In reality, Bill Sigler had lost his humanity by acquiring the taste for human flesh, but he was once a stellar dad and taught his children how to be good human beings, and to be resourceful.

In Mandy, Jack would have much more than a love partner, he would have someone to rely on in times when it got tough, and someone to figure things out when he hadn't a clue. She would be his yin to her yang, which would make the love he had for her even stronger down the road.

Mandy was settling in with her new family of survivors and was spending most of her time with Jack, but when she wasn't with him, she spent the rest of her time with Kate, getting to know her and helping her out with things she had difficulty doing herself.

Kate was getting to be very big with the baby only a couple of months away, and Mark could not do certain things for her that Mandy could. Girl things.

Mark knew his wife was in good hands with Mandy, knowing her resourcefulness and her pragmatic mind.

Kate knew that something was happening between Mandy and her older brother, and she was very pleased that it was Mandy and not the other girl Tracy that was their same age.

Kate didn't much cotton to Tracy, all the way back to the very beginning back at New Hope. She didn't out and out dislike her, but she didn't have anything in common with her either.

She suspected that Tracy liked girls and boys both, so that alone was a big obstacle for Kate to overcome, so she never sidled up to her. Besides, she had always been busy with Mark being a new wife.

Mandy had hinted around the subject of her and Jack a few times to see how it would fly with Kate, so Kate was pretty sure that they would be together if they weren't already.

Little did Kate know, but Tracy had tried to put a subtle move on Mandy the first week she was there, which was rebuffed and would have given Kate more fodder for her ambivalence toward her.

Mark was looking forward to being a father and having his mom and dad so close in the mix was the icing on the cake. Mark was Webster's definition of a family man and wanted to remain as close as he possibly could to all his family members, including Julie, Jack, and Rocky.

In actuality, they were the biggest family in the Peaceful Valley clan, having the Jenkins and Price families joined as one, making them eight and soon to be nine, and that wasn't including Mandy yet.

In the back of everyone's mind, they all were still on edge, the remnant of being attacked a second time by hunters.

Though it had been discussed over and over in group discussions that the probability of hunters ever again showing up was nil to none, they still held out the possibility that it could happen again, odds be damned.

Unfortunately for them, that fear, even as remote as it was, lingered like a bad taste in their mouths, and it would in some way dictate what they did for months, if not years, to come.

Though they never saw the bodies of Henry and his wife, other than Bill and Conrad, they got the details through the grapevine of gossip of Henry's beheading and his partially eaten wife on the grill, and it was enough to give them nightmares, especially the children.

Certain supplies were running low, and though they still had a couple of months before the cold weather would begin to set in, they needed to make a trip to the Burlington Coat Factory in Colorado Springs to get winter coats, boots, gloves, scarves, and anything else winter-related, so sizes would be gotten from everyone in camp and several of the women would make the trip this time to procure these items.

They had almost forty to shop for, so it wouldn't be a walk in the park, meaning they would need more than a couple of gals.

The bus pulled out of Peaceful Valley and headed into the heart of Colorado Springs, uncharted territory for all of them, but they didn't expect it would be any worse than downtown Denver.

Of all the possible scenarios they could have run into, this was not bad at all.

Viv, Mrs. Jennings, two of the other women along with Mandy made the trip, all of them having their assigned clothing to shop for. Bill, Randy, and Burt made the trip along with the women for protection.

While they were all in the store, a Chinese assault vehicle had pulled up a couple of blocks away, unnoticed by all of them until Burt had stepped out of the store with a brand-new down winter coat and gloves.

He saw it parked up the street running and stood there for a minute staring at it, not knowing what to do.

Not only did he see them, but they saw him as well, and he knew it.

There would be no point in drawing his weapon and shooting at them.

For one, they hadn't done anything.

For two, they would gun him down before he even got off a shot.

FIFTEEN

Jack Price, DDS

T hey'd been in the store for close to two hours and had shopping carts full of winter clothing for everyone in camp, right down to things for the baby that had yet to arrive.

Burt had gone back into the store to alert Bill to the Chinese parked up the street.

"Looks like we've got company. There's a Chinese military truck parked up the street about 2 blocks, and they know we're here" said Burt.

Bill went outside to take a look, and he could see two Chinese soldiers in the front of the big truck, both of them staring him down, and like Burt, he wasn't quite sure what to do.

Everyone else in the store was unaware of their presence, so when they all started coming out with their full shopping carts and noticed the truck as well, they were each taken aback, looking at Bill, wondering what they should do.

Bill thought the best thing would be to proceed as if they didn't notice them and instructed everyone to load up the bus with the things in their carts, so one by one, they filled the seats of the bus with coats, snow pants, gloves, boots, and everything else they had gotten.

While they loaded the bus, the vehicle just kept sitting there idling with its inhabitants eyeballing the group with great interest.

Once everything was on the bus, the group followed suit and got on the bus as well, with Randy behind the wheel, and he began to slowly pull away from the curb and head back the way they came, with the Chinese following, staying a safe distance behind them.

Every turn that Randy made, the Chinese duplicated.

"It looks like they're going to follow us to where we live Bill. What should I do?" asked Randy.

"Just keep driving and let's see what they do," said Bill.

"Should I run them on a wild goose chase?" asked Randy.

"If we do that, we might make them angry, plus we can't be wasting fuel. No, just head back to Peaceful Valley like you normally would," said Bill.

And so they did, heading back on all the backroads they had taken to get there, crossing I-25 toward Elbert.

After about ten miles, the vehicle eased back and they were alone on the highway, but Bill noticed they had a tail.

It was two Chinese helicopters far above them, keeping an eye on them to see where they would go, and once they turned into the scout ranch off of Elbert Road, the helicopters disappeared.

"Well, they know of our existence, and they know where we live. Maybe they just want to be aware of us and keep tabs. Who knows." said Bill, hoping this was not a precursor to something bad happening to them in the future.

"There's nothing we can do about it except go on living our lives."

Even though they hadn't yet reached the dog days of summer, they were well prepared now for winter when it made its arrival.

Lots of wood had been chopped, maybe a cord for every cabin, and they now had plenty of winter clothing to be able to function outside in the coldest of weather.

The garden had produced a ton of produce for the camp, and all were happy to be eating ears of corn, though without any butter, but they were still happy to have it.

A lot of the vegetables they canned for the winter, and soon the pumpkins would be ready for harvest, just in time for Halloween.

This was the epitome of living off the grid, and since there was no grid anymore to live off, they adapted nicely.

Their lives of leisure were a thing of the past, and everyone had to chip in some way for things to run smoothly.

Burt had changed since Henry and his wife's passing, and he wasn't the same old gregarious man that loved playing with the kids like he used to or riding his horse as much.

He seemed to be spending less time around the village they had created and more time at his place, and he barely made it over for meals, with Viv sometimes bringing him a plate to his house.

The death of the superintendent and his wife hung over the camp like a damp dirty rag, and the spring in everyone's step seemed to lessen.

Whiskers was very glad to return to the dining hall from the bunk house after the attack on them, wanting as little to do with Andy as possible, instead chasing field mice that had gotten in from outside, and occasionally bringing a mouse head to Julie as a trophy of his kills.

Andy was just Andy, and when he wasn't at the side of Mandy, he was chasing ground squirrels outside or fetching sticks thrown from the boys,

Andy was also known to steal an occasional fish off the stringer when they were fishing in the lake, much to the chagrin of the fishermen, whomever they would be at the time. He had gotten adept at taking the fish and not getting his mouth caught on the hook.

Every night though, the two animals would be with their adopted humans, Andy in the headquarters with Mandy at the foot of her bunk on a pillow she laid down for him, and Whiskers sleeping on the bunk with Julie upstairs over the dining hall.

The village finally had its first bout with illness, though nothing that couldn't be cured.

Terry had a really bad toothache, one that he'd been dealing with off and on ever since the Jenkins and Price families joined up with them, but it was now to the point where it was affecting his health.

After lunch one day, seeing Terry struggling to eat because of the pain, Bob Hawkins had urged him to see Jack about it, not knowing what he could do, but Jack was better than leaving it alone entirely.

When Jack looked into Terry's mouth in the Health Lodge, he could immediately see the affected tooth, as Terry didn't have many left in his head. He had always suffered from having bad teeth and had many of them pulled over the years, so this one was easy to identify, mostly because there wasn't another tooth in the vicinity of the pain, plus the condition of the tooth itself. Jack could see a gaping hole in the side of it, and after reading about it in his PDR, he figured Terry now had an exposed nerve, but the real telltale sign was the gum around it.

It was bright red and swollen, meaning his tooth was abscessed, so before doing anything else, Jack prescribed him Clindamycin to get rid of the infection and would wait five or six days until the infection had gone away before proceeding to remove the tooth.

Everything up to this point was nothing Jack couldn't handle, but he was not sure he could handle this.

He had never given anyone a shot, especially in their mouth, and he had never done anything even remotely close to surgery, which is what removing a tooth is, but he had a few days to figure it out.

Jack consulted with Bill, then with Viv, and finally read his PDR for anything tooth related.

When Terry's infection subsided, Jack would attempt to give Terry a shot of lidocaine in his mouth, hoping that it would numb him up enough to try to pull his tooth.

Mandy agreed to assist him, though she had no experience in these matters, she nevertheless would try to the best of her ability.

Six days later, Terry came into the Health Lodge feeling much better, as the pain had gone down significantly due to the lack of throbbing from the previous infection, so they all decided that the time was right to attempt to remove the tooth, and along with lidocaine, Terry decided to be half-lit with a bottle of whiskey.

After half an hour of drinking a quarter of a fifth of whiskey, Terry was pretty well buzzed and laid down on the table for Jack to begin.

In there to assist was not only Mandy but Bill and Bob as well, to hold Terry down if need be, especially when Jack was extracting the tooth.

Jack knew from reading the PDR that no more than four and a half mg of lidocaine could be given, which meant he had to be sure where he would be injecting the gum, making sure he was hitting the right nerves.

He first drew up a tiny bit to squirt into the hole of the tooth, hoping to numb it enough to stick the needle in the surrounding gum. When he did this, Terry jumped a little from the lidocaine hitting his exposed nerve, but within a minute, Jack was able to touch his tooth and gum without Terry feeling it.

So far, so good.

Jack then drew up two mg more of the lidocaine and was able to stick the needle into the gum just below the tooth, with no major reaction from Terry. He then put another two mg in the gum on the other side of the tooth, and after waiting five minutes, Terry could not feel a thing and could barely speak because his mouth was now paralyzed from the numbness, and that is when Jack began to remove the tooth.

The only thing Jack had to do this with was a pair of needle-nose pliers he had gotten from Burt out of the quartermaster building.

Beforehand, the pliers were boiled in water to sterilize them, then cleaned with alcohol.

Jack put the pliers on Terry's tooth, but he could not feel them until Jack began to move the tooth back and forth to loosen it, and that is when Terry became unglued.

Jack had not gone deep enough to hit all the nerves, so he gave Terry another shot, but this time underneath the previous shot, going deeper than he had before.

Waiting another five minutes, he attempted to remove the tooth again, and this time Terry could feel nothing at all, and after a twist of the pliers, the tooth came out intact, with a very long root.

Mandy applied gauze to the gaping hole where the tooth used to be and had Terry bite down to stop the bleeding.

All in all, Terry's extraction was a complete success, and though Jack did not go to school for dentistry, he had earned his title of Camp Dentist.

Bill and Bob were both very impressed with Jack and told the rest of the camp as much.

Mandy was beside herself with pride for Jack, and Terry was glad to be out of pain and was very appreciative.

Jack was sure to tell Terry to finish the medicine he had been prescribed, and after Terry had left to go lay down for a while, Jack let out a big sigh of relief and thanked God for giving him the ability to perform this act without messing it up.

Jack couldn't fill a cavity or give a teeth cleaning, but he certainly could remove a bad tooth, and that was worth its weight in gold.

No one had to remain in agonizing pain as long as Jack was there to remove the source of the pain.

His best advice to everyone was to brush their teeth regularly in order not to be in the position of having to have a tooth removed, because once a cavity was gotten, removing the tooth was how it would eventually end up.

The difference between now and the days before Lidocaine and antibiotics was stark, making Jack's successful extraction one of timing.

July had now turned into August, and the leaves were beginning to change color.

It wouldn't be long before they got their first frost, with autumn being right around the corner.

The boys continued to chop wood for the cabins and the cooking fire, and the kids resumed their schooling after taking a break for the summer.

The sun was going down earlier each day, and soon they would attempt their version of daylight savings time. The only thing they had now to keep time was an old-fashioned wind-up clock, as there were no more electric clocks to be used, so they kept time the best they could with what they had.

It was almost 6 PM on a Sunday after an early dinner when they heard the sound of trucks out on the main road, stopping in front of the entrance to Peaceful Valley.

They could hear them, but not yet see them, but from the sound, they knew they were coming up the dirt road toward them.

No one ran to hide, but instead just stopped what they were doing to prepare for a possible confrontation with the unknown.

As soon as they got up to the lake, they could be seen by the whole community.

It was a long caravan of Chinese military trucks, about eight or nine, led by an American military vehicle, an MRAP. When they got to the headquarters building, they stopped, not knowing exactly which direction they should go, as the roads went in several different directions.

Out of the MRAP stepped out two American Soldiers, dressed in battle gear, as if they were in Iraq.

One of them walked back to the Chinese vehicle behind them and spoke to the driver, then went back to the front of the MRAP with the other American soldier.

Bill was at the dining hall with mostly everyone else and decided to walk over to the caravan to see what they wanted.

As he walked up to the soldiers, they both put their hands on their holstered firearms, just in case Bill was bringing trouble with him, but when he got up close to them, they both eased their stances.

"Mr. Jenkins? Long time no see Sir" said one of the soldiers.

"Sergeant Sanchez. Yes, it has been a while, hasn't it?" answered Bill, remembering the two soldiers from when they escorted him home from Base 12.

Sergeant Sanchez was accompanied by Sergeant Halliday; the other soldier Bill knew.

Bill shook hands with both men, then walked over to inspect the MRAP.

"I'll tell you boys, there have been a couple of times when I sure wish we had this vehicle," said Bill.

"I'm surprised to see you are still alive Mr. Jenkins. We've been hearing stories out here. Surprised you haven't been eaten" said Sergeant Halliday.

"We've come close a couple of times, believe me," said Bill. "What are you doing with Chinese soldiers? And why are they on American soil?"

"It's not American soil anymore Sir. Hasn't been for about three months now," said Sanchez. "They've been on the west coast for about six months, and they made their move on D.C. They were able to breach Mt. Weather and took the President and killed most of Congress, at least all the Republicans. The Dems laid down to them and surrendered everything, meaning the military and everything else. Halliday and I have been assigned to escort them around Colorado, mostly to our bases to see what was valuable to them. We just came from Fort Carson and NORAD."

"NORAD let you in?" asked Bill.

"They had to. As I said, they have the President, so they must do what he says. It's done Mr. Jenkins," said Halliday.

"The Chinese are very curious about you. They know practically everyone is dead now because of the hunters. That is what you folks call them, right?" asked Halliday.

"Yeah. I don't know who stuck that name on them, but that's what we call them. They hunt humans the same way we hunt animals, and for the same reason, a food source," said Bill.

"How have you managed to survive this long?" asked Sanchez.

"After you guys dropped me off, we loaded up a bunch of shopping carts with supplies and headed to a state park with a reservoir about fifteen miles away. We were looking for a water supply with hunting and fishing capability, so we decided on there, and we weren't the first ones with that idea. We met up with a bunch of people that got there first, so we joined up with them.

Three months ago we were attacked in the night by a small group of hunters that discovered us, but we were ready for them and killed most of them.

We were able to secure one of their vehicles, believe it or not, and we decided we were too exposed there, so we decided to look for a bigger vehicle that runs and we found that city bus over by the dining hall. It ran, so we loaded up all of our stuff and the people, and we came down here off the beaten path.

This used to be a boy scout ranch, and me and my son had been here a lot, so it had everything we needed, and we came down here in May.

Everything was fine until a month ago when we were attacked again by a traveling group of hunters that found us by accident I suppose, and they killed two of our members that lived away from us.

We were tipped off by that and had a good feeling they would be attacking us that night, so we waited in the dark and saw them coming from the direction we figured they would be coming from, all in the moonlight, and we picked them off one by one.

That's how we got here and what we've been through to survive" answered Bill.

"That's a remarkable story, Mr. Jenkins. How many of you are there?" asked Sanchez.

"Close to forty of us. One of the women is pregnant, my daughter-in-law, and we are just trying to survive. We don't want any trouble with anybody, and we don't intend to cause any trouble for your friends. I hope they understand that and will leave us alone" said Bill.

"I used to come here in the summer when I was a Boy Scout,' said Halliday. "We used to come here from out of state. Came here two summers in a row. I know this place. I don't think they want any trouble either Mr. Jenkins. The only reason they are here, first and foremost, is the oil. They are already pumping oil out of the ground in North Dakota. They rebuilt all the electrical infrastructure up there and are using the existing pipelines to shuttle it down to the gulf, where they are loading it onto tankers, going through the Panama Canal, and shipping it over to China.

Their whole economic infrastructure has changed, and as powerful as they used to be, you can say they've increased that by a hundred-fold.

They plan to utilize every source of oil there is to be had in the United States, so they've been doing reconnaissance missions here in Colorado, Wyoming, and especially Oklahoma and Texas.

America is practically a dead country now, but it still has resources, lots of them, and the Chinese see America the same way they'd see an uninhabited planet out in space, full of resources.

They just want to mine it, not populate it.

I'll bet there are not more than a million people left alive in America, and most of them are out here in the mid-west or somewhere around the coast, but not near a major city."

"They aren't interested in hurting anyone that has managed to survive. From what I'm told, they feel if you've gotten this far, you deserve to live your lives the best way you can but don't expect any help from them either. I guess what I'm saying is if you leave them alone, they will leave you alone," said Sanchez.

Bill let those words sink in and was relieved to hear them. He already assumed that America would not be coming back, at least not in his lifetime, so if the Chinese were exploiting the resources here, there wasn't a damn thing he or anyone else could do about it, especially if we had surrendered to them.

"Why don't you come with us so I can introduce you," said Sanchez, so Bill and the soldiers walked to the front vehicle behind the MRAP, to the passenger door, and out of the vehicle stepped out an officer of the Chinese Army.

"This is Captain Lee with The Chinese National Army. Captain Lee, this is Bill Jenkins, and he speaks for a small village of people that have managed to survive several attacks from cannibalistic hunters in the area.

I have explained America's situation to Mr. Jenkins and your reasons for being on American soil. He understands everything and does not wish to engage your army or interfere in any way. They just want to be left alone" said Sergeant Sanchez.

Captain Lee then extended his hand out to Bill, and Bill accepted his handshake.

"You are a survivor. There are not many of you" said Captain Lee. His English was perfect as if he were born and raised in America.

"So I'm told" answered Bill.

Jack and Mandy had by this time joined Bill, Captain Lee, and the American soldiers.

"We will not be in this area for very long. You were discovered by one of our helicopters, so we wanted to introduce ourselves and see what your intentions are. We have no designs for you and your community. We do not want to be interfered with, and that is all we ask. In return, we will not interfere with you" said Captain Lee.

Mandy was becoming increasingly uncomfortable at the way the driver of the truck was staring at her, looking at her like she was a bowl of pork fried rice, and he hadn't eaten for days.

It wasn't the look of a cannibalistic hunter, but instead a sexual hunter.

An understanding was come to, with everyone bidding each other a good day, and the trucks made a wide birth in front of headquarters and turned to exit the camp the way they came.

SIXTEEN

Mr. Stork Comes to Call

Mark was getting increasingly agitated, not knowing what he should do, if anything.

All the women were in the vicinity of their cabin, with Kate inside in labor.

The baby was going to come when the baby decided to come.

There would be no inducement of labor, and no epidural when it was coming.

Kate would have to tough this one out, and there wouldn't even be an episiotomy to help the delivery.

This was going to be an old-fashioned frontier birth, with plenty of hot water and rags.

The crib was already set up and waiting for the miracle child to come into the world, and the hope now was that when it came, it wouldn't reject Kate's breast and would take her milk, but only time would tell.

Viv and Julie were with Kate, trying to make her as comfortable as possible, and they were her designated midwives.

Viv had been practicing stitching up an elk carcass, so she could stitch up Kate when the time came, but Viv was still nervous, no matter how much practice she had under her belt because it wasn't the same thing.

With all of Julie's detachment issues she'd been suffering, she came out of her malaise at just the right time. She was there for her daughter in her hour of need, and soon she would be a grandmother.

"I know you're nervous son, but you are just going to have to relax and let nature take its course. There's nothing you can do from this point, so just hang out here with us and let the women figure it out. Everything's going to be all right." said Bill to Mark.

Mark felt helpless and wanted to do something to help his wife, as he could hear her in distress from inside the cabin.

This was going to be an afternoon birth, not a wee hour of the morning birth, like so many have been in human history.

Burt was super excited for Mark and the community. They were bringing in new life, signifying progress for their existence.

Burt had become attached to everyone there, but especially Mark and Kate, because he remembered Mark from the past, attending camps at Peaceful Valley. He wanted nothing but the best for him and would do anything necessary to help the new parents out.

Mark asked Burt to be the baby's Godfather, and though Burt knew nothing about how to do that, he graciously accepted that responsibility.

One thing was for sure. The baby would have plenty of men in its corner.

It was September and the weather was still warm, with no sign of winter on the horizon, and that was a good thing seen by all. Winter would come soon enough, and no one was looking forward to its arrival.

It was close to 4:00 P.M. when the baby started to come, and the screams that came out of that cabin could have been heard from miles around.

Julie was behind Kate holding her upright in a sitting position, whispering in her ear and comforting her with cold compresses as she pushed the baby out, and when he arrived, he was as beautiful as you can imagine a baby would be.

Covered in vernix and blood, the baby lay on the bed between Kate's legs after Viv held it up and smacked its little butt, letting it clear its lungs with a tiny cry. She then began to rub the vernix into the baby's skin while waiting for the placenta to come out, and when it did, another woman held it up above the baby to allow the blood to drain into the baby while Viv cut the umbilical cord and tied it in a knot.

Kate did not tear much at all and would only require a stitch or two, and Viv began the stitching while two of the women cleaned the baby up, swaddled it in baby blankets after putting on a diaper, and placed it in the arms of a crying Kate Jenkins, so happy to have her pregnancy end in the delivery of a perfect baby boy.

It was then that Mark was allowed in the cabin to be by her side and with the baby, and he kissed them both over and over again, and he was crying too.

Viv was exhausted, but exhilarated at the same time, and so happy she was able to help with her new grandbaby and not screw anything up that she was entrusted to do.

The baby took Kate's breast like a fish to water, and everyone was relieved.

He was so perfect, so righteous, and he was a gift from God.

Bill, Jack, Burt, Bob, Terry, and Randy were outside the cabin smoking cigars that Burt had brought out from his house, relishing this monumental moment in the history of Peaceful Valley.

To the best of Burt's memory, he was pretty sure this was the first baby delivered on the property, as he made it one of his hobbies to know the history of that piece of land.

It was now dinner time and thankfully two women had taken care of the cooking while the rest were in the cabin with Kate, and they had something simple in beans and cornbread.

Jack had given Kate some ibuprofen and did not want to give her anything stronger since she was nursing, for fear of passing it on to the baby.

They decided to name the baby Paul, after Kate's dad, and this made Julie very happy,

He even had a nickname because they called the baby Pauly.

Julie walked out of the bunk house cabin and sat in a chair, so overwhelmed by what had just happened, and she began to sob in her hands while talking to her husband, knowing he could hear her.

Jack left the group of men he was with and came up behind Julie and put his arms around her, talking sweetly to his mother, comforting her with words of his dad in heaven looking down upon them, pleased with Julie and Kate, and the new baby boy that had come into the world.

Julie had a purpose again.

Dinner was brought to Kate and Mark, and everyone left them alone to go eat in the dining hall, and they were all so excited about the new member of their community. The dining hall had not been that loud with conversation in a while.

Everyone slept a little better that night, knowing that life always finds a way, and their lives were all now refreshed with the new blood that had arrived.

Mark and Kate barely touched their dinner and slept with the baby for the remainder of the night.

Jack sat on the front porch of the headquarters building with Mandy, professing their love for one another, and Mandy secretly wished she was pregnant with Jack's baby.

She wanted to be a mother too, which is something she hadn't thought of until Jack came into her life.

She knew it would be her responsibility as well to bring new life into Peaceful Valley, and with Jack, she could make that happen.

She only wished her mother and father could be a part of it when the time came.

Jack knew that Mandy was who he would be with for the rest of his life, and he was torn inside about asking her to marry him.

It had only been a couple of months since he first met her, so it seemed premature to ask her for her hand in marriage, but these were not normal circumstances, and he battled within himself why he should not pop the question to her now.

Why should he wait?

He knew she loved him as he loved her, and it wasn't like either one of them would be holding out to see who else could come along for either of them.

It was meant to be, he thought, and it was God's plan.

This was what was on Jack's mind first and foremost.

Maybe it was the birth of his sister's baby, but he would pray about it and ask God for a sign.

The next day there was still excitement in the air, and everyone wanted to know how the new parents made it through the night.

At breakfast, Mark came out of the cabin to be with everyone else and relayed the news that Kate and the baby were doing spectacular. After retrieving Kate some breakfast and bringing it to her, he came back out to the dining room to eat and answer everyone's questions.

They all wanted to see Kate and her baby, and they were reassured they would be able to once she was feeling up to it, possibly as soon as tomorrow.

After breakfast, the men were all around the campfire outside the dining hall, relaxing while having their morning coffee, and chatting about the possibility of a harsh winter. No one could know what the weather would be like, but they all agreed to prepare for the worst.

One of the things that came up in conversation was the showers, and how it would be rough to take a shower in the dead of winter.

There were no roofs on the showers, but Burt came up with the idea that they could build the roofs and heat them with five-gallon tanks of propane and heater coils, which sounded like a fantastic idea.

It was then that Randy saw the horses riding toward them from the east, carrying two men they had never seen before, both looking to be in their thirties, and he alerted everyone else around him to their presence.

They were about 300 yards away and coming up to them slowly.

Bob grabbed his pistol, hoping this wasn't going to be a replay of past encounters with hunters.

All the men got up and began walking out toward the horsemen, and Bob pointed his pistol at them when they were forty yards away.

"Stop right there," Bob said as he had his pistol trained on them. "What's your business here?"

The men were carrying rifles with them, but they were holstered on their horses.

"We aren't looking for any trouble. We just want to talk with you. We've ridden about fifty miles to find you" said one of the men.

"Is this Peaceful Valley?" asked the other man.

"It is. Did you come looking for us? How can that be? How do you know about us?" asked Bill.

"Sergeant Sanchez told us about you. Can you stop pointing that pistol at us? You're making me nervous." said one of the men.

Bill looked at Bob, nodding at him to lower his gun.

"You guys want some coffee?" asked Bill.

"We'd love some. Can we dismount?" asked the other man.

"Sure, but leave your rifles holstered. You can tie your horses up to that tree" said Terry.

The men got down off of their horses and led them to the tree Terry pointed at, tied them up, then walked over to Bill and the rest, extending their hands out to introduce themselves.

"My name is Miles Wilkerson. Next to me is Jeff Fraley. We're from Simla, due east of here" said Miles as he was shaking the hands of all the men that came out to greet them.

"Don't know that town," said Burt. "I'll go get you fella's a cup of joe and you can grab a seat around the fire."

After everyone had sat down, all the men in the camp were eager to hear what these men had to say.

"How do you know Sergeant Sanchez?" asked Bill.

"He and his partner showed up at our camp with a bunch of Chinese soldiers in trucks. He told us about you and your village. They were just traveling north on highway forty and we are pretty visible from the road, so they pulled in to see what was what." said Jeff. "He told us about you guys, how you have a township of some sort here. We came looking for you because we want to join up with you."

The men of Peaceful Valley didn't know what to say and looked at each other expecting someone to say something.

"You say you are from Simla? Where exactly is that?" asked Bill.

"I figure it's about fifty miles from here. It took us two days and nights to get here," said Miles. "How many people do you have here?"

"We've got forty-one people now, thanks to the baby that was born yesterday, "said Bob. "How many people do you have? It's not just the two of you, is it?"

"We've got four families, nineteen people in all including us. We are set up in tents next to a small lake. We've really had a rough go of it this past year, and one of our women is pregnant. We've been living off of anything we could catch and eat, even prairie dogs. There isn't much game to be had out there. The army guys saw how bad we were having it and suggested we hook up with you. I don't think we will make it through the winter" said Miles.

"Have you run into any hunters out there?" asked Bill.

"You mean other people hunting for food? No, it's just been us" replied Jeff.

"I'm talking about people hunting other people for food. Cannibals," said Bill.

The two men looked at each other in shock, not believing they were being asked this.

"What the hell are you talking about, people hunting people?" asked Jeff.

Being out as far as they were with not much population to contend with, they had no experience with hunters and had no idea what Bill was talking about.

"Most of the people in Colorado that survived the initial EMP, especially in the urban areas, are now dead because of them. A lot of people started hunting their neighbors for food, killing them and eating them. We've had some experience with them ourselves. When you came riding up, that was the first thing that crossed my mind, as I'm sure it was for the rest of us," said Bob.

"Oh hell no. Are you kidding me? I'd starve to death before I'd eat a person. Oh my God!" said Miles.

"Jesus Christ. What the hell is wrong with people?" said Jeff.

"Yep. Do you even know what happened? Why we are all in this situation?" asked Bill.

"We didn't until we talked with them soldiers. We figured someone would have to come by and rescue us. We went into town, which is nothing more than a gas station and a post office, and nobody there knew either. We figured it was something that had to do with the electrical grid, that's all. We kept on waiting and hoping, and then the next time we rode the horses into town, the few people that were there were either dead or gone.

If those soldiers hadn't of come by and told us what they told us, we'd have just kept waiting for help and we would have died out there," said Miles.

"Listen, men. Me and the men from camp need to talk among ourselves for a few minutes. Why don't you just get some more coffee from the pot there on the fire, and we'll go inside the dining hall? We'll be back out in a few minutes" said Bill, and the men from camp walked single file into the dining hall to discuss their proposal.

"We've got to help these people," said Burt.

"Any objections to growing Peaceful Valley?" asked Bill.

Everyone immediately agreed that the Christian thing to do would be to help these people in any way they could.

"We still have three unoccupied forts, so there's plenty of room. These men look like they could help us in a lot of ways, namely shooting elk and other projects around camp. The most important thing is they have a woman getting ready to have a baby. We can't leave them out there exposed to the elements. We can drive the bus out there and get all of them" said Bill. "There's still three quarters of a tank of fuel in the bus. We can send Randy and one of the other men to the Walmart and siphon another fifty gallons of fuel, then we can go get them. Randy, are you up for making the drive?" asked Bill.

"You can count on me. I will do it," said Randy.

"Those men can leave their horses here and ride with us. I'll go, along with Burt?" said Bill, waiting for an affirmative from Burt.

"You bet. I'll go too," said Burt.

"Well, let's go out there and tell them what we've decided," said Bill, and they all walked back out to the campfire.

"We'd love to have you all join us. You probably didn't see the bus on the other side of the dining hall. It runs and tomorrow morning, me, Burt, Randy, and the two of you are going to drive out there and get them" said Bill, and the two men jumped out of their chairs and began hugging anyone that would allow them to.

"Thank you. Thank you. Thank you so much. I can't believe it, and neither will they when we pull up on a bus!" said Miles.

"We've got three forts, buildings with bunks in them that are empty. You've got four families, so two families will have to bunk together," said Burt.

"We need to get some more fuel for the bus, so we will do that today and we'll leave first thing after breakfast tomorrow, and we should be back here by early afternoon. I'll bet you guys are starving. When's the last time you ate?" asked Bill.

"The day before yesterday," said Jeff.

"Come on in the dining room and I'll have the women feed you. I'll put your horses in the corral with my horse, then we'll get you situated in a bunk upstairs above the kitchen," said Burt.

The men were overjoyed that they had found Peaceful Valley and that their families were about to be rescued.

God was alive and well, and present in the hearts and minds of the two weary travelers who had almost given up on finding refuge for their families.

SEVENTEEN

To the Rescue

" **D** ang, it sure is nice feeling that air conditioning," said Miles Wilkerson, as the bus hauling him, Bill, Burt, Jeff Fraley, and Randy behind the wheel went up Elbert Road to Highway 86.

"We found the bus in an underground garage in Boulder. It was spared from the EMP because it was underground. It literally saved our butts. We used to be located at Cherry Creek Reservoir outside of Denver, but we were attacked by hunters and decided we needed to move, so we found this, and it transported all of our people to Peaceful Valley, the same way we are going to transport you and your folk," said Bill.

"I'm sure glad we never had to contend with cannibals. I don't know if we would have made it this long," said Jeff Fraley.

"It definitely changes the way you think about things, that's for sure," said Bill. "Tell us a little bit about your crew."

"There are two men still at camp with the women and the kids, one of the men is older, in his fifties with his wife. His name is Mike Dilbert. The other one is Jake Riley, and he's in his twenties with his wife, and she's the one that's pregnant. She's due in a couple of months, and they got two kids already.

There's my wife and my three girls, all teenagers, and there's Jeff's wife and his six kids, and they range from five to fourteen." said Miles.

"My second to the oldest is a down's syndrome baby. He's twelve and his name is Sonny. He's a good boy and he takes care of his momma when I'm not there," said Jeff.

"You got a big family Jeff. You are definitely doing your part to repopulate civilization" said Burt, and they all had a good laugh.

It took about an hour, give or take ten minutes, to get to their encampment, and when they got there, they were amazed these people lived as long as they had.

There were several small tents pitched next to each other about ten yards from a small fishing hole, with no trees or anything else around them to give them protection from the elements.

As soon as they pulled up on the side of the road, the people in camp just stood amazed at the bus, not having seen a vehicle other than the Chinese military trucks and the MRAP.

When Miles and Jeff exited, they all started jumping up and down and were glad to see them. In the back of their minds, they must have been worried sick they'd never see them again.

There was nothing these two men had said to Bill and the boys that prepared them for what they were seeing.

These people were close to death, some worse than others. They were all skinny as a rail and hadn't looked like they'd eaten for a long time.

Bill and Burt exited the bus behind Miles and Jeff and walked over to the campsite through the tall grass. They began introducing themselves to their new neighbors, and each and every one of them, including the men, began crying tears of joy to meet them. They had long since given up on living, and instead were counting the days left before they died.

It was no wonder to Bill why the soldiers told them about Peaceful Valley, and it must have killed Sanchez and Halliday to have to leave them there in this condition.

This wasn't just a rescue mission. This was a lifesaving mission.

The hardest thing for the men to see was the pregnant wife of the man that stayed behind with her. She was horribly skinny and did not look seven months pregnant, maybe four or five months at the most. They knew they had gotten there just in the nick of time, because had she gone another week, she may have miscarried, and she still might, depending on how quickly they could get her to birthing weight. Only time would tell.

There was no point in taking down and packing away the tents, as they wouldn't be needed. The only things these folks needed to take with them were their personal effects, sleeping bags, and their clothing, and most of them were too weak to carry their belongings, so the men carried most of it to the bus.

Burt was standing outside next to the back door when Bill came out, and Burt pointed over to a cross sticking up out of the ground, back about fifty yards from where they were camped.

"You see that cross Bill?" asked Burt.

Bill nodded his head and looked around, then asked Jeff to come over to him.

"Is that cross from your people?" asked Bill.

"Yes. Yes, it is. That was Miles's youngest son Timmy. We lost him about eight months ago. He was diabetic and he had no insulin. He lasted longer than most of us thought he would. I don't think he has gotten over him yet. He really loved that boy and cried by himself out on the prairie for days. That's why he volunteered to go looking for you guys. He wouldn't have been able to take seeing another one of us go."

Bill stared at Miles, walking toward the bus with a suitcase full of clothes, and he couldn't imagine having to live through the pain of what that man went through. He wiped a tear away, not wanting to make this man relive any of it, not wanting him to feel like he had to explain anything. Someday if he wanted to talk about it, Bill would be there to listen.

"I think that's about it. I think we are ready to go," said Miles.

When the bus started up and all the people and their things were loaded, they all said goodbye to their campsite, and Bill couldn't help but notice Miles and his wife, and his kids not looking at the campsite, but instead looking at the cross with tears rolling down their cheeks.

Bill couldn't remember ever seeing anything as heartbreaking as that, and he had to turn away, otherwise, he would begin to cry as well.

They were leaving their dead son behind so they could live, but Bill wondered how much the family cared about living at that moment. To lose a child is the most unnatural thing a parent can go through, and to want to keep on living would be a struggle if it weren't for their three daughters, so as tragic as it was, they still had children to look out for, and that's what kept them going.

Bill knew that once they got to Peaceful Valley, the women would tend to all of their needs and get them all healthy again in no time.

If he remembered right, Jack had also snagged all the prenatal vitamins he could find on his last trip to the pharmacy. Hopefully, he had enough to put the whole damn bunch of them on vitamins for at least a month, so they could catch up on their health.

By the time winter hit, they would all have an extra layer of fat to ward off the cold weather, and before anyone knew it, they'd all be back up to snuff.

Bill took an immediate liking to Miles Wilkerson from the moment they shook hands.

The fact that Miles never spoke about his son told Bill everything he needed to know about the man. He didn't want to use his loss as a gain, making everyone feel sorry for him.

He was a straight shooter, and Bill knew how hard that was to come by.

He would make it a point to sidle up to him, befriend him, and make damn sure that if he needed anything, Bill would move Heaven and Earth to make it happen.

It was just after lunch when the bus pulled into Peaceful Valley, and all of the new residents were shocked at the beauty of it. Trees and buildings all around, and they would be sleeping under a roof for the first time in over a year, on a real mattress and not on the hard ground.

All of the women made it a point to be at the door of the bus to greet their new residents, and by the looks on their faces, they were also shocked at their condition as they slowly exited the bus, but still, they tried not to make spectacles of themselves.

"All of you, welcome! Follow me into the dining hall and let's get you fed" said Viv, introducing herself to everyone and giving hugs to the women and kids.

It had been days since they had eaten, and weeks since they had eaten a real meal.

Special attention was given to Jake Riley's wife, as she was the weakest of the bunch, and needed help getting up the dining hall stairs.

"I don't think it's a good idea putting her out in one of the forts, so far away from the rest of us," said Bob. "She doesn't look so good, especially for someone getting ready to have a baby."

"I think you are right Bob. I was just thinking the same thing and I might have an idea. I have to run it by Viv, Mark, and Kate," said Bill.

Bill's idea meant moving Mark and Kate in with them and moving the boys back upstairs in the dining hall and moving Jake Riley, his wife, and his two boys in where Mark, Kate, and the baby currently were.

It would put the expectant mother a whole lot closer to everyone else and keep her walking to a minimum for meals and the latrine, especially with winter coming.

Bill got no argument from Mark and Kate, and Viv was happy to have the baby in Trail Boss with her and Bill.

Brian and Rocky loved the idea of staying in the dining hall again, away from his parents, giving them a feeling of independence.

Miles and his family would share Ft. Vasquez with the older man and his wife, while Jeff Fraley, his wife, and his six kids would inhabit Ft. Lupton.

Jake Riley was very appreciative of Mark and Kate giving up their cabin for him and his family, and Mrs. Riley was beside herself with the generosity and kindness everyone was showing toward them. It felt good to feel safe and not concentrate on when you were going to die, but instead live and prepare for the birth of your child.

"Looks like we're going to have to make another trip to Walmart for baby things," said Viv as she laid next to him that night, whispering so as not to wake the baby in the bedroom next to theirs.

"Miles, Bob, and I are going to hunt in the morning. A family of elk was seen hanging around Bent's Fort yesterday morning while we were getting the families. We're going to need more food now. Our township has grown by half. We're right at sixty people now if my math is correct," said Bill.

"Wow. It's amazing how far we've come in the last year, despite all the obstacles we've had to overcome. Just think Bill, if we hadn't decided to head to the reservoir, none of this would have happened, and all of this led up to you guys throwing these families a lifeline because we were here. It's funny how God leads people to each other" Viv said, then she gave Bill a big squeeze and turned over to go to sleep.

Viv was right.

It all seemed like Providence, and God was leading the way for them to follow, and as long as they listened for his guidance, they knew everything would turn out ok for them.

Burt had a few more wood stoves in the quartermaster building and he would need to install one in each of the new forts being occupied before the cold weather hit, so he got busy on that first thing the next morning and had several of the boys chop wood for each of the forts.

The women had more food to prepare now, so they got up a little earlier than normal to take care of that, and the three new women were corralled in to be given kitchen duties to help out. One of them elected to help with teaching the children as well, and as luck would have it, Mary Dilbert, the oldest woman, was a nurse at one time in her life, and she would be a welcome addition to help Jack out in the Health Lodge.

Margaret Riley was not asked to do anything yet, as it was important for her to rest and gain weight for the baby.

Everyone was very concerned for her and checked in on her constantly, almost to the point of annoyance. The woman now had more caretakers for her than she was used to, and she had to adjust to being around a lot more people willing to help her. This was welcomed for sure, but at times it was a little overwhelming, but she would come to appreciate the concern, especially when the times came when she did need more help.

Soon meals would be brought to her the closer she came to having the baby.

The men that went hunting that morning could find no trace of any elk, so after sitting for an hour with no elk appearing, Bill thought it would be a good idea if they did something they hadn't done previously, and that was to go across the road to the Magness camp where the cub scouts went.

There was plenty of land over there and a lake for the elk to drink from, so maybe they'd find a new honeypot for hunting.

When they drove up to the lake in the police cruiser, they saw several herds around the lake drinking, so they parked down the dirt road from it and walked up with rifles in hand, careful not to spook any of them.

Bob bagged the first one, knocking down a massive bull elk, which turned out to be all they needed. They field-dressed it right then and there and cut it up into sections to fit into the cruiser, then brought it back to the dining hall for butchering and salting.

Just about all the vegetables in the garden had been harvested, except for the pumpkins, which would make lots of pumpkin pies when the time came.

Between baking bread and desserts, the women that did most of the baking were in the kitchen practically every day…all day, so they had little time to do much else in the way of chores around Peaceful Valley, but that was ok. They were providing a critical service to the camp already.

In the afternoon after lunch, Bob, Randy, Bill, Viv, and Mary Dilbert, along with Brian and Rocky, all loaded up onto the bus to make their trip to Walmart again.

The boys came along specifically to siphon diesel fuel out of the semi-trucks on the loading dock because the fuel gauge on the bus was showing below half a tank.

Viv and Mary were there to get another crib, bassinet, and things the new baby would need, plus replenish what little Pauly was starting to run out of.

The men went along for the ride to scan the store for things the camp needed, like matches, more propane tanks, and anything else they could think of, but they were there mostly to provide cover for the women.

The boys filled up ten five-gallon fuel cans twice, getting 100 gallons for the bus, bringing the bus almost to the full mark, and this took most of the time they were at the store.

The ride to and from was uneventful, other than the pack of dogs they had seen down the street coming their way as they were boarding the bus for home.

Bob fired off a couple of shots toward the dogs, ricocheting off the concrete next to them, scaring them away. There was no telling what the dogs had been living on all this time, but a pack of wild dogs with limited food sources coming your way was most likely not a situation you'd like to be a part of.

When they got back to Peaceful Valley, they dropped off the crib and bassinet, and other baby stuff at the Riley's cabin. Jake was more than capable of assembling the crib and bassinet, leaving the men to attend to other things on the ranch.

By that night, the new residents had a few meals under their belts and were looking a hundred times better than the day before when they arrived.

The camp had a busyness to it now. There were more people, and with that came a lot more conversations and longer lines, but it was all welcome and made them feel like civilization instead of a few people out on a campout together.

Jack had spent a great deal of time with Mary Dilbert in the twenty-four plus hours she had been to camp and was so relieved to have an actual nurse on the premises that would be able to assist him and give him advice should a situation arise that would normally be above his pay grade.

Of all the new people that arrived, her husband Mike was the most entertaining. His stories around the campfire after dinner had the community in an uproar of laughter, and he could be counted on at least once each night to tell a story so funny, you had to wonder if he had missed his calling by not being a standup comedian.

They all felt fortunate to have each other, and in their way, everyone contributed something vital to the community, almost like they were cogs in a well-oiled machine.

They all hung on to each other and became one big family, which was an experience none of them would have had if the EMP had not done its damage.

Out of tragedy and hardship came love and unity, and in its own way, was a symbol of what could happen if the right people got together with the same mindset, with all wanting to do their part in making everyone's life a better one.

Mandy could not keep her eyes off Jack and grew increasingly more attached to him by the day.

How long was he going to wait until he popped the question to her, she thought?

What was he waiting for?

She thought that if he didn't do it soon, she would have to ask him.

All she knew was that she wanted to be with him, and she knew damn well that's what he wanted too.

Maybe he was concerned about how his mother would react.

It was a waiting game for Mandy, and she was getting impatient.

EIGHTEEN

Not Smokey the Bear

B rian and Rocky had their eyes on the two oldest daughters of Miles Wilkerson since the day they came to Peaceful Valley. The girls were sixteen and fifteen, both Brian and Rocky were fifteen, and both sexes teenage hormones were raging.

There wasn't a whole lot to do once their chores were done, so they found themselves wandering over to the vicinity of Fort Vasquez where the girls stayed with their family whenever they had free time on their hands, usually after lunch.

The oldest girl's name was Amanda, and her younger sister was Eleanor, and both could usually be found together reading anything they could get their hands on outside while the weather was still favorable.

The boys would sneak up on them through the woods and spy on them from a distance, never revealing themselves, and talk about the things boys talk about girls once their interests have been piqued.

Rocky had his eye on Amanda, leaving Brian to fantasize about Eleanor, meaning whatever crazy things they could think up with not an ounce of experience in such matters, their adolescent imaginations would run wild.

The girls never paid attention directly to them, but they knew they were being spied on from the woods by them, and they just pretended like the boys were not there, giving the boys a false sense of security in their covertness.

In the week the girls had been there, they had filled out considerably, having a steady diet of good food, and instead of looking like the sickly rails they looked like in the beginning, they had both blossomed into beautiful healthy girls, really catching the attention of the boys.

The boys also had the attention of the girls, but the girls couldn't let on that they were interested, because they had to be cool. They liked the idea of being pursued, so the less attention paid to the pursuer, the harder the pursuer tries.

On this particular day, the two boys were hiding behind a boulder by a pine tree off to the side of Fort Vasquez, and the girls were playing jump rope out away from the Fort.

Rocky was the one who saw it first.

"Brian, look!" Rocky said as he pointed to the side of the cabin.

It was a huge black bear, and it was acting strangely, with foam coming out of its mouth.

"Holy moly! That bear is sick! Look at all the foam coming out of its mouth!" said Brian.

The bear seemed disoriented and perturbed, growling and pawing at the air, as if it was seeing something it didn't like in front of him.

"HEY! WATCH OUT FOR THAT BEAR!" yelled Rocky at the girls.

The girls stopped jumping rope, then looked over at the boulder where the boys were.

"What?" said Amanda.

Rocky stood up from behind the boulder and pointed at the bear, and when the girls saw it, they both screamed. Mrs. Wilkerson was inside the cabin, and when she heard the girls scream, she opened the door, and the bear was just six feet from her and growled at her, causing her to scream and slam the door behind her, leaving her girls out there to fend for themselves.

The bear then spotted the girls and began moving toward them.

The girls screamed again and stood frozen not knowing what to do.

"GET IN THE CAMPER! RUN! GET IN THE CAMPER NOW!" screamed Rocky.

There was an old camper shell on the other side of the cabin from where the bear was, so the girls both ran to it, opened its door, and locked themselves inside.

The bear then walked over to the camper shell, and you could hear the girls screaming bloody murder at the top of their lungs, but this only seemed to agitate the bear even more. The more the girls screamed, the madder the bear got, and he started swatting at the camper shell, hitting the door with its paw, making the girls scream even louder still.

Brian and Rocky were frozen in fear but snapped out of it and tried to get the attention of the bear by yelling at it.

The bear turned and looked at them, now growling and roaring like never before, torn between the girls in the camper and the boys behind the boulder, but the girls' screams were more shrieking and louder, garnering the full attention of the bear now, and it got on its hind legs and began rocking the camper shell back and forth, knocking the girls around inside.

Without thinking, Rocky ran out from behind the boulder and confronted the bear, getting only a few feet away from it.

"ROCKY! WHAT ARE YOU DOING? GET AWAY FROM THAT BEAR!" screamed Brian.

But it was too late. The bear charged Rocky and knocked him down, then bit his hand.

And then a sound cracked the sky. It was a bullet fired from Bob Hawkins's rifle, shooting the bear in the side of its head, dropping it to the ground, and falling on Rocky's legs.

"GET THIS BEAR OFF ME! GET IT OFF ME" Rocky screamed as Brian flew down to where Rocky was laying on the ground.

The bear was deader than a doornail, so the immediate danger of Rocky being mauled by the bear was over, but there was still danger to be dealt with.

Rocky's hand was bleeding profusely, but it wasn't anything life-threatening.

Bob came running up to the bear to make sure it was dead, and after confirming it, he turned his attention to Rocky.

"Look at that bear's mouth. Do you see all that foam? This bear is rabid. It's got rabies, and it bit you, which means now you've got rabies. We need to get you over to your brother Jack right now. We don't have any time to waste." Said Bob as he handed his rifle to Brian, then pulled Rocky out from under the bear.

Bob then picked him up and threw him over his shoulder in a fireman's carry and started running down the road toward the Health Lodge.

Brian opened the door to the camper and told the girls it was ok to come out, then told them about the bear being rabid and how Bob Hawkins shot it and was taking Rocky to the Health Lodge, then Brian began running down the road after them.

Naturally, the girls started chasing Brian because they wanted to know everything that was happening in real-time.

When Bob got close to the Health Lodge, many of the other residents saw Bob carrying Rocky and rushed to see what was going on.

Once inside, he laid Rocky down on the examination table and stepped aside, letting Jack take over.

"What is this? What happened?" asked Jack.

"He was bitten by a rabid bear. He needs a rabies shot" said Bob.

Jack began to panic because he had no rabies serum to give him, nor would he know how much to give him.

"Somebody go get Mary Dilbert, and hurry!" he said to the crowd.

"I'm here Jack," Mary said as she was already there and walking in the door.

They filled her in as to what happened, and she then jumped into action.

"We have to get some anti-rabies serum into him, and I'll bet you don't have any, do you?" she asked.

"No. It's not something I thought of. Can we go to get it at the pharmacy?"

"They wouldn't have it there. It would be in an emergency room in a hospital. There's one in Colorado Springs, so Bill is going to have to drive me. I'll go because I know what I'm looking for and know where it would be. You stay here with your brother and treat his wound" she told Jack, with no argument from him.

Someone went and got Bill and told him what was going on, so he, Bob, and Mary piled into the police cruiser and hightailed it for Colorado Springs.

"Where are we going?" asked Bill.

"There's a hospital on Woodmen Ave I used to work at, and I know where they keep everything in the emergency room" she replied. "If you can get us on I-25, I can direct you from there."

"Where the hell did that bear come from Bob, and how did you get on it so quickly?" asked Bill.

"I was over by the junkpile on the other side of camp looking for some of that metal roofing they have over there. I'm making a rabbit cage. My kids want me to catch some cottontails and they want to take care of them.

Anyway, I came up on this monster paw print, and I knew it was from a bear, and it was fresh. I started looking all around me and followed some tracks I thought belonged to it, and then I saw it running through the trees toward the cabin Miles is in, so I started following it.

At one point, I thought I lost it, then I heard these kids screaming and I heard the bear growling, and you know me, I always carry my rifle.

I got up on Miles's cabin just in time to see this bear knock Rocky down to the ground, so I took aim right there and shot it in the head just as he was biting Rocky's hand. Had I gotten there one minute later, that bear would have ripped his throat out. Thank God I chased that bear. I almost was going to leave it alone," said Bob.

"My God. If it's not one thing, it's another. Welcome to frontier life. Well done, Bob, well done," said Bill.

They were coming up to the Woodmen exit, so Mary told Bill to get off and hang a left. After driving about a mile, they came up to the hospital and drove to the emergency doors. They were closed, but not locked, and Bob slid the door sideways so Mary could gain entry.

After a few minutes, she ran back outside with some small vials and a few Hypodermic needles, jumped in the car, and they sped off toward home.

"This stuff is supposed to be refrigerated, but some studies were done on it and it doesn't lose its effectiveness at room temperature, but it's been at room temperature for quite some time, so hopefully it will still work. If not, that boy's in serious trouble," said Mary.

Mary was right about Rocky being in trouble if the vaccine didn't work.

It meant certain death, and the death was horrific for those that die from it.

Fortunately for Rocky, and Jack, Mary knew what she was doing when it came to stuff like this, and she would be administering the dosage to Rocky with Jack's assistance.

When they pulled back into camp and up to the Health Lodge, they found Rocky sitting up on the examination table admiring his bandaged hand, not aware of the danger he was in. Jack, Mandy, and Julie were chatting about the bear in camp, but they all moved into action when Mary came in with the medicine.

"Jack, why don't you sterilize the area at the end of the bandage with some alcohol, and I'll get this shot ready," said Mary.

"I'm going to give you this shot Rocky at the base of your hand by your wrist. I'll give you another one in three days, then four days after that, then again a week later. You need to be monitored by someone these next couple of days. Jack, can he spend the next couple of nights with you here in the Health Lodge?" asked Mary.

"Sure thing. I'll make sure someone brings a bunk in here" answered Jack.

After Jack swabbed the area where she was going to administer the shot, she pushed the needle in his hand and gave him his dosage.

Jack then grabbed Mary and Mandy's hands, with Julie and Rocky in the circle as well, and they all prayed for a speedy recovery and healing of Rocky. These next forty-eight hours would be telltale if the serum was working, otherwise, it was going to be some long days and nights until Rocky finally succumbed to this disease,

"How are you feeling?" asked Jack.

"I feel fine. My hand is a little sore, but other than that, I'm good" Rocky answered.

Bill, Viv, and Brian then walked into the Health Lodge, and it was beginning to get a little crowded in there.

They all hugged Rocky, and Brian greeted him with their special handshake.

"Damn dude, that was crazy what you did. Brave man, just brave," said Brian.

Rocky tried to play it off, but what he did was astounding, and may have saved the lives of the girls in the camper shell.

"Amanda was really impressed. I think you got her attention bro," said Brian.

"I heard what you did Rocky. That was truly a stand-up man kind of thing to do," said Bill.

While Bill and Mary were retrieving the serum, Viv had come over and offered to stitch up Rocky's hand, and she did an excellent job before his hand was bandaged.

"How does your hand feel? It's not too tight, is it?" Viv asked Rocky.

"No. It feels good. No worries" Rocky answered her. "I'm spending the next couple of nights in here with Jack. They want to keep an eye on me" said Rocky.

Then in walked Miles Wilkerson with his wife and three daughters, Amanda being one of them.

"I heard what you did son," said Miles to Rocky, putting his hand on his shoulder. "I can't thank you enough. You probably saved the lives of my two daughters. Anytime you need something, you come to ask me, ok?"

Then Amanda stood next to him and whispered in Rocky's ear, something that made Rocky smile, and then she kissed him on the cheek, and all had not gone unnoticed by Brian, who was smiling from ear to ear.

Rocky Price was a bonafide hero at Peaceful Valley, and in the next few days he would be lauded eventually by every single resident in camp.

During meals, Amanda Wilkerson was now sitting next to him, and before long it was obvious to all that they were becoming an item, spending more and more time with each other, not just at meals, but at other times during the day.

Rocky had gone through his first two nights at the Health Lodge without even so much as a giddy up, so it was safe to say that the serum was working on him, and he would stick around to live another day.

Three days after getting his first shot, he got another, and soon his bandage came off and they removed his stitches. Mary was amazed at the job Viv had done on his hand. There would be a scar, but it would be minimal.

The day after the bear attack, Miles and Burt chopped up the bear so they could move it away from Miles's cabin, and they moved its pieces to a place over by the junkyard, where it could rot away and the smell wouldn't affect anyone in the camp.

Normally the bear would have been added to the camp menu, but because it was rabid, the meat was useless.

The men were all sitting around the fire after breakfast the next day sipping coffee, and reminiscing about the bear attack.

"I can't ever remember a bear coming onto Peaceful Valley. Not in all my years being here, and I also can't remember ever having a kid being bitten by something rabid," said Burt.

"It must have come down from the mountains and been here all summer. It must have eaten something rabid, like a bird or a bat. Crazy," said Mark.

Over the Rocky Mountains, they all noticed some dark clouds that seemed to be moving their way.

"We might get our first snow tonight by the looks of the clouds heading toward us. We'll know more as the day goes on. Just the same,

I'd make sure all of you have some wood in your stoves prepared for lighting tonight. Better to be prepared," said Burt.

The presence of the bear had given the residents a wake-up call, that not all their potential dangers came in the form of a human being.

They would all be reminded that living in this new world they found themselves in brought new challenges to their survival.

One of the things the men discussed was the repopulation of gray wolves to Colorado, and they wondered how long it would take for them to make an appearance at Peaceful Valley.

Wolves were a whole different thing to contend with and were natural-born carnivorous predators that hunt in packs.

It could take years for them to come down from the mountains, or they might not come down this far at all.

Rocky and Amanda were becoming very close, much to the chagrin of Brian, who now had to share Rocky with her, and Rocky spent most of his time, not with Brian, but with her.

Mrs. Riley had made leaps and bounds in her weight and health recovery, and the vision of her being emaciated was a thing of the past. She looked ready to have that baby when the time came, and no one saw any potential issues with the birth.

Jack and Mandy were still living apart, but Jack was getting ready to ask Mandy to marry him, but the question in his mind would be who would perform the ceremony?

He was waffling between the mayor, Terry Pryor, or Burt, but all things considered equal, he decided on Burt because he was the oldest member of the Peaceful Valley clan.

NINETEEN

Mercy and Murder

❧

T he two Chinese soldiers that had been driving Captain Lee had
been assigned to deliver a truckload of food and medical supplies
to Peaceful Valley, unbeknownst to its residents.

The shipment originally was sent to the people rescued from Simla,
but when the shipment got there, they discovered the campsite empty.
Captain Lee had been touched by their sheer will to survive and was
impressed that they had made it this far, but also believed they were on
their last legs and needed help to continue.

After speaking with Sergeants Sanchez and Halliday and discovering
the people of Simla were told to find Peaceful Valley, it was obvious
to Captain Lee that they went looking for the scout camp and were
hopefully rescued by the residents of Peaceful Valley, now residing at
the camp there with them.

The only way the residents would all be gone was if they were picked
up by the bus he had seen there, so he sent the shipment out again, this
time to Peaceful Valley to reward their kindness and to help.

It was not customary for the Chinese army to assist in any way the
indigenous people of America, but Captain Lee was a man of great heart
and could not stand by and do nothing, letting those people die a slow
and horrendous death, so he broke protocol and sent the shipment out,

knowing that if the word had gotten back to his superiors, he would have to answer for it.

Had Captain Lee known of the bad character of the men he sent to make the delivery, he would have dispatched another two soldiers, but there they were, driving down Elbert Road getting ready to turn into the scout camp, and both men were anxious to see Mandy Sigler again.

The camp had gotten a lot of rain in the past week, and even had their first frost, but they had yet to get any snowfall. The dirt roads were muddy, but passable, as the military truck found out once they entered Peaceful Valley.

The residents saw the truck well before it descended on them as it stopped at the headquarters building, and they all ran up to it through the grass, then the mud.

The driver of the truck addressed them in broken English the best he could.

"I need to speak with your leader. Can you get him for me?" asked the driver.

"Yes. Just a minute. Someone will fetch him," said Amanda Wilkerson.

Her younger sister Eleanor ran for the dining hall to get Bill. Even though Terry was the mayor, the camp looked to Bill as their leader.

A minute later, Bill could be seen jogging through the tall wet grass toward the truck.

"Hello. What can I do for you?" asked Bill.

"Captain Lee has sent us. We have food and medical supplies that he has instructed us to bring to you. Where would you like them unloaded?" asked the driver.

"What? Are you serious?" asked Bill.

"Yes sir. Very serious," said the driver. "The medical supplies are in the back to be unloaded first, then the food."

"Wow. Please give Captain Lee our regards and our deepest thanks. We can sure use them. The Health Lodge is your first building to the right, so the medical supplies can go there. The food can go up to the big building through the trees on your left. I will get some men to help unload the food while you are unloading the medical supplies," said Bill.

The driver then put the truck in gear and drove up to the Health Lodge.

Mandy had been inside the headquarters building and had a watchful eye on the driver through the window, remembering his creepy stare at her the last time they were there, and was glad to see him move away from the building she was in.

Jack had come out to meet the truck and was thrilled at the delivery of medical supplies, knowing these were fresher than anything they currently had, but there was just one problem.

Everything was written in Chinese, meaning he had no idea what medicines he had, but if he could get his hands on a Chinese/American dictionary translating Chinese into American, he could use the medicines for what they were.

There were several cases brought into the Health Lodge, so he stacked them in a corner until he could figure out what everything was.

The bulk of what was in the truck was food items and a lot of tea.

It took about half an hour for several of the men to unload the truck, but once again, everything was in Chinese, so they too would have to get a Chinese translation to find out exactly what they had.

They knew a lot of it was freeze-dried, meaning they might have things they had all but forgotten about, such as eggs, certain kinds of meat, fruit, and vegetables, and they were more than appreciative to receive this generous and timely gift from the Chinese military.

After the last box was unloaded from the truck, the Chinese soldiers had desserts brought out to them from Mrs. Jennings in the kitchen. The soldiers ate them and approved, thanking Mrs. Jennings for thinking of them, and they then boarded their truck and headed out the way they came in.

On the way out of camp, they both noticed Mandy Sigler on the veranda of the headquarters building, sitting in a rocking chair petting Andy and reading a book. They stopped their vehicle and just stared at her, wanting more from her than a look back, and the driver motioned for her to come to the truck, but she refused.

The more they tried to convince her, the more she refused, until she finally got up from her chair and walked into the headquarters building, shutting the door behind her.

These men were not going to take no for an answer, as they had an agenda that would put Mandy at serious risk of harm. Begrudgingly, they put their truck in gear and left the ranch, but five miles out, they pulled the truck over and just sat there waiting for the sun to go down.

They intended to go back to the ranch when it got dark and have their way with her.

It had been much too long for the men. They had not had carnal knowledge with a female since being deployed to America, especially one as pretty as Mandy.

They would not be going back there as far as they knew, and Captain Lee would be none the wiser if they took by force what they desperately wanted and felt they needed, so they waited for their opportunity.

These were not men of good character. If they had a moral compass to begin with, it had been broken long ago, but more importantly, these were not men of God.

In Communist China, worshiping anything other than the government was highly frowned upon and forbidden, so these men had no foundation in Christ or his teachings, leaving their souls hollow from the time they had been born, meaning darkness was all they knew and understood.

Though they were subservient to their government, they would use this opportunity to exercise their power and control over this American woman, the same way their government did over them.

In all honesty, this was the way they preferred it.

Taking something that was not theirs to begin with made them feel omnipotent.

In the meantime, Mandy had unlocked the door, thinking they had left for good, and let Andy out to go to the bathroom and chase ground squirrels, as Burt and Jack talked next door in the Health Lodge.

"I have something to ask of you Burt, and it's really important to me that you say yes to it. You are the only one I feel comfortable asking this, so I hope you will say yes," said Jack.

He certainly had Burt's attention, as he had never seen Jack as serious as he was then.

"Well go on…ask away," said Burt.

"You know Burt, I've been interested in Mandy ever since she got here," said Jack.

"I think everyone knows that. You two have been inseparable. Everyone knows you two are love birds. Have you laid down with her yet?" asked Burt.

"Oh no…no…I wouldn't do that unless we were married," said Jack. "I love her Burt, and I want to ask her to marry me."

Burt smiled, thinking he knew what was going to come out of Jack's mouth next.

"You're going to ask me to be your best man, aren't you? Well, of course, I will. You can count on me," said Burt.

"No Burt. That's not what I was going to ask you. I'm going to ask you to marry us if she says yes. I need you to lead the ceremony," said Jack.

Burt needed a minute for what he was just asked for to register in his head.

"What? I've never married anyone before. I'm not a priest or a pastor. I never even went to church that often," said Burt.

"That may be true, but you haven't missed a single service I've led since we've been here. I've seen you in church, and I know you are a man of faith. You can do this. I know you can," said Jack. "I need you to say yes."

Burt knew he had to say yes to Jack because he couldn't say no.

Jack had given so much to the people of Peaceful Valley, and he deserved to be happy, and if Burt could help to give him happiness, he would of course honor Jack's request.

"Sure, Jack. I'll do it, but you're going to have to teach me how" Burt answered.

Jack was beside himself with joy at Burt's willingness to preside over his marriage, but he still had to ask Mandy, and she still had to say yes.

"Thank you, Burt. I will write it all out for you. I've only done it once myself, so I know you can do it," said Jack.

Burt whipped out his flask, which he kept with him at all times, and offered Jack a sip.

"This calls for a drink. Here you go" said Burt as he handed over his flask to Jack.

"I'm not much of a drinker, but here goes nothing," said Jack, then he hoisted back the flask and took a generous sip.

"Atta boy. Here's to Mandy saying yes too" said Burt, then he sipped as well.

Burt gave Jack a big hug, congratulated him, and walked out the door over to the dining hall, as it was getting close to suppertime.

It was dark now and the camp would be having dinner in about half an hour.

The days were getting shorter, and the nights came faster.

Jack was studying his PDR as he often did, trying to get a handle on all the different medicines there were and their uses.

The Chinese soldiers had parked out on the paved road and were walking up the dirt road toward the camp in the dark, namely toward the headquarters building where Mandy was finishing up the book she was reading earlier in the day, with Andy at her feet.

The soldiers were standing outside of the headquarters building now, about a hundred yards away, discussing how they would proceed.

They did not want to alert the residents of the camp to their presence, so they planned to quietly walk in the door and jump her, quickly stuff her mouth with a rag to prevent her from screaming, and then tie her up and have their way with her.

After a few minutes, they would be done with her and make their way back to the main road and no one would be the wiser until they were already long gone.

Andy started to growl a low, but intense growl, almost under his breath, because he heard something outside that didn't seem quite right.

Mandy didn't pay much attention to him because Andy growled at anything he heard outside. It was a ritual with him every night and had been since they had been together.

His growl continued and became a little louder and a little more intense, causing her to look down at him as he was focused outside of her front door.

She figured it might be Jack sneaking up on her, coming to get her for dinner.

She would let him surprise her and not get up and spoil it for him.

Just then she saw the door handle begin to turn, so she put the book down on the floor, getting ready to fake a scream in anticipation of Jack bursting through the door, but when the door opened, her giggly anticipation turned into stark terror as she saw the two Chinese soldiers enter the room and quickly bum rush her, stuffing a rag in her mouth before she could even let out a scream, pulling her up from the chair and tackling her to the ground.

Andy was beside himself, and as little as he was, he had a heart bigger than dogs ten times his size and began to tear at one of the soldiers' arms, trying to get him off of Mandy. The other soldier grabbed Andy by the head, then twisted and broke his neck, causing the little dog to fall into a lifeless heap on the floor.

One of the soldiers pulled off her jeans, then her panties, while the soldier on top of her put himself inside of her, and there was nothing she could do about it except cry into the rag in her mouth.

She was being raped mercilessly by this Chinese demon while the other one held down her arms and head, making sure the rag did not fall out of her mouth.

This went on for several grueling minutes until the soldier had enough, then got off her and switched positions with the other soldier, so now she had to endure another rape while crying her eyes out from the brutality and violation of her body, as if she were not even human, but instead nothing more than a receptacle for their demonic seed implanted in her.

By the time the second one had finished, the first soldier was ready to go again, but this time they turned her over to face the floor, and the first one jumped on her and took her from behind with the other soldier laying over her upper back and head, muffling the sounds of her screaming through the rag in her mouth.

In the dining hall, people were starting to line up for dinner, yet the food had yet to be brought out.

Everyone was looking forward to that night's dinner, which would be mulligan stew with macaroni, freshly baked bread, and blueberry pie for dessert.

With everyone inside, no one could hear the muffled screams from Mandy nearly half a mile away, and Jack's doors and windows were already shut because the weather had been chilly as of late.

After the first one was done raping her backside, the other soldier resumed for his second go-around, not skipping a beat. Mandy had no more fight left in her and just laid there enduring the excruciating pain she had gone through for close to half an hour.

She drifted off to memories of her childhood, playing with her friends, birthday parties her mom had spent hours preparing, and her Eagle Scout ceremony, anything to keep her mind off what was happening to her.

Halfway through the soldier's second round, she mentally and physically numbed herself out, praying that God would either make them stop or that he should take her life and bring her back home to heaven where she belonged.

It was the epitome of evil she was being forced to endure, and she kept asking God in her mind why this was happening.

There were no more tears left for her to cry, and it wasn't until she heard one of the soldiers giggling that she started to become mad. She counted the minutes until he was finished when he rolled off her and pulled himself off the floor, pulling his trousers up and buckling his belt.

She turned over to face her abusers and kicked the one that had just gotten off of her between the legs, almost causing him to vomit, but he instead pulled his service revolver from its holster and shot Mandy in the forehead, right between her eyes just over her nose, and she was instantly dead.

The shot was heard all across Peaceful Valley and the dining room emptied onto the veranda, with Bill, Bob, and Burt trying to determine where the shot had come from.

The soldiers immediately ran out of the headquarters front door and continued running down the dirt road toward the main road where their truck was.

Jack had run out of the Health Lodge toward headquarters to see two men in uniform disappear into the dark running down the road, then he ran inside to find Mandy and Andy, both dead.

He was in disbelief, and he couldn't register what he was seeing with the reality of what had just happened.

He then let out a big scream, and this told everyone on the veranda which direction they should run.

When they all showed up at once at the headquarters building, they found Jack in the doorway sobbing into the dead body of Andy, with Mandy naked from the waist down, bleeding from a bullet wound in her forehead, also dead.

The women began to scream, and Vivian grabbed a blanket from the couch and covered Mandy up.

Burt was stunned and didn't know what to say.

He had just talked to Jack about marrying him and this girl not more than an hour ago, yet here she lay dead, and their beloved Jack sat in the doorway shaking his head, asking God why?

TWENTY

Test of Faith

J ack Price was shattered, broken into a million pieces, and there was nothing anyone could say to him that could console him.

There was a dark cloud over Peaceful Valley now as tragedy had struck again.

Some of the men ran down the road after the two soldiers, but by the time they had gotten to the headquarters building, the soldiers were just yards away from their truck and were off into the night, but the men could see that it was the same truck that had made its delivery earlier that day.

Captain Lee had given them his assurance they would be left alone, as long as they left the Chinese alone, but that was a lie.

Bill could not fathom Captain Lee knowing anything about this and was sure that if he became aware of what had just happened, the soldiers would be punished severely, maybe executed.

First, there was Henry and his wife, now Mandy, and both were as horrific as the imagination could conjure.

Not only did they have to be at the ready for hunters, but the Chinese would be added to that list now.

The village wanted retribution, but there would be none to be had, at least not at that time.

There was no way of knowing where the Chinese were or how to get in touch with Captain Lee, so this would have to be an unpunished crime committed by the very people that had shown them mercy earlier in the day.

The men carried Mandy out of the building and onto the far side of the veranda and laid Andy next to her, covering her up from head to toe, out of sight of the Health Lodge so Jack would not be able to see her.

The one man that could bring solace to the camp was the man most in need of it, and there wasn't a single soul that wouldn't have taken Jack's pain away from him if they could have.

Julie and Rocky did their best, along with Mark, Viv, and Bill, but no one could do anything except help him back to the Health Lodge and just sit with him, be there for him to let him know he was not alone.

Bob and Burt, along with Miles, Jeff, and some of the other men, all sat around the fire later that night, discussing the day's events.

'They raped the hell out of that poor girl. Why did they have to kill her? Evil bastards!" said Bob Hawkins, as he was fit to be tied.

"They did it because they could. That's why. There's no other explanation. Those Chinese aren't like us," said Burt. "They don't view life the same way we do."

"They're just going to get away with it. I can't believe it," said Miles.

"Well, you better believe it. In case nobody's noticed, we live in a different world now, and justice just isn't there like it used to be. Had we caught up with them before they made their getaway, we would have given them all the justice they deserved, but there's no one to call for help anymore. We are on our own and will be for the rest of our lives from here on out," said Burt.

"It's God that's gotten us this far, with no help from anyone else. As long as we stick together and put one foot in front of the other, we will do the very best we can and keep things like this happening to a minimum. There's no magic answer. Who would have seen this coming? No one, that's who, and yet, it happened. We can't bring that girl back, but we can do everything we can do to make sure it doesn't happen again. We must."

Eventually, everyone left Jack that night and went to bed, leaving him to lie awake on his bed most of the night, wanting to understand why God had allowed this to happen.

The next morning Jack awoke after not getting much sleep and laid there for what seemed like hours, not understanding why God would allow those men to take from him the one woman in camp he loved and wanted to spend the rest of his life with. It seemed mean and cruel to him.

Jack got up from his bunk, took a deep breath, and dressed himself to walk over to the dining room for coffee, and the denizens of Peaceful Valley were glad to see him up and around so soon.

At the crack of dawn, some of the men had put Mandy on a stretcher and carried her out to the field in between the lake and the dining hall and set her and Andy on top of a massive pile of wood, to be used as a funeral pyre when the time came, in the same spot where they burned the dead hunters.

As Jack walked into the dining hall, he could see her covered body resting on top of the pile of wood, and he resolved himself to her death once again, as he would do many times in the coming days.

There was no getting around seeing her out there, and he did everything he could do to not look in that direction when going to the dining hall for coffee and meals.

It was his faith in God that still allowed him to carry on and function, to keep the fire of Christ burning in his heart, and the hearts of others around him, leaning on Christ as he never had before because he knew without him, he would be lost. At the same time, he questioned whether God loved him the way he loved God.

He needed to talk with someone desperately because he was losing his grip on his faith, so he went to his friend Mark, who was instrumental in his path to knowing and loving God.

"I don't know why God would do this to me, Mark. She gave me hope in this horrible nightmare we are living in, and he took her away from me. She made me feel alive. She made me feel like I was wanted and needed. I can't understand. Was it because I paid too much attention to her? Was it because I loved her too? Why?" asked Jack of his friend.

"Jack, he didn't take her away from you. Those men did. God loves you just as much today as he always has, and he wants you to be happy. He's always wanted nothing but happiness for you. He is hurting right now for you. You can believe that. Satan took her away because those men were evil. You know this as well as I do. God didn't intervene because he gave all of us free will to do the things we do, good or bad.

Why do little children get abducted and murdered by evil people? It's the same thing, Jack. It doesn't make any sense to us, but it happens just the same," said Mark.

"How can I continue preaching the word of God when I can't even believe it myself? I have given everything to the Lord this last year, praying hard for his guidance, to show me the way forward, and I've done everything for him. Why couldn't he intervene and save her?" asked Jack.

"What about when your father came to you in my living room? He told you there would be difficult times ahead. Your faith in God is most important during times like these Jack. It's easy to believe in God and trust in him when things go smoothly, but then when things go sour, we want to blame him for all the things that go wrong in our lives. You can't lose your faith in him.

Not now. This is when you need him the most.

Your faith is being tested Jack, maybe more than it ever will be in your life.

Read Job and see how his faith was tested. He didn't buckle Jack, and neither should you. It is God that is going to get you through this and out to the other side of it.

My best advice to you is to pray about this. Pray super hard that God will send you a sign and give you comfort. I'm so sorry for your loss my brother, but you can't give in to the Devil, because it's him that wins if you turn your back on God" said Mark.

While Jack and Mark talked, the rest of the men gathered at the headquarters building for an emergency meeting called by Terry Pryor and Bob Hawkins.

"We lost a member of our village yesterday, so we have to discuss what our weak points are and what our strong suits are. This can't happen again. We lost Henry and his wife a few months back. That makes three of our folks lost before their time.

The way I see it, we have three known enemies. First are the hunters. Second, are wild animals, and the third are now the Chinese. Anything else anyone can think of?" asked Bob.

Everyone agreed that those were the three things they needed to keep an eye out for.

"We almost lost Rocky the other day due to that rabid bear, so things could be worse. As far as I can tell, the animals are the enemy we will have the hardest time preparing for. There's no way we could have been prepared for that bear, but now that we know it's a possible threat, we have to think differently in the camp.

I think the men, and the women too, need to be strapped at all times when moving about from one place to another.

The chances of that ever happening again are nil to none, but we must be ready just the same. Burt tells me he can't remember ever seeing a bear on the property in all his years of being here, and he's been here for a long time. Nevertheless, it can happen again.

We haven't seen any wild dogs, but if they did make it onto the property, they'd have to be considered dangerous. Then there's always the possibility of a mountain lion. Though we haven't seen one since we've been here, those have been seen here every so often, so there's always the chance one of us could get attacked by one of them.

Lastly, I want to mention wolves.

Up until a couple of years ago, there were no wolves in Colorado, but somebody thought it would be a good idea to reintroduce them to this state, so they began just before the blast hit. I have no idea how many of them are in Colorado now. They are gray wolves and pretty ferocious, but they were released up in the mountains, very far away from us, so the likelihood of us ever seeing one down here is almost zero. Having said that, Murphy's law always applies.

That's it for the animals, and that's all I've got to say for now.

Everyone should be strapped in my opinion," said Bob.

Bill then began to speak.

"So, let's talk about hunters. We've had two major experiences with them. We were lucky the first time because no one was hurt, but as you all know, the last time was different. There's not a whole lot we can do differently than the way we prepare for animals, except that no one should be going anywhere outside the immediate area of the living areas of the camp, and no one should be alone. That means not going over across the road or going over to the other campground on our side of the lake.

We've been leaving that gate out on the road unlocked since we've been here, but I think it's time we start locking it. We definitely don't want the Chinese driving up in here again, and we certainly don't want any hunters on an expedition looking for fresh meat.

The bottom line is this. We are vulnerable no matter how we look at it. We're a whole lot less vulnerable than we use to be at New Hope, but we still are exposed to the outside world, and if someone or something wants to get at us, it wouldn't take much, so we must change our way of thinking now to survive anything that comes our way.

Bob is right. Everyone needs to carry a weapon when they are traveling through the camp, otherwise, you are exposed unnecessarily to potential danger.

It sucks to have to live like this, but these are the cards we've been dealt," said Bill.

All agreed with what both men had said and committed to start carrying a firearm with them around camp and would escort their children from one place to the next.

Burt grabbed a padlock from the quartermaster building and ran it up to the gate on the road with a chain and locked the gate securely so no vehicle could enter on its own.

"By the way everyone, I believe Jack is preparing a funeral ceremony for Mandy in the morning after breakfast. I'll know for sure tonight at dinner, but Jack will probably announce it to all of us then. Just wanted to give you a heads up," said Bill.

That night at dinner while everyone stood in line, Jack made his announcement.

"I want to thank everyone for the kindness you've shown me. Some of you know I was about to ask Mandy for her hand in marriage, so this was a great and unexpected loss for me personally, as it was for many of you that knew her, but I know she is at peace in heaven with the Lord Jesus.

She is at peace and waiting for all of us when it's our time to be in heaven." Jack said, then continued.

"Tomorrow morning after breakfast, we will have a memorial service for her, and anyone wishing to speak about her can do so then. The funeral pyre will be lit, and her body will be cremated in the eyes of God. I hope all of you can make it."

Later that day, Jack attempted to write a service for Mandy but stopped short every time he thought of something to write down. He decided he would not prepare but instead speak from the heart whatever words came to his head.

It would be natural, as it should be, and he would probably break down in tears anyway, so why prepare something?

Everyone had plenty to eat that night, as most did not eat dinner the night before because of the shooting.

They warmed up the mulligan stew and it was probably even tastier the second day.

After dinner, the whole clan gathered around the fire, where most other nights, only a few did.

Fall was definitely in the air, so it felt good to be outside around a roaring fire, and then something interesting happened.

One of the men brought out his guitar, which he didn't do too often, and before you knew it, the camp started to break out in song.

Many old familiar tunes were sung, and not so old, and it made everyone escape their realities for a while, going back to a time not so long ago when concerts were attended, and CDs were played on the stereo.

Some songs everyone knew and belted out with the conviction of experience, relating to times in their lives they cherished and refused to let go of, and they were happy to be reliving them again.

Some of the women teared up, and so did some of the men.

The children tried to sing along too but didn't know most of the words.

Most of the people had all but forgotten how it felt to not have to worry about the simplest things that concerned them now, like getting sick, cutting themselves, breaking a bone, or God forbid, something worse.

They had all been born with a safety net in the way of police, fire engines, and hospitals, but those were a thing of the past, and would someday be a distant memory of days gone by.

There were none of those thoughts present around the campfire that night.

They sang as if their lives depended on it, and in a very real and human way, they did.

No matter how primitive their lives had become, they could not succumb to a nonexistent sense of being, of only staying alive and nothing more, because there had to be more.

Their lives had to have meaning, and for that night around the fire, they found their meaning again, and it felt good and authentic.

For that night, death had brought out the best in them.

Death had given them back their lives for a fleeting moment.

The next morning after breakfast, everyone slowly meandered their way to Mandy's body on the tall stack of wood in the field by the lake.

They all sat in the tall grass around the clearing and began to share a fond story they had about Mandy, starting with Jack, and yes, he did break down in tears, which was to be expected.

Many of the constituency talked about their dealings with her, a lot of them being the new people, who did not know her well, but she had certainly left her mark on them.

Kate, holding her new baby, talked about how Mandy used to ask her what it was like to be a mother at such a young age, and Kate sensed that Mandy wanted that for herself, to be a mother and raise a child, and this brought Jack to tears again.

Miles's three daughters also talked about Mandy, and how they admired her and looked up to her.

This went on for over an hour, until finally Bob Hawkins and Burt walked around the perimeter of the body with cans full of gas, sprinkling the fallen tree limbs to add fuel to her fire. Conrad then struck a match, and the funeral pyre was fully ablaze after about a minute.

It didn't take long before she was completely in flames, and as the sheets covering her began to expose her, everyone began to turn and walk back toward the dining hall, and they all began singing Amazing Grace as they walked.

Everyone except Jack.

He couldn't bring himself to release her through song. He was still full of anger at God.

He would continue to pray and ask for God's help to resolve this in his mind.

The memorial was beautiful and rustic at the same time, and for this particular service, anything else would have been insufficient and trite.

TWENTY ONE

Sixty to Fifty-Nine to 102

❧❧✦❧❧

I t was the beginning of October, and though they still had yet to get their first snowfall, the air was chilly at night, with the mornings downright cold.

The cabins were fine, but there were no stoves in the dining hall because of its expanse, something Burt and the men would work on in the coming days.

The pumpkins were ready to harvest, and there would be a slew of pumpkin pies baked in the coming days.

The plan was to have a fall festival, not so much for Halloween, but to celebrate their continued survival.

Burt still had cases of candy bars in the trading post, so on the night of the festival, he would pass out candy bars to the kids.

Mrs. Riley was very close to giving birth to her baby, and Viv, Mary Dilbert, and Mrs. Wilkerson would be her midwives. The crib and bassinet were ready, so everything was a go when the time came.

In the month and a half she had been at Peaceful Valley, you would never know she had at one time been seriously underweight and malnourished. She was now at the perfect weight for having her baby and there were no signs that there would be a problem, much to the relief of everyone, especially Jake Riley.

Jack Price had pulled himself up by his bootstraps and pressed on through his pain, resolving himself to a life without the love of a woman, and instead would give all of himself to the community.

He had baptized little Pauly, who was turning into a handful already for Kate and Mark, and he had been leading the charge to bring everyone there into the fold of the church he had created.

Up until now, he had wished he knew more about the teachings of Christ and tried to study any piece of literature he could get his hands on.

They had made a trip to the library in downtown Colorado Springs to get a Chinese American translation guide, and it was there Jack grabbed as many books as he could find on theology and biblical teachings, and a few more Bibles.

Had things not gone off the rails, he could have seen himself going to seminary school to learn how to be a pastor. He wanted to know everything there was to know about Jesus Christ, his background, and his history leading up to his crucifixion.

He knew this was not possible, but he wished he could know more than what he did and prayed constantly for wisdom and understanding concerning the message of God.

Now his thoughts of God were all-consuming, but not in a prayerful way.

He was still angry with God for allowing Mandy to be taken from him.

All in all, though, Jack Price was doing a remarkable job for the community, and they did not see him as lacking, but instead saw him as their spiritual leader.

Even Mark, who helped lead Jack to Christ, saw Jack as a divine creation of God and was brought to the earth for this exact moment in time for healing and direction.

Jack didn't see himself that way and now wondered if he could continue to go down the path he had been on. He needed to understand what his true purpose was. Was it just to make God happy?

The camp had breakfast as they always did, and as they congregated outside of the dining hall around the fire before going off to do their various chores of the day and to school the children, they all heard the sound of a motor coming up Elbert Road, so Bill and Bob got in the police cruiser to take a closer look, thinking it might be the Chinese, but they would not be able to gain entry with the front gate now locked, which was the way they preferred it after what had happened to Mandy.

They parked far enough back from the main road to not be seen and exited the vehicle to stand behind a tree to take an unobstructed look while hidden.

Amazingly enough, it was not a Chinese vehicle, but instead, a school bus, an older school bus that was filled to the brim with people on it, and the bus pulled into the scout ranch and stopped at the locked gate.

"What in the hell? What do you make of this?" asked Bill.

"It looks like a lot of people are on that bus. Other than that, I don't have a clue" answered Bob. "I suppose we should probably go down there and take a look-see."

The two men got in the cruiser and drove down to the locked gate and sat there not getting out of their vehicle, but instead looking through the bus's front windshield to see its occupants.

Upon closer inspection, they could see that this was a church bus converted from a school bus, with the words *"New Church of Christ"* painted on the sides.

When the bus driver exited the vehicle, both Bill and Bob exited the cruiser with weapons drawn on them.

"What's your business here? Who are you and what do you want?" asked Bob.

The bus driver put his hands up and slowly walked to the men on the other side of the gate.

"We are not here to cause you any trouble. I've got a bunch of thirsty people on that bus and we'd like to come inside and get a drink from your well" said the driver.

Bill and Bob looked at each other puzzled.

"How do you know we've got well water?" asked Bill.

"We've got a few people on the bus that used to come here during the summer. This is a scout ranch, isn't it?" asked the driver.

"It is indeed. How do we know you aren't hunters? How do we know you aren't here to hunt people to eat?" asked Bob.

The man was in shock to hear that question asked of him.

"What? Why in blazes would we want to do something like that? We've got our own food, and we certainly don't eat people, even if we didn't have food of our own." said the driver. Bill and Bob lowered their weapons and told the man to put his hands down, then walked around the gate.

"How many people do you have on that bus?" asked Bill.

"Forty-three, including me. Wanna take a look?" asked the driver.

Bill and Bob walked over to the door of the bus and stepped up inside and were amazed to see all the men on the bus standing up and pointing rifles at Bill and Bob, so now the tables were turned, and it was them that had their hands up.

"Put down your weapons. There's no need for that" said Bill, and the men lowered their weapons to hear what Bill was going to say.

"Who's the leader of your group? Who speaks for you?" asked Bill.

An older man in his sixties stood up from the back of the bus and introduced himself.

"I'm Pastor Wally Jorgenson and I speak for my congregation. I've led many scout troops here over the years for summer camp. Is Henry Williams still running this place?" asked Pastor Wally.

"He was when we first got here, but I'm afraid he and his wife passed away a few months ago," said Bill.

"I'm sorry to hear that. How about Burt? Is he still alive?" asked the pastor.

"Yes, he is," said Bill. "Would you like to see him?"

"Yessir. I would love that" the pastor answered.

"Ok then. You all just sit tight, and we are going to drive up and get Burt to unlock the gate" said Bill, and the two men got off the bus and told the driver what they were doing, then they jumped in the police cruiser to go retrieve Burt.

"Burt, there's someone at the front gate that knows you! He says his name is Pastor Wally Jorgenson. Do you know him?" asked Bill.

"Know him? Heck yes, I know him. He's a scoutmaster out in eastern Colorado and he has a church. Is he by himself?" asked Burt.

"No, he's got a whole busload with him. Why don't you come with us and unlock the gate so they can come in and get watered up" said Bill, and the three men headed back out to Elbert Road.

After unlocking the gate, Burt went to the bus just as Pastor Wally was stepping down the stairs.

"Hey, you old buzzard...how are ya'!" asked Pastor Wally.

The two men hugged and laughed that they were both still alive.

"We've got a whole community of people living here. Follow us to the dining hall. That's where you all can park and get all the water you need," said Burt.

After getting to the dining hall, all the residents of Peaceful Valley surrounded the church bus and greeted everyone as they came off, directing them to the freshwater.

All the men grabbed some water, and some coffee, and sat down around the fire that had since gone out after breakfast.

"So where are you heading?" asked Burt, but in the back of his mind, he thought he already knew the answer.

"To be truthful, we were heading here, hoping to set up camp. When we ran out of water we had stored, we decided it was time to pack up and head somewhere we knew there was fresh water. You know how many times I've been here over the years. I knew there was well water, and I knew there were a lot of bunks and buildings, plus there is game to be had here, but it looks like you guys beat us to it. How would you all feel about us adding to your community?" asked Pastor Wally.

"We aren't coming empty-handed. We've still got over a year's supply of freeze-dried food for the forty-three of us, and we've got a police officer, a master carpenter, and a doctor."

The thought of having a doctor among them was music to their ears.

Jack had filled in nicely as the camp doctor, but there was no substitute for the real thing, and Jack would be relieved, not only at having a real doctor but also having a real pastor that could mentor him.

"Where are you all from, and how did you make it this far? Where did you find a running school bus? I have so many questions" asked Bill.

"All of these people are my parishioners, coming from all walks of life really. I always knew this day would come and I've always been a prepper. I knew that once this happened, there would have to be people like us together as a community to continue life.

I have a big aluminum building on the church property that I covered in lead, which is where the bus was parked, so it was not affected by the EMP. I had been using a lot of the donation money we would collect every Sunday to begin compiling stores of food and water, enough to feed all of us for a couple of years. I miscalculated on the water, and that only ended up lasting us for a little more than a year, which was when we decided we had to go someplace with a water source.

When the EMP happened, I had already assembled some families that I knew could contribute to our survival, so they knew to come to the church where we would be ready" explained Pastor Wally, then he introduced some of the men.

"This is Officer John Ordman. He was with the Strasburg Police Department. To my right is Doctor Marv Kinsley. He's been a general practitioner for Strasburg for the last fifteen years, and to my left is William McHenry. He had his own construction company in Strasburg for twenty-five years and built a lot of homes there.

Now, Doctor Kinsley's wife is also a registered nurse and has assisted him throughout the years in his practice. The rest of the men here are not afraid of hard work and are related to the ones I introduced either by blood or friendship, plus they have a lot of kids, which will be needed later on in life" said Pastor Wally.

"We have a township, with Terry Pryor as Mayor, Bill as City Planner, Bob Hawkins as law enforcement, and I take care of everything that needs fixing, but all of you would be welcome to share in those responsibilities. What do you have to say Jack?" asked Burt.

"This is Providence, that's what I think. Doctor Kinsley, I've been ham-handedly taking care of the sick, but I will gladly step aside and assist you, handing everything over to you." Jack respectfully responded.

"The Health Lodge is just past the headquarters building where you drove in, and I have a ton of medicines at your disposal, anywhere from heavy-duty narcotics for pain to antibiotics. I have been staying in the Health Lodge, but I will happily hand it over to you and your wife. I can find a bunk over the dining hall.

As for you Pastor Wally, I have been praying for something like this to happen regarding a man of the cloth to appear, and here you are. I have been leading church services, but I would much rather have you take that over and I can learn from you. I am new to Christ and his teachings. I can't tell you how happy I am to meet you" Jack said as he walked over to Pastor Wally, then gave him a great big hug.

Without even having a side meeting, it had been agreed upon that the New Church of Christ would join forces with Peaceful Valley and become a larger community.

"We had sixty people until Mandy passed away, which brought us to fifty-nine, and now with forty-three more, that brings us to 102 people. Wow. We are growing in leaps and bounds" said Terry, and he then continued.

"The first order of business will be to determine where everyone will stay. We still have a couple of unoccupied forts, so we can put 4 families in those, maybe more, and we will just have to squeeze more families together, at least until the spring. It will be cozy for sure, but we will survive and get to know each other a little better."

There were hundreds of cases of freeze-dried food to be unloaded into the dining hall, and it took all afternoon to place families where they would be and add more bunks to each dwelling to accommodate the new people.

Some of the older kids volunteered to stay above the dining hall, making room for the adults to be with the smaller children. The dining hall bunks had to be reorganized to separate the boys from the girls as much as possible.

The only living quarters unaffected by the residents were Trail Boss, Cook's Roost, and Doc Holliday because all the rest had to be expanded to accommodate everyone.

Life would become very different for all of them now.

Shower Fridays would become twice as long and would require twice the wood for heating the water, which meant a whole bunch more wood would have to be chopped.

With twice the people, there were now twice as many to do the chores, making life easier for everyone.

Dr. Kinsley was very impressed with the Health Lodge and could not believe that Jack had thought of stocking the shelves with all that he had, not until Jack told him that his dad was a pharmacist at a hospital in Denver. He was also glad to see a PDR on the premises, a book the good doctor frequently referred to when treating his patients.

The Health Lodge made Dr. Kinsley feel right at home, as it had been a while since he had practiced any kind of medicine in a controlled facility with medicines at his disposal.

This was one step closer to normalcy for him, and his wife concurred.

Mary Dilbert was sure to introduce herself to Dr. Kinsley and his wife, giving him two qualified nurses and an assistant in Jack, should he be needed.

In the coming days, it was decided that a couple of big trees would need to be cut down on the outer perimeter of Peaceful Valley, allowing them to age for a year to be used for firewood, so the men carefully studied the trees to be cut, determining how they would fall and what they would need to do to make sure all safety precautions were met, then felled the trees, leaving them where they landed, not to be addressed until the following spring at the earliest.

Burt had given Bill McHenry the grand tour of everything they would need in making repairs, and also for new construction.

A plan was made to build a new string of row houses similar to the bunkhouses, just up the road next to the trading post, big enough for seven to eight families, giving most of the families a place of their own.

Construction would begin after the last snowfall the following spring, and they would need to make a trip or two to the closest Home Depot to get everything they needed. There was probably enough in the junkyard to piecemeal something together, but since this would be built to last for years, they elected to do it right and get everything they needed new.

Dr. Kinsley was also introduced to Jake Riley's wife, and he gave her an examination just a few days before she was expected to give birth to her baby and gave her a clean bill of health.

The birth would take place in her own dwelling, just like Kate gave birth to her baby, and nothing out of the ordinary was expected to take place. This meant the mid-wives would play a less critical role in the delivery, and Viv would not have to do any of the stitching.

Viv had outdone herself in that department, but she was more than happy to turn that over to Dr. Kinsley now.

Mrs. Riley was close now, almost four centimeters, and the baby would be here shortly.

Everyone was excited for another birth in Peaceful Valley, and Mr. Riley was especially anxious for his wife. Though she'd already had two children, this would be different.

Dr. Kinsley was in the bunkhouse apartment, ready to catch the baby, along with his wife and Mary Dilbert to assist in the birth and the immediate care of the child after.

The good doctor was also able to give Mrs. Riley an epidural, something Kate did not have the luxury of having, making this a much less painful birth for the baby. It was a little girl, and she was healthy as could be.

The official resident count of Peaceful Valley was now 103.

Pastor Wally had been brought up to speed on Mandy's death and how it was affecting Jack, so he thought he would visit Jack up to his bunk above the dining hall, where he found Jack in deep meditation.

The two men talked for over an hour, discussing the world, our place in it, and God's purpose for us.

Jack confided in the pastor that he was having a hard time with his faith, and that the loss of Mandy was almost too much to bear. He wanted to understand why God had allowed this to happen, and the pastor almost repeated verbatim what Mark had told him.

He reminded Jack that our time on earth is finite, and no man knows when it's his time to go, and only God can understand why people die when they do and the way they do.

The hardest part of death is the people that are left behind, such as Jack, who are filled with loss and sorrow, and it is our faith and belief in God that helps us to heal from our brokenness.

They both then kneeled at Jack's bunk and prayed for understanding and acceptance, asking for a miracle to heal Jack of his broken heart and revive the holy spirit within him.

TWENTY TWO

Faith Renewed

There was a lot of ruckus up above the dining hall, as some of the boys were playing grab ass amongst each other, and it wasn't until Julie threatened to give Rocky a beating that they stopped.

There was a new energy with the addition of the folks from Strasburg.

Whiskers wasn't very happy with the boys either, but boys will be boys, even the older ones.

Jack was oblivious to it all, as he lay on his bunk, silently asking for God to show him something, anything to help the pain subside.

He wanted to know that God loved him as much as he loved God, so he needed a sign.

Sometime in the night, he fell asleep, and that's when Mandy came to him in a dream.

It was clear as day, and she came walking to him out of a brilliant source of light and sat next to him, put her arm around him, then kissed his cheek.

She told him that she was sorry she had to leave him, but God needed her, so she had to go. She told him that she loved him, and she would be waiting for him when it was his time as well. Jack protested in the dream, telling her that his life would be meaningless without her, but she stopped him and assured him that the life he was living was just a blip compared to the eternity he would spend with her. She told him that his life mattered on Earth, and he was there to do many good things, but more importantly, this was a test of his faith in God.

Then his father came out of the light and sat on the other side of him, telling him how beautiful it was there and that he would be waiting for him as well, and in the end, they would all be together forever.

He told Jack to remain strong and persevere through the pain, that it would make him stronger. He told his son that he was proud of him and loved what he was doing for the Lord and that the Lord loved it too.

He told Jack that when it was his time to be there, he would understand all the things that confused him now. The world around him was suffering greatly, and it was never more important to speak the gospel of Christ than it was then.

They both then got up with Jack and hugged him tightly, telling him they would see him again, and they both walked back into the light from where they came, and then he woke.

His tears were streaming down his face, and he knew this was more than a dream.

He had just been visited again, and he could not deny the impact of their visit on him.

He laid back down hoping to resume, but instead slept a restful and peaceful sleep, unlike any he could remember having before, but when he woke in the morning, the visit he had was just as real to him then as it was when he had it.

This was the sign that Jack was looking for, and he would continue to profess the beauty of the Lord, knowing that he couldn't possibly know or understand why God did the things he did, but he would have to trust in him and accept all things as Providence.

He also knew that God had nothing to do with Mandy's death, just like he had nothing to do with his father's death, that because of the free will of man, the gift given to us by God, God would not intervene and would not prevent the things that man does, otherwise it would be God's will and not mans.

In just a few days, Jack's outlook had changed, and his grief, though still there, was now manageable, because now he had a sense of peace, and his belief in God and the hereafter had taken another leap toward his commitment to Christ.

He knew, without a shadow of a doubt, that Mandy was right.

This life is just a blip compared to the eternity that follows, because there is a heaven and he had seen it with his own eyes, both in a woken state and in his vivid dream.

He knew that he had spoken to his father, just as he had spoken to Mandy, and he felt their touch upon his skin.

He knew that he would be with them again, and just knowing that gave him the strength to carry on and move forward on his path to knowing God.

It was the night before Halloween when they got their first snowfall of the season, and they all had mixed feelings about it. Some welcomed the snow as a cleansing, a new beginning to a new season, while others could do without it.

The cold brought with it dark, dreary days and less time outside, but the dining hall did get its share of use on those days, turning it into a noisy den of children playing hopscotch, jump rope, and tag, and on Sunday would double as a place to have church services.

The community was thriving with good cheer and merriment, as much as you could expect in this new world they found themselves in, and the adults were looking forward to making a difference in their children's lives by finding new ways to enlighten, entertain, and teach them about America and what it once stood for.

There was no telling what was in store for their kids down the road, but they knew they had to instill in them a sense of pride for where they came from, the love of Christ for purpose, and the moral fiber to discern right from wrong, never purposely hurting anyone and always being willing to help those needing it.

They were starting over again, creating a new generation of Christian warriors ready to make the world a better place than what they had found.

They had not seen any evidence of the Chinese since the end of summer, and no hunters had been a threat to them since Henry and his wife's passing.

In all practical purposes, it felt to them as if they were the last ones on the face of the earth, so they lived their lives embracing the responsibility of carrying on as if they were, making sure they kept their end of the bargain by being the chosen ones that got to live.

Margaret Riley's baby was doing famously well and thank God for that because it would have been more than the village could bear should the child be having issues on top of all the tragedy they had already endured.

She and Jake decided to name the baby Promise because she was the promise of a new tomorrow.

Pauly was only a couple of months older than Promise, so they often played in a playpen together, bringing Kate and Margaret closer together. Margaret was older than Kate, but their common bond broke through any age difference, and Mark and Jake also became close, and it was not uncommon for the two families to sit together at night and play cards, and occasionally have a few beers.

Mark and Kate were not much for drinking as they were much younger but did imbibe from time to time.

Jack spent a great deal of time with Pastor Wally, picking his brain and asking a lot of questions, trying to get a handle on the whole theology aspect of the Lord and his teachings, and taking notes of the pastor's sermons, which were enlightening and informative.

Jack also continued to contribute to the sermons by speaking to the congregation about his personal growth, his love and respect for everyone in attendance, and thanking God for bringing Pastor Wally into his life to teach him what he needed to know, enabling him to be better prepared in dealing with the everyday problems that arose regarding faith and love, and their relationships in it.

The community was so focused on God and their appreciation of what they had; it was as close to a perfect society as there could be.

They were all, each to a man, living for the Lamb of God, in constant prayer for direction moving forward, wanting to serve him the best they could.

Jack sometimes asked himself if what had happened to America was punishment for its Babylonian ways, even though he knew that what had happened had been from the hands of man, but he wondered if somehow the two were not connected in some way.

There was no way to know for sure, but it was a question that nagged at him from time to time.

It was frustrating for him not to know some of the answers he had to his questions, but he always reverted to what Providence is, and that he cannot know the heart of God or his true intentions, but instead would have to always trust in them, regardless of what he thought he knew or understood.

The night of the fall festival they had planned went on, and they had most of it in the dining hall that night.

Burt had raided the trading post and distributed candy bars to all the kids and even some of the adults with a sweet tooth and used more of them for prizes to games they had set up throughout the night.

The adults had a time of their own, modestly drinking whiskey and gin, using cans of Pepsi and Mountain Dew for chasers.

No one got hammered, but all had a roaring good time, and for a few moments, they forgot their stations in life, and instead relished in the laughter and excitement of their children, knowing everything they did revolved around them and their well-being.

They were the future, and whatever happened going forward, it would be them and only them that would determine the direction the community took.

It was about them because it had to be.

The world they would inherit would be ultimately theirs to decide.

Their community had expanded to over twice its size in a matter of a couple of months, and they wondered aloud if it would get any bigger. As it stood, they would be building a series of new homes by the trading post, but what if they have more people find them down the road?

How many people could Peaceful Valley support, and for how long?

The game was still abundant, but the fishing in the lake would soon dry up regardless.

The lake was a lot smaller than the reservoir they had left, and fewer fish were being caught.

Their supply of canned goods was starting to dwindle, meaning they would have to find other sources. They knew there was plenty more to be had, but they needed to find them.

A big food warehouse somewhere should and would be their next target but finding a location would need some serious research through phonebooks, and maybe the library.

Whatever it took to find these places, however, they would do it.

They also started to consider giving the vehicles a long overdue oil change, so that was part of their itinerary going forward.

There would be much to do when springtime rolled into camp, and fortunately for them, they had plenty of bodies with skills that could get these things done.

One of the things great about Peaceful Valley was the abundance of wild turkeys, so when Thanksgiving rolled around, they had plenty of bird for their tables, even though the meaning and significance of the holiday had virtually vanished with the downfall of the America they once knew.

Still, they celebrated it, because, in all honesty, they needed as much to celebrate as they could.

In a greater sense, this Thanksgiving had much more personal meaning to all of them because they were extremely grateful for the things they had, not concentrating on all the things they had lost.

When December came, with Christmas around the corner, it was harder for a lot of them.

Most had family in other parts of the country, people they would normally be shopping for, but they had to assume that after a year and a half, they were most likely dead, so their memories of them were ever-present in their minds, creating a hollowness inside of them.

Pastor Wally and Jack did their best to keep their spirits up, inventing new ways to involve them in church services, even incorporating the guitarist into songs sung by the congregation, giving a light that shined upon them, elevating them all to a higher consciousness of being.

The adults that had children were able to travel on the bus to Walmart and select gifts that did not need batteries, making that Christmas similar to ones in the past, setting up artificial trees with ornaments, and having presents under the tree for them on Christmas morning.

Christmas cards became a rediscovered custom, with everyone wanting to give a card to someone in camp, and by themselves, they created a needed distraction by weaving their way throughout the holiday season, bringing them into the new year of 2024.

The snows of January were the hardest to get through and made everything they did become a chore, especially paying a visit to the latrine.

The dining hall throughout the month became the go-to place, where food was always available and togetherness was the word of the day, even though there was no heat, but with all of them in there at once, they created their own heat, which made their time spent inside tolerable.

The food supplies brought to them by the Chinese were very good, providing them with freeze-dried chicken, beef, pork, and a lot of different fruits and vegetables, which were appreciated along with what they had canned themselves.

There was no flu being spread among the citizens, and it appeared that the flu would be a thing of the past, as would other communicable diseases.

This was at the top of the list of good things that came with the change in their lives.

Whiskers had become the town cat, as everyone got to know him as they spent so much of their time in the dining hall.

He became accustomed to everyone and wanted something from everybody, whether it be a scrap of food or to be petted into submission, and he was rarely denied, but at the end of the day, he always ended up with his soulmate, which was Julie Price.

She had grown to love that cat almost more than her kids, and he knew and understood her love. They were in this together and that's how they would leave, together.

February was a sign that there would be an early spring, as most of the snow had melted, leaving a muddy, but sunny Peaceful Valley most of the days.

There was even fishing to be had, and sometimes enough were caught to provide dinner, but these days were few and far between. They figured they had at most, a couple more years of the lake providing any fish for their dinner tables.

At that time, they would have to concentrate on the smaller lake across Elbert Road in the cub scout camp.

March roared into camp like a lion, with a snowstorm coming in the second week that dwarfed all the previous snows by comparison, dropping a whopping twenty-three inches on to camp, almost paralyzing them for a couple of days until they could dig themselves out, which was done primarily by the teenage boys and girls. It was wet and heavy snow that was exhausting to shovel, so the elders gladly let the teens do the brunt of the hard work, leaving the elders to supervise and concentrate on the back pain they were avoiding at all costs.

Before they knew it, it would be springtime and a time for planting the new seed to begin, and they were all chomping at the bit to get out in the elements and contribute to bringing forth new life into Peaceful Valley.

April, just like the saying goes, brought a lot of rain showers to camp, almost daily, and brought a greenness to camp no one had seen since they could remember. As far as the eye could see, everything was green and beautiful, and waiting for human feet to be traipsing around in it, just as it would normally be with pre-summer campouts from various boy scout troops across the state.

The winter had come and gone just like any normal winter would have, and the spring was in full bloom, with prairie flowers standing at attention across the valley.

The days were becoming longer and the mornings warmer, and before you knew it, the summer they had said goodbye to the previous year would soon be here again.

Fortunately, they had cut enough wood to get them all through the winter, and the two trees they had cut down in the fall at the outskirts of Peaceful Valley would soon be ready for chopping into the wood for the fires.

Some of the men, along with all of the boys old enough to swing an ax, were at the trees inspecting how far along they had become in getting seasoned, trying to get a timeline of when the boys should begin chopping.

That is when they heard them from a distance south of them.

In an instant, the sky became full of Chinese military choppers heading north, and overhead them were large transport planes heading in the same direction.

There were hundreds of aircraft in total, and the best guess from Bill and the men was that they were heading to Wyoming, or even North Dakota, where most of the oil drilling was being done.

Then on Elbert Road, they saw a small caravan of Chinese trucks heading north tailed by an American MRAP, which turned into Peaceful Valley and stopped at the locked gate as the trucks continued on.

Bill and Bob, along with Miles, jumped into the cruiser to meet the MRAP, knowing it had to be Sanchez and Halliday, which it was, and they had much to tell the soldiers about what had transpired since the last time they saw them.

TWENTY THREE

The End of the Rainbow

"Sergeants Sanchez and Halliday! Good to see you again!" said Bill as all the men got out of their vehicles.

"Mr. Jenkins. Good to see you as well!" said Sergeant Sanchez.

"Let me unlock the gate and you guys can follow us back," said Bill.

As the MRAP pulled up to the dining hall, Sanchez and Halliday could see a lot more people than they remembered since the last time they were there.

"Your name is Mr. Wilkerson, correct?" Sergeant Halliday asked Miles.

"Yes. We met in Simla. We took your advice and sought these people here out, then joined up with them. It saved our lives, thanks to you fellas" answered Miles.

"We've actually grown in leaps and bounds. We took the bus out and picked these people up, then when autumn was about to hit, we had a whole busload of people show up and join us as well, so we've got quite the community going now. There's over a hundred of us" said Bill.

"You know Mr. Jenkins. You said the last time we saw each other you'd wished you had your hands on an MRAP like this. We'd like to join up with you as well" said Sergeant Sanchez.

"We've got no place to go except back with the Chinese, and we've had enough of that. No more. We don't want to serve under them anymore and to be honest with you, I don't think they are going to miss us. That caravan you saw is headed back to DIA to board some cargo aircraft and head back to China. They've fulfilled their mission here. They've been pilfering everything they could from Ft. Carson and NORAD, and there's nothing left here for them to do.

There's no more U.S. government left to speak of, so once they take off, there's nothing for us and nowhere left to go. Base 12 is completely empty now, as that and the underground railroad was taken over from the beginning.

Our families are dead, and we are just two soldiers looking to belong somewhere, so if you'll have us, we can contribute," said Sanchez.

Bill was beside himself because he felt these soldiers belonged there with them and wasn't afraid to say so.

"I'm sure we can arrange that. I personally would love to have you here with us. You can talk with Bob here about helping him with the law enforcement part of our camp. It's going to be lunchtime here pretty quick, so why don't you boys wash up over by the picnic tables over there, grab a cup of coffee over by the fire, and we'll sit down and catch up, and we can introduce the two of you to everybody.

I'm sure anxious to hear about what's been happening in this country," said Bill.

Burt came around the corner of the dining hall, carrying a hammer, hand saw, and a tool belt as he'd just repaired the balcony railing on the dining hall veranda.

"Hey fellas. Good to see you again" said Burt to the two soldiers. "Let me get both of you a clean coffee cup."

The men sat around the fire and were joined one by one, as other men from camp wanted in on the conversation.

"From what we've been told, the President has turned over everything to the Chinese, and our military has completely disbanded, handing over all our working military equipment as well. America is now nothing more than a landmass. There are estimated to be less than 500,000 people left alive in America, with most of them being former government officials.

The Chinese have set up an infrastructure where the remaining representatives and senators that weren't killed are now working for the Chinese government, primarily running the operations of oil pumped from the ground, then piped down to Louisiana and Texas to be loaded onto tankers, and eventually shipped to China and other countries that are buying the oil from China.

They've also taken over offshore drilling.

The Russians had come in to take that over, but the Chinese quickly took that from them, so now China is the number one producer of oil, and practically the whole rest of the world is their customer.

Russia is still piping oil to Germany, so the EU is getting some of their oil there, but that will be a thing of the past soon.

Russia is almost belly up, so soon they will be in dire straits as well.

China has completely taken charge of anything that used to be America, and there's been no other country willing or able to stop them.

For all practical purposes, China has become the rulers of the world, because the world's economy revolves around them and everything they do," said Halliday.

When he stopped speaking to take a drink of his coffee, you could have heard a pin drop.

To the circle of men that were his audience, you might as well have told them that God was dead. It was unbelievable what they were hearing, and none of them could speak because they had no words.

None of the men in Peaceful Valley had given up on the idea that America would someday make a comeback, but without any of its citizens left alive, there was nowhere to even start that conversation, let alone follow through.

'So now what?" asked Jeff Fraley. "What are we supposed to do?"

"You are doing it, right now. What you are doing is what you are supposed to be doing, and that is staying alive" said Sanchez.

"The Chinese see the ones like yourselves left alive in America the same way they see the tribes in the Amazon Forest. There's not enough of you to be a problem for them, so they basically have no interest in you at all," said Halliday.

"You know, Captain Lee sent a truck down here late last summer full of medical and food supplies, which we were damn glad to get. If they didn't care about us, why would he do that?" asked Bill.

"Captain Lee did not speak for the Chinese Government when he did that. He did that on his own. I'm sure he was able to get away with it by burying the manifest for it as some sort of loss or damage. Who knows?

After seeing the people you brought over from Simla, his heart was touched by their desperation, because he knew that if they didn't get some kind of help, they would all die. His conscience weighed on him greatly, so he sent the truck down to them, but when the truck came back and the soldiers told him no one was there anymore, he assumed your camp went to rescue them, which you did, so he sent the truck here.

Captain Lee is different from the rest of the officers and soldiers we have met. He has a good heart and compassion, unlike the rest of them.

How he made it to be Captain in that army is anyone's guess, but thanks to him, that truck made its delivery," answered Halliday.

"The rest of those people were the most cold-hearted sons of bitches I'd ever met in my life," said Sanchez said with clenched teeth.

"The way you've been living will slowly but surely become harder. The gasoline and diesel fuel you've been using will eventually go bad, as will the canned goods. Everything that we will eat will either be hunted or grown. What we do now will determine just how hard it will be in the future," said Halliday.

"I've been thinking about that as well, especially with the food items. I figure we've got another five years before we have to start taste-testing every can of food to make sure it's safe to eat. And the fuel? I don't know for sure how long we have before that starts to turn" said Bill.

"Maybe a couple more years tops," said Sanchez.

"Whatever new additions or construction you are planning, the time to do them is now while you still have operating vehicles," said Sanchez.

"Speaking of new construction, we are getting ready to build a new bunkhouse of sorts, only these will be separate living units for families.

We are planning a major trip to a Home Depot around here to get everything we need to do it, so we are already on top of it in that regard. You've arrived just in time to help with the building of it," said Burt.

"I have a question. Have you had any more run-ins with cannibals? The last time we saw you, you had just been attacked by a bunch of them" asked Halliday.

"No, thank God. I think they may have died out, especially because of what you said about there being less than 500,000 people left in America. They've probably eaten the rest that used to be alive, then started eating each other.

I'm hoping and praying we will never see any of their kind again." Bill paused for a moment to collect his thoughts.

"Now I have a question for you," Bill continued.

"Those soldiers that brought the food supplies here. Whatever happened with them?" he asked as he looked around to make sure Jack was nowhere in earshot.

The soldiers looked at each other and shook their heads.

"Not sure which soldiers you are talking about," said Sanchez, but genuinely curious as to the question.

"After making their delivery, they left and waited up the road until it got dark, then parked their truck out on the road. They snuck up to the cabin of one of our women, then raped and murdered her.

When we heard the gunshot, we all ran up to the building where it happened, but it was too late to catch them. They were long gone down the dirt road, got in their truck, and drove down the main road, making their escape. The girl they murdered was going to get married to our pastor. It was a very horrible thing to happen to us and took us a while to get over it, especially our pastor.

I was hoping to hear something about them, anything. I'd like to believe that something happened to them, that they paid for what they did to that girl," said Bill.

The soldiers standing before him were devastated to hear the news about Mandy and hung their heads in sorrow, not knowing what to say.

"I wish we had known. We would have brought them down here to you if we had known about this and known who they were. We are truly sorry," said Halliday.

"We've reached the end of the rainbow and there's no pot of gold," said Burt.

The dinner bell rang, and everybody got in line for lunch, but most of their appetites had been lost at the tragic news of America.

One of the hardest hit was Burt, who was a true-blue patriot that served in Vietnam, doing two tours.

He didn't even talk about it, but he was spat on like so many soldiers after they had come back from the war.

He was raised to love America and believed in everything she stood for.

He believed in our forefathers and the sacrifices they made.

He believed that the injustices done to the black community were a stain on our country, and also believed we did the right thing by fighting to end slavery, where a million soldiers were lost in battle. He believed we were heading in the right direction to right the wrongs of our past.

He believed in free enterprise and a man's right to be whomever he wanted to be, to carve his way and make his mark, to be a truly free man in the eyes of God, and to worship the God of his choice, or worship none at all.

He believed in everything that made America great, and he would have died for his country, and still would.

To be told that the land he had always loved and believed in no longer existed was like a knife driven deep into his heart, and though there had been no evidence of anything close to a government since this whole thing began, he still held out hope that we would rebound and someday come back stronger than ever before.

Everything he had believed in was now gone in a matter of minutes, and he felt like a man without a country for the first time in his life, and the truth was just that.

He had no country anymore, so that meant to him that all of his energy, desire, and love would be directed to the survival of Peaceful Valley, but more importantly, to worshipping God and his son Jesus.

But there was still a denial in him that America was over, and a part of him refused to accept it.

"Bill. I want you to do me a favor. I want you to meet me by the flagpole in the morning right around 8:00 after everyone's been up for a while and outside. Will you do that for me? And make sure Mark is out there as well" asked Burt.

Bill agreed, then went about the rest of the day wondering what Burt was up to.

The next morning at 8:00 sharp, Bill and Mark were standing at the flagpole, with Pastor Wally and a couple of boys from his troop making their way across the field from the Headquarters building where Pastor Wally was staying.

In the distance rode Burt on his horse, carrying an American Flag that had not been flown for many years.

It was folded in its proper presentation, the same way it had been given to his mother off his brother's casket after giving his life in Vietnam.

That was why Burt didn't talk much about his war days because that meant he would have to talk about his brother.

He handed the boys the flag as he got off his horse, then swatted the horse on the butt to shoo him away, and then he asked the boys to unfold the flag and raise it on the pole.

Many others in camp saw what was happening and rushed down to be a part of it.

As the flag started going up, Burt raised his right hand in salute, and others followed his lead.

Sanchez and Halliday were moved to tears as they saluted the flag they served under as well, and then Sanchez began singing the Star-Spangled Banner, and he was joined by Halliday, then Burt, until the whole camp was singing in unison, bringing tears to the eyes of Burt.

He was afraid this would be the last time he would ever salute the flag or sing the National Anthem.

ABOUT THE AUTHOR

J amey O'Donnell's world view comes from a lifetime involved in politics based on his work involving two presidential campaigns, being a recovered homeless methamphetamine addict that used from the time he was 13 to the age of 45, and being a single father that raised his son alone from the time his son was one years old.

As a father, Jamey's main objectives were to teach his son the value of hard work by instilling in him a work ethic, enlisting him in scouting and helping him achieve the rank of Double Silver Palm Eagle Scout, and the importance of giving his life to Christ.

His son was awarded both athletic and academic scholarships to Benedictine College. He is now beginning his senior year for his degree in Journalism and Mass Communication.

To date, Jamey has written five books and is one of America's most prolific writers of our time.

Printed in the United States
by Baker & Taylor Publisher Services